BREAKING CURSES

M. A. FRÉCHETTE

FOREWORD

An eye for an eye, a curse for a curse...or the poison in her blood will consume her.

To my family, friends, and readers: thank you for your continued support!

PROLOGUE
THREE MONTHS AGO

Namika sat on the edge of a cot she'd called her bed for the past few... she wasn't sure how long it had been. It could've been days, weeks, or months, even. The room itself wasn't bad, considering it was inside the basement of a nightclub, but it definitely could've been worse. They could've thrown her into a cell, considering she was part of the Venatores, a group of demon and vampire hunters. And this nightclub, called the CrowBar, was owned by a demon.

And she was under the protection of a Sanguis demon. Demons who were originally human, tortured and twisted until they became demons. It sometimes took years before they were made anew.

There was a knock at the door, but she'd sensed him before she heard the sound. She swallowed hard, trying to get her mouth to work. "Yes?" It was always strange that a demon was giving her common courtesy, but she reminded herself they were charming until they weren't.

Adam Ashton.

"Miss Strang," he said with a curt nod.

As always, he wore a tailored suit, giving him an air of sophistication not belonging in any place that didn't ooze with wealth. He'd combed his brown hair back; everything about him was meticulous. Not a single wrinkle. Calm emanated from his pristine appearance until it reached his gaze. A predator lurked behind. Unmerciful once he pounced for the kill.

She got to her feet and wrapped her arms around her waist, trying to put any distance between them. The demon king, Mekaisto, had stripped away her people's magic as punishment for their uprising against him. After the Venatores were defeated in the war against the demon king, Mr. Ashton informed her what had happened so she wouldn't panic about the sudden loss of her powers. Namika had felt it extinguish from within, but her natural-born magic quickly filled the emptiness—a secret she hid from everyone. The loss wasn't likely as great to her as the other Venatores, who'd had everything taken away from them.

Mr. Ashton had even told Namika of her boyfriend's fate: dying in battle when they attacked demons inside the demon realm itself. He informed her gently about the war's outcome, surprising her.

"Celina is here," he said with a smile.

She stiffened, trying her best not to give any of her hopeful emotions away, since he might use them against her if he wanted to. "And can I see her?"

"Of course." He stepped aside and waved his hand toward the open door. "After you."

She eyed him, unsure if she should turn her back on him, but after a few seconds, she decided that if this was her chance to see Celina, she wouldn't chance stalling too long.

They walked in silence down the corridors beneath the

CrowBar, and soon enough, reached a living area where Celina and a demon she didn't know stood waiting.

Namika ran to her best friend as Celina rushed forward as well, and the two collided in a tight hug.

Celina pulled her away, gripping Namika's shoulders. "Are you okay?"

Adam scoffed. "Are you insinuating I'd break my word and harm your friend?"

"I'm saying no one reads the fine print."

Both demons laughed at that, but Celina pulled Namika away. They went through an archway leading into another area where rusted chains hung on the wall over a small wooden table. Namika took a seat, wondering why they'd bothered trying to get privacy since, if either demons really wanted to, they'd easily eavesdrop.

Namika pointed at Celina's abdomen. "How's your baby?" The last time she'd seen her best friend was when she'd been in labor. Since then, although Adam had assured her Celina was fine and so was her child, Namika wanted to hear it from Celina herself.

"He's well. A boy. His name is Fenrir." She took a deep breath. "There's something… well, lots of things I need to tell you."

Namika's pulse sped at the seriousness of her friend's tone. "Oh?"

"I… made a deal for revenge with Mekaisto after Thomas died."

Namika's eyes widened, but she pressed her lips tight together; she needed time to process the insanity. Her friend had made a deal with the demon king himself. And for revenge?

"Wait… are you serious?" she asked, unsure what she was feeling; definitely shock, but there was a strange sense of betrayal at the same time.

Celina had been a descendant of the Lumen, after all—a branch of Venatores who hunted demons as well.

But demons had destroyed both groups.

They'd won.

Namika took a deep breath. "So, does he own your soul now?"

"No. As crazy as it might sound, Kai... Mekaisto and I fell in love."

"But he's a demon," she said louder than planned.

Celina gave her a sheepish smile. "I know it's hard to understand, but it's simple for me. Especially since... well, I was half demon, and now—"

"What?" Namika leaned back as though her friend might suddenly attack. "You're half demon?"

Namika tried coming to terms with that. After all, she wasn't one to judge since she herself was a mystic; the name they went by for centuries, despite being called many other names. Witches, wizards, sorcerers. And Namika had never told anyone about it.

"I'm a full demon now so that I can live in the Dark Realm with my family," Celina said slowly, as though it would make the shock a bit less bad.

"Your family..." she repeated, letting the words sink in. "Wow," was the only word that came to Namika's mind.

"Yeah."

Namika shook her head, but smiled. "Sounds insane."

"You're telling me," Celina muttered. She bit her lower lip. "Did Adam explain what happened?"

"The demon king took away our magic source. I felt it leave me. It was horrible... like I'd lost a part of myself. But Adam talked me through it." She stared at her friend, the memories of the time they'd spent together filling her with warmth she'd missed. "I don't mind it so much anymore."

"What are you going to do now?" Celina asked.

"I found out my boyfriend died during all the attacks. A lot of my friends are gone, and the group I called family are either dead or they've dispersed out of fear. I was doing my Master's degree in business, but that was being paid for by the group… they figured I could help with the business side of things."

She gave a half-shrug, but the heaviness of her situation weighed down on her. "Adam said I have to stay here until things settle down."

"I'll try to come visit you with Fenrir as soon as I can."

They both stood, and Celina pulled her into a hug. "Take care of yourself, and if you ever need anything, tell Adam. He can pass the message along."

"I will. Thanks." She smiled. "And same to you. If you need me, I'm just an Adam away."

"I don't think the Sanguis leader will appreciate being used as a messenger," Celina quipped, walking back toward the main living area.

Namika inched closer to Celina as she tried pointing to where Adam and the other demon were speaking. "Wait. He's the… first Sanguis? The leader?" Her pulse throbbed in her ears.

"I am, *buttercup*," Mr. Ashton said with a wink.

Namika's whole body seemed to be engulfed in flames. He'd glimpsed the tattoo she had on her shoulder blade once, and since then, had occasionally called her buttercup as a pet name.

"I have to go," Celina said a bit suddenly. "Remember what I told you. Anytime you need me, okay?"

Namika nodded, and they embraced one more time before Celina vanished in front of her.

The other demon rolled his eyes. "Great. I'm supposed to keep an eye on her," he said with a sigh. "Mekaisto will have my head." And he disappeared as well, leaving Namika and Mr. Ashton alone together.

"Nice visit?" he asked in an exaggerated, innocent tone.

She clenched her jaw. "Wonderful."

"Well, I had an interesting one with Brihan." When Namika arched an eyebrow, he grinned. "The demon who just left."

"Oh… What did he say?"

"Mekaisto wants you to remain here for now since there is still some of my kind hunting yours down. It'll be safer for you at the CrowBar, where I can keep an eye on you. Just for a little while longer."

A shiver shot down her spine. "And if I refuse?" she asked quietly.

"You can take it up with my king, if you'd prefer…" He didn't say more because they both knew she wouldn't do any such thing. "In the meantime, I think you need a new place to call home than that tiny room I had put you in temporarily." He motioned with his head. "Follow me."

They arrived inside a new room, and Namika gawked at the place; it was bigger than the studio apartment she'd been living in before all this. How big was this basement?

She stared around. The living room wasn't immense, but it had the essentials. A loveseat was next to a cozy armchair facing a flat-screen television. There were even a few gaming consoles plugged in for entertainment. A soft red rug lay in the middle of the area. The kitchen was the smallest part, but it was complete with refrigerator, stove, and microwave. Beyond the curtains up ahead, a double bed stood against the wall with plenty of space on both sides for nightstands.

"This will be your room from now on," he said, his voice taking her out of her daze at how nice the place was.

She opened and closed her mouth, trying to think of something to say until the only two words came to mind. "Thank you." And while she truly meant it, she knew, deep down inside, that this was all just an illusion. It may look beautiful, but it was a prison, no less.

1

A BEAUTIFUL CAGE

*N*amika checked the numbers a third time.
This can't be right.

Someone was stealing from the company, and where she worked, that meant torture or death. Maybe both.

She checked the numbers yet again, this time manually, biting her lower lip. On the one hand, if she reported this and a demon suffered, it would be one less monster to prey on humans. However, things weren't as black and white anymore after she found out her best friend, Celina, was part demon herself. They'd known each other since high school, and nothing in the world—not even being a full demon—would change how Namika felt about Celina.

That had meant accepting that not all demons were evil—not an easy feat for an ex-demon hunter. But she wasn't one to judge since she herself had a hidden truth. Witches, wizards, sorcerers… They had many names, but whatever they were called, Namika was a mystic.

Namika stretched her arms above her head while leaning back in her chair. Her office had a lack of windows, but it was nicer than her quarters with the Venatores. She shivered, recalling the last time she was back there, when the demon king himself destroyed it in battle. She was lucky to be alive, though she had the feeling it had less to do with luck and mostly because the king was in love with her best friend.

She couldn't blame Celina for having fallen for a demon. They were everything a person wanted, just waiting for their chance to go in for the kill.

Humans do that, too.

Shaking her head, she got back to the laptop and ran the numbers one last time. If she was going to put out an accusation like this, she'd be a hundred percent sure about it.

But she hadn't made a mistake.

Her shoulders slumped as she clicked over the print icon, and the printer started whirring. She didn't like the idea of having someone's death linger over her like that, demon or not. Still, Mr. Ashton had given her this job, and she'd do it properly. When he'd found out about her educational background, he'd offered her the work, and she was thankful for the distraction while forced to stay in the nightclub's basement. Her stay was supposed to be temporary, but after the demons won the war against Venatores, the king had given strict orders that she remain here for her own safety.

She snorted as she grabbed the paperwork and slipped it into a folder before leaving her office. Safer with Adam Ashton?

It was a bit earlier than when she usually ended her day, but considering the importance of this discovery, she decided it was best to bring them directly to her boss.

The hallways below the nightclub looked like something out of a gothic mansion, with wine-colored walls and candelabra every few feet. Thankfully, they were the electrical types and not real candles, or it may have been a fire hazard to have this many. Her footsteps echoed against the black marble flooring, and she slowed as she approached a fork. One way led to Mr. Ashton's office, while the other went upstairs to the club. Towards the exit. To freedom.

Without thinking, she took the one towards the stairs, her pulse speeding. Doubts of actually being able to escape flooded her, but she pushed them aside, focusing on her instincts to run. But when she got to the bottom of the steps, she stopped.

She had to pretend to have lost her powers, which meant being vulnerable. Escaping would be beyond difficult.

And where would she even go? She had no one left in this world to run to for help. She was alone. No family, no friends, no boyfriend.

Her heart squeezed at the thought of Yasuo. They'd been friends for so long, but it was no secret among the other members that it had been an arranged pairing by the higher ups. They wanted people to have as many children as possible in order to grow the group. Namika and Yasuo were around the same age, so it had been logical to get them together in the hopes she'd have children of her own one day. She loved him as a friend, and he shared those feelings, but neither had been in love with one another. It's why she hadn't even minded the fact that he had fathered eight other children with other women in the group. It had given him so much joy to become a father, and he'd been celebrated and given a higher position because of it.

And now, they were all gone or stripped of their magic, unable to help her.

"Lost?" Mr. Ashton asked from behind her, and she spun, heart racing.

"I took a wrong turn," she whispered, bringing up the

folder against her chest as though that would protect her somehow.

She may have been under his protection, but it didn't always feel like it with the way he looked at her. They were natural enemies, after all.

He took a step closer, and she pressed her back against the wall. "Is that right?"

She quickly put out the folder. "Someone's been stealing from your company." When he arched an eyebrow, she explained, "They're not huge amounts, but it's been going on for a few years, and it's likely why no one noticed before."

"I noticed." He took the folder from her. "It's why there was a job opening for you. I had to let the last one go…" A slow smile curled his lips. "Permanently."

"Oh…"

"In the meantime, we need to speak about your…living arrangements here. Make a few details clear." He sounded bored, which was never good. She'd heard this tone before he turned demons to piles of mush.

He stared at her like he was daring her to defy him. She felt compelled to disobey him, wanting to gain any kind of control of the situation, but she decided it would be dumb on her part.

He wants a rise out of me, and I won't give him the satisfaction.

Without a word, she walked past him, ignoring the way he watched her; something dangerous always lingered behind his gaze.

He moved to her side. "Did you really think you'd be able to just walk out the door?"

"I thought you said I was a guest. Not like I'm confined to a specific place, right?"

He laughed, a breathy rumble that sent a shiver up her

spine. "Guest, prisoner, employee—the title doesn't matter. You're required to follow my rules."

They took a turn towards his office, and she kept her focus on the demon walking beside her. They approached a large wooden door, which swung open with Mr. Ashton's power alone. The hairs on her neck rose as he motioned inside.

"Come in," he said, his voice sending her pulse into a frenzy.

Mr. Ashton strode to his desk as the door closed with a resonating click. Namika kept her attention on the exit while part of her magic searched for any other way out in case she had to run.

Nothing.

His essence surrounded her, and she stiffened, realizing she'd stopped focusing on him. A deadly mistake to make.

"Have a seat," he said in a quiet voice.

She stared up and froze as his gaze locked on her. Like he was measuring her movements. He sat on an antique office chair, leaning back as though comfortable with the whole situation. Yet nothing was calm in his gaze; a storm brewed in their depths.

She glanced at the two matching armchairs facing his desk and decided on the farthest from the door in case someone came in. At this angle, no one could sneak up on her.

The ghost of a smile touched his lips as though he was reading her mind. She couldn't deny the man was handsome, but this was the danger with demons. They looked like everything people wished for, but beneath the pleasing facade lurked horrible nightmares.

And the bastard had so much patience. He sat there, watching her as though silence would cause her to admit anything. Well, he would find out how stubborn she was.

The lights buzzed overhead, and she glanced up for a second before focusing on his desk. New and bought at an expensive office store. Except for the chairs, the rest fit with today's styles. His hands came into focus as she lifted her head, and she swallowed hard when she met his gaze.

"How long have you been here with us?" He drummed his fingers against the surface. "Three months?"

"Too long," she said over him.

"You've known your fate for some time. Why are you suddenly surprised by it?"

"Why are *you* surprised I'd try to leave no matter how you decide to brand me?" she shot back.

It wasn't the right answer. His irises turned a dark shade of red, and she braced, ready to fight. But he didn't move. He stilled completely, as though staring through her. Into her mind.

"Very well. No more games." He leaned his elbows against the surface. "I gave you a job, and you're allowed to come and go as you please in the living areas of the basement as long as someone is accompanying you. But you *are* correct. I'm not letting you leave."

"Then why let me believe I'd be able to?"

"The illusion of freedom is precious." He played with his cufflinks. "But no matter how beautiful it is, a cage is still a cage."

An honest demon who didn't use sweet lies to comfort his victims. This was a switch from what Namika had experienced as a hunter for the Venatores. "Okay..."

"And if giving you an inch means you'll constantly take a mile, then perhaps joining the other prisoners beneath the basement is a better idea." His icy stare froze her to the core. "Although it isn't as comfortable."

She put in her best effort to keep her expression neutral, stopping herself from pleading for mercy.

The corner of his mouth curled into a small grin. "What intrigues me is you don't actually try to escape. Why is that?"

"I'm trying to find a way to leave without a trace.

"Leave without a trace?" he repeated. "We both know I'd find you easily. I have your scent."

Her stomach tightened at the concept of being hunted. Especially by this demon. "Your king may have won the war, but my people are still out there. They're likely looking for me."

He tugged open a desk drawer and retrieved a thick folder.

"Let's see, shall we?" he said with indifference. "Your father is dead. You haven't spoken to your mother in years, and you have no siblings."

Her heartbeat pounded in her ears. "Where——"

"You were attending Carleton University, but in the past year, you began to skip classes." He glanced at her. "And you didn't register for the last semester. Not planning on finishing your master's degree in business?"

She parted her lips, part of her desperate to explain, but quickly pressed them together as he continued.

"We already know what happened to your former lover, Yasuo." He spoke so matter of fact, as if his words weren't a knife straight through her. "The other people you've had contact with recently were Venatores, and I doubt I need to go into details about what happened to them." He closed the folder and placed it on his desk. "Don't fool yourself. No one is looking for you. You are very much alone."

She swallowed hard through the lump in her throat, desperate not to cry. The very last thing she wished for was to give him the satisfaction he'd hit home.

"My king's orders about your stay here were revised a

few weeks ago when your people were discovered to be holding meetings in secrecy. There's unrest, and many of my kind are out for blood, wanting to destroy what's left of you." He replaced the folder inside the drawer, a cold smile curling his mouth. "I told my king to exterminate you all for the sake of thoroughness, and it seems I was right."

She tightened her grip on the armrest, pretending it was his neck. "Good to know you see us as such a threat."

The red in his irises glowed brighter, but the smile never left his lips. "Do you think provoking me is easy?" He shook his head. "Still as fearless as the day we met. And just as foolish," he finished, his voice lowering.

Namika recalled that day all too well. Her best friend, Celina, was in labor but also wounded. A demon helped and brought them both to the CrowBar club, and when Mr. Ashton showed up, Namika was determined to protect Celina. No matter what.

Although she hadn't known who Mr. Ashton was when she'd punched him in the face.

She narrowed her eyes. "Can I go back to work now?"

"Finish early for today since it's Friday."

NAMIKA CURLED up onto the couch, glad she was finally in her cozy pajamas. Her new living situation was definitely better, but being unable to leave made her uneasy. Months had passed, and she'd hoped she could eventually leave, but Mr. Ashton had pulled the rug under her feet by refusing. How much longer would she be stuck here? Until she died?

And why did he have to be so cruel when describing her life like that? Like she had nothing to live for on the outside; was her past so dull to him?

Who cares what he thinks?

She gritted her teeth as she grabbed the book on the side table, trying to focus on anything else. Her vision blurred as his words repeated inside her mind over and over. Father dead, mother estranged, boyfriend killed, what was left of her people scattered. The war against demons had taken everything away from her. And he expected her to sit still like a good little prisoner?

No. She wouldn't take this imprisonment lightly. There had to be a way to contact Celina... even if it meant using a spell with the magic no one knew she had.

But first, she needed to get away from here. Get away from *him*.

2

———

PRISONER

*N*amika eyed her reflection. "I am *not* going upstairs naked."

Linda, the demon in charge of watch duty for Namika this evening, approached, her hips swaying like she walked to music only she heard. Her blonde hair fell in thick waves, her red lipstick matching the color of her irises. And although she was beautiful, Namika saw the woman for what she was; a vile monster needing to be exterminated.

The demon scoffed. "Keep complaining, and I'll give you an outfit that shows a lot more skin." Her gaze darkened as she leaned closer, her Playboy bunny costume barely covering her chest. "Now, stop running your mouth and finish getting ready."

When Linda found out it was her turn for guard duty, she'd thrown a fit about missing the party tonight. After all, Namika couldn't leave the apartment beneath the nightclub. But a few remarks from Namika as they sat in her living room persuaded Linda to bring her upstairs. Besides, as Namika had pointed out to the demon, where would she even run?

That was the final little push, and before Namika knew it, Linda had thrown her an old Halloween costume to wear.

Namika took the police cap off and tied her hair in a high ponytail, doing her best to tuck the unruly curls into the elastic.

Linda licked her lips as her gaze swept along Namika's body in the mirror. "Besides, you look yummy. You should dress like this next time I have to babysit you. It'll make being around you fun."

Namika's face heated. She was never comfortable wearing anything other than clothes that covered most of her skin, but arguing too much about the costume choice had the potential to have the demon change her mind. But it also meant donning a leather police outfit with a zipped-up jacket so tight her A-cups appeared to have doubled in size. The pants weren't any better either since they looked painted on.

"Let's get this over with," Namika muttered, following Linda to the living room.

"Don't cause me any trouble tonight, and I promise I'll tell my master how much of a good girl you were while I took care of you."

Master. Anytime people mentioned him—and not even by name—a shiver ran down Namika's spine.

Power tingled along her skin, and her stomach clenched as a knock on the door sounded. It opened on its own, and Mr. Ashton leaned against the door, arms folded as he stared from Namika to Linda, his expression stony.

Linda bowed her head, but Namika held the gaze, threatening to burn her. One of the key lessons she learned as a Venatore was to never show fear, but with certain demons, it wasn't easily done.

"Miss Strang," he said.

She tried her hardest to ignore his power as it moved across her body. He took a few steps closer, and she stiffened as he leaned into her personal space, his smell invading her senses as his breath tickled the side of her head. She curled her hands into fists, attempting to overlook years of training as a hunter. Both wouldn't need much of an excuse to strike against one another.

A clinking sound caused her thoughts to freeze. He straightened, the handcuffs that went with her costume hanging from his finger.

"I'll be confiscating these," he said as he retreated. "Unless you needed them for something, buttercup?"

Linda let out a small laugh but glanced at the floor when Mr. Ashton shot her a side look, warning her she was in enough trouble.

"As for you, Linda," he placed the handcuffs on the coffee table, "I'm leaving for a meeting, so we'll speak about this later."

She nodded, biting her lower lip as though more disappointed than nervous.

Mr. Ashton turned his attention back to Namika and smiled. "Just remember what we discussed. Each time you try your little escapades, I *will* catch you." A deadly calm crossed his features. "I suggest you make each attempt count."

An icy chill shot down her spine, her pulse speeding so quickly she wasn't sure her cloaking spell would work entirely. "I don't know what you're talking about."

He chuckled at that and walked away towards the door. He paused, then glanced over his shoulder. "Oh, and Miss Strang?"

"What?"

His smile was wolfish. "I like your costume."

Her whole body warmed, and she was thankful he'd

left before she'd felt the heat burning her face. She slumped in the armchair, digging her fingernails into her palms until they throbbed.

How dare he comment on my outfit like that?

This couldn't continue. Adam kept drawing closer as though trying to wear her down. What would happen once she gave in? She had to leave. And she had to deliver a message to Celina.

Linda frowned. "This isn't fair. Why am I being penalized for your mistakes?"

"Trying to make life better for humans was never a mistake. The only thing we did wrong was trust deceitful monsters." She let out a sigh. "I'm surprised he didn't give us both an earful since it's obvious by this stupid Halloween costume that you were planning on bringing me upstairs."

"The only reason is because my master has more important business." She glanced at the ceiling as though the matter in question would fall through the tiles.

"I can't imagine he'd like anything more than to destroy me; he didn't hide his hatred in that little meeting yesterday."

Linda waved her hand dismissively. "I didn't say he likes to meet with Viscus demons, only that they take priority over you. You're barely a threat without your magic, and at this point, you're really just a nuisance."

Namika shivered at the mention of Viscus demons. Powerful and cruel, they'd never been human. The demon king's second in command was rumored to be one, but she had her suspicions he was something else entirely.

Namika rubbed her face. "I know my situation could be worse... I mean, I'm free to come and go as long as I'm accompanied by one of you... but still."

Linda opened her mouth as though wanting to shoot

something nasty back, but instead, she cocked her head. "Wait. You're allowed to leave on the condition that a member of our group is with you?" She grinned. "Damn straight it could've been worse. If it was me in charge, I'd have killed you already."

"If it makes you feel any better, your boss said the same comment to me. The only thing stopping him is your king's orders. Until he changes them, anyway." Namika's stomach churned at how easily her fate could be altered; would she be ready to fight back when it did?

Linda clapped her hands, and Namika jumped at the sudden noise.

"That's great to hear, but tonight is about me since I planned for this party for a long time, and I'm not about to let some washed-up amateur on death row ruin it for me," she said, marching to the door. "Let's go. We're leaving."

Namika stood slowly, unsure if she was satisfied with how effortless it was to trick the demon or how much her words about being on death row scared her.

If I can escape permanently, I won't need to wait for my demise.

"I REALLY HATE HALLOWEEN," Namika muttered, even though no one would hear her over the sound of the blasting music playing in the nightclub. Well, except for the demons and vampires present.

They were the tricks, and the humans who came here for a good time were the treats, their costumes the candy wrappers that the supernatural beings couldn't wait to peel off.

Namika kept on high alert as she turned a washcloth back and forth inside a mug, not actually cleaning it. Not that it mattered since her work at the bar wasn't a matter of life and death; paying attention to who or what approached her was.

The base thumped throughout the room, blasting Halloween-themed music. People grinded together to the beat while fog from the machine partially hid them from view.

Namika studied the scene in front of her; if only the humans knew that the red glowing eyes, silver irises, and fangs weren't props.

Linda leaned against the bar. "Don't forget what happens if you try anything stupid."

Namika gave a curt nod; the last thing she wanted was to be sent back downstairs before she could go through with her plan. Although Mr. Ashton suggested there would be many escape attempts on her part, she wanted this to be the sole occasion.

"You can relax. Your threats aren't something I'll forget anytime soon," Namika said.

Linda twirled a finger in her hair. "I almost wish you'd try running off. I'd love to see my master catch you."

At the thought, Namika dropped the glass she was cleaning, and it fell with a crash that managed to be heard despite the noise. She quickly crouched and began picking up the larger pieces. "Go back to dancing. Isn't that why you wanted to be up here so badly?"

Before Linda responded, Namika shifted her attention to her mess. She had to be careful not to cut herself on the edges since that would draw notice from the wrong people.

"Excuse me? Do you serve any banana daiquiris with real bananas?" a woman's voice shouted over the techno music.

Namika straightened, and her pulse sped as she recognized the customer who'd asked the question.

Emma, dressed as some sort of sexy military woman,

was part of the Venatore group and had fought alongside Namika several times. That phrase was a code to get the attention of another member without detection, and so far, Linda's reaction didn't show she knew that information. The demon just looked annoyed.

"Of course we don't," Linda spat. "Are you drunk or something?"

Emma giggled as she straightened her Army jacket and nodded, not once catching Namika's gaze and keeping up the charade. "Where are the restrooms? I think I'm gonna puke."

Linda pointed at the back. "If you make a mess, I'll use your hair to clean it."

Emma stumbled off, heading towards the line for the washrooms as Namika did her best to slow her heart rate, not wanting to give anything away. Her magic flowed through her extremities, warming her as her pulse slowed. She checked that her spell to shield her powers remained strong and shifted her focus to Linda.

But the demon had vanished without a word. Namika rolled her eyes as she stepped out from behind the bar, scanning the dance floor. It wasn't difficult to spot Linda with her bunny ears rocking back and forth. Plus, the attention she attracted by grinding against two other women certainly created a crowd.

Namika pushed through, not bothering to excuse herself since no one would hear anyway, and stepped into the circle that had formed around the ladies. Linda's jaw clenched for a second, but a slow smile curled her lips.

"Come to play?"

"I need to use the toilet!" Namika shouted over the sound.

She did her best to ignore the warmth filling her as a few people laughed, keeping eye contact with the demon's scowl. "You sure know how to ruin my fun, you little brat," she said, seething.

"I can go by myself," Namika crossed her arms, "I didn't want you to have a fit if you suddenly don't see me at the bar." She pointed at the two women who'd kept dancing as though not realizing their third partner was in conversation. "Keep enjoying yourself. I'll be right back. Threats and all not forgotten."

Linda scoffed and motioned her hand for Namika to go away, and she obliged. While walking towards the queue of people waiting their turn, Namika grinned at how simple it was to get out of the demon's sight.

Now she just needed to find Emma and see why her old friend was here, of all places. And on the same day, Namika had planned to run for it.

Emma wasn't in line, so Namika pushed her way to the door as a woman yelled at her to wait her turn. Among other obscenities.

She grabbed Namika's arm and spun her around. "Who do you think you are, bitch?"

Namika straightened, despite her five-foot-five height with the heeled boots she wore. "My friend is in there puking her guts out. Want to be the person to clean up after her?" Without waiting for an answer, Namika stepped inside, this time ignoring the continued shouts of the indignant women.

I'm lucky they avoided trying anything physical.

The washroom only had three stalls, and each one was large enough to fit a single bed. Why they designed it so poorly, Namika didn't know - or really cared - but it certainly created quite the wait time.

As expected, Emma stood near the sinks, waiting for Namika to join her. The ex-Venatore Namika had fought alongside on many occasions smiled ear to ear, grabbing hold of Namika's wrist and pulling her quickly to the side of the room with a small nook. Nothing that hid them out of sight completely, but at least enough to keep focus off them.

"I didn't believe him when he said you were still alive," she muttered, her gaze darting around Namika as though ensuring she was real. "I thought for sure you died. You were here this whole time..."

"Not like it was my choice."

"So they're keeping you here as a captive?" Emma waved her hands dismissively before Namika had the chance to answer. "It doesn't matter. I'm here to rescue you. We can work together tonight, and you'll come back with me."

Namika arched an eyebrow, glancing over her shoulder as a woman entered the washroom, the music blasting inside the room as the door swung open. "Wait. What do you mean, work together? Go back where? And who's *him*?" That was the question that burned her the most; someone told Emma she was held here as a prisoner; who?

Emma bit her lower lip, and Namika instantly put her guard up. "I know that look," she said in a low tone, "every time you do that, it's because you're trying to find the right words, so I won't tell you whatever you're planning is a bad idea."

"Promise not to be mad——"

"Tell me."

Emma let out a sigh and leaned closer. "Okay, fine. We've grouped up after a few of the members were contacted by someone willing to help us."

A knot in Namika's belly tightened. "What's the rest of the story that's supposed to make me convince you not to do something foolish?" Namika asked, wondering what her people were up to in the last few months.

"We're working with..." Emma glanced towards the stalls, "a vampire who offered to help us."

Namika waited for her friend to say something else, but when Emma remained silent, Namika did her best for her next words not to be too loud. "This is the part where you add that you obviously didn't fall for that trick, considering what happened last time we trusted monsters."

The war was lost for many reasons, but two of the major causes were identical; an angel who'd been the one to grant powers to the Venatores eons ago in order to fight darkness and a demon who wanted the world altered to have supernatural beings ruling it. Both turned out to be the same person with their own agenda, and his betrayal cost them everything.

"Look, I get that trusting Gabriel was stupid," Emma said quickly, her blue eyes haunted by what had happened. "I was there in the Dark Realm during that last fight." Her voice grew thick, and Namika suppressed a shiver at the thought of being in that place—the place humans referred to as hell.

Namika took a deep breath. "I'm sorry you were there. It couldn't have been... pleasant."

Emma scoffed. "You think?" She shook her head, her sandy short hair flicking from side to side. "It was carnage. We didn't stand a chance. When I was dragged into those cells along with a bunch of our people, I was sure I'd be killed. It was horrific hearing screams constantly."

The door to the washroom opened once more, and three women rushed in, shoving against each other as they fought for a stall. Namika pushed her magic around her, trying to sense if anyone was pissed off and looking for her. So far, it still seemed alright.

Movement caught Namika's attention as Emma rummaged inside her purse and pulled out her cell.

"After everything I went through, do you honestly think I'd trust so blindly again?" Emma asked. "Especially another supernatural being?" She checked the phone's screen quickly before putting it away. "He promised to give us our powers back—"

"And you believed that lie?"

Emma's eyes gleamed as she lifted her palm in front of Namika's face. Orange lights swirled between her fingers, creating an eerie glow between the two women.

Namika's eyes widened. "That's..." she wanted to say impossible, but the proof was right there.

"I'll accept your apology now," Emma said with a laugh as she closed her hand and straightened. "And it's not only me," she added quickly. "He's given magic to all of us who joined up. It's why I'm here; he sent me to rescue you. He'll give you the same powers, and we'll be even stronger when you come back."

Namika stiffened. Members of her group had often called her one of their most powerful hunters, but they never knew it was because she had more than the Venatores' magic flowing through her veins. If she returned with Emma, would this vampire realize this?

It doesn't matter if it means finally eradicating the world of demons.

Her wish was always simple; once most demons fell, the ones who remained could stay in the Dark Realm to rule as they pleased. Vampires would return to the parallel world where they were originally from. The human world would be out of bounds for them, and people could live without fearing the darkness.

Namika frowned as the information Emma provided sunk in. "Wait. A vampire? They don't have magic. Not unless it's a nightshade?"

Emma shook her head. "Just a vamp, but he has powers, somehow."

"So what exactly did you mean by work together tonight? What is it you have to do here?" Namika asked.

Emma beamed, bouncing on her heels. "I'm so glad you're on board."

"I'm not agreeing to anything until you tell me the plan," Namika pointed out, but her friend didn't lose her smile, knowing Namika would help no matter what.

"Well, I need to go to a storage room that's apparently in the basement of this place. It's past the torture rooms, so I guess pretty far down."

Namika's brows snapped together. "In case I wasn't clear before, I'm a prisoner here. They don't exactly let me roam around the corridors." But with her magic, she'd had a few occasions to track demons with her sight and knew the layout of some sections.

"Yeah, but you're always resourceful." Emma gave Namika a hopeful look. "Any ideas?"

If Namika went through with this, there was no way she could fail this escape, or it would mean certain death for her. "I know exactly how."

3
____

DANGEROUS CRIMES

*N*amika dusted herself off while staring at the ceiling. Not that there was any debris to get off her costume since they'd used magic to go through from the floor above. It was a tricky spell requiring the user to know for sure there was space below; if Namika wasn't certain there was a storage room there, they would've ended up fused within the solid wall and died.

At the thought, Namika rubbed her arms and turned to Emma. It also required someone who was skilled at the enchantment, and Emma was the best. Namika was one of the top magic users, but as far as everyone knew, she'd lost her powers the day every other Venatore had. And it would stay that way. The last thing she needed was for anyone to discover what her ancestry held.

As soon as they'd suffered defeat in the war against demons, she'd sealed her mystical abilities away, only leaving a small shield to help keep her emotions grounded and not as obvious to others in her presence.

Emma glanced around the compact closet. "I'm glad you were right about where this place is." She pulled out a piece of paper and stared at it. "Okay, so I know where we're heading once we get to the sub-basement and what I need to grab from the storage." Her gaze fixed on Namika. "Any suggestions on how to reach that area and how to unlock the way down?"

"Actually, I do, but it's not going to be easy..." Namika opened the door and peeked out into the long hallway. "It'll require blood magic if you're up to it," she finished quietly.

Emma pushed past her with a scoff. "It's my favorite kind. Let's go."

Namika frowned but didn't comment about Emma's recklessness; it wasn't like her to go into a dangerous situation without some level of caution. Namika wondered if this had something to do with the Venatores' newfound magic; was it affecting them?

A figure rounded the corner up ahead, walking towards them. Namika's heart sped as she recognized the demon. Marc was on watch duty a few times for her, and although he'd never tried anything with her, he'd given her the creeps when he just stared at her.

Marc frowned. "What are you doing down here? Isn't Linda supposed to be with you?"

Namika was never a great liar, but Emma had it down to a science. She turned towards Namika, sliding her arm around her neck and cuddling close. "Ah, we got caught, babe," she giggled.

Before Namika reacted, Emma pulled her closer, pressing her lips against hers in a deep kiss. Heat rose to Namika's cheeks, but she played along, trusting her friend had a plan. When they pulled away, Namika cupped Emma's cheek. "It's fine."

Marc cleared his throat, and they both turned to look at him. A small grin curled his mouth to the side. "You're going to be in so much trouble with Linda. And once she's done with you and she's told the mas—the boss, not even your connections will help you."

Emma pulled away and shot daggers from Namika to the demon. "Done with..." She slurred her words, obviously pretending to be tipsy. "Hang on. Wait." She pointed at Namika. "You said you wanted to-to...fuck. Now I find out you...you want to, what? Have a threesome or something? Wow. Ew. No." She raised her hands in the air, walking straight past Marc and heading in the direction where the stairs back up to the club were located.

Namika put on her best angry expression she could fake and marched towards Marc. "Thanks a lot! You couldn't have given me a break this one time? You've ruined my chance at finally being able to hook up!"

The demon had the decency to look like he actually felt remorseful for a few seconds as he rubbed the back of his neck. "You could've cleared it with Linda—"

"You're kidding, right?" Namika spat. "On the rare occasion I get close to finding myself a nice girl, Linda notices it and swoops them off."

Namika was so glad the demon she ran into didn't know her well. If this was Linda, Haku, or Mr. Ashton, they would've known she was lying through her teeth. Even pretending she had trouble talking about anything remotely sexual.

Marc opened his mouth as though to say something, but light shone around him from the back, and he fell to the floor with a loud thud. Emma lowered her hand as she stared at the demon, and Namika suppressed a small shiver. Darkness swam behind her friend's eyes as she looked at him, and for a second, Namika almost didn't recognize her.

What kind of magic had she used?

Pushing her unease away, Namika returned to the closet they'd exited a few minutes ago and opened the door. "We can put him in here so if anyone——"

A sickening sound sliced through the air, and Namika spun as Emma's blade impaled Marc in the back. Fire-red veins traveled from the wound around his body, and within seconds, the demon turned to ashes.

Namika bolted to where Emma stood, eyes wide as she stared at what was left on the floor. "Why did you do that?" she nearly shouted the words. "You didn't have to destroy him."

"If we'd put him in the closet, once he woke up, he would've sounded the alarm and told everyone what happened." Emma twirled the handle of the weapon, the only remaining part after the blade had melted into Marc. "Besides, since when do you care about killing these monsters? The less, the better, right?"

Namika was unsure why she had reacted the way she had. It could be she'd been around demons too long and had started to see them as people. Or maybe having her childhood friend become one of them had changed the perspective she had of them.

She shook her head, turning her gaze away from the remains. "It's just that... if we do get caught, destroying one of their own won't work in our favor when we plead for mercy."

"Mercy? They wouldn't give us that in the best of times." She slipped the hilt of the dagger back into one of her Army pants' many pockets. Lifting her hand above the ashes, she murmured a spell, and they vanished. "Anyway, as long as we aren't discovered, it won't matter," she said with a wink before continuing down the hallway.

With one last glance at where Marc's remains were a mere few seconds ago, Namika caught up to Emma, unsure if she'd made a huge mistake in following her friend down this path.

THE BASEMENT WENT deep beneath the nightclub, but the dungeon seemed to go further still. Namika focused on keeping her breath steady and her footsteps controlled. Each step brought the risk of being discovered, and after what they'd done to Marc, not even Celina could save them. A nauseating sensation rose in her throat at the thought of what Mr. Ashton would do if he found out. He was the lowest of demons in terms of sub-race, but being the first meant he had powers she didn't know about.

Dripping water echoed around, and Namika tried her hardest to tune out the moans from nearby cells; they had to focus on the plan. Once they returned to the rest of the members, they'd prioritize finally sending demons back to the Dark Realm and rescue all the people down here. She wanted to believe it would work, but trusting another supernatural being sounded like insanity. If they lost again, this would be the last time the demon king would spare any of them.

"It's this room." Emma's whispers brought Namika out of her own mind, and she refocused on their goal.

"What's the name of this item you need?" she asked, waiting by the door. She could've used her own supernatural abilities to make sure the coast was clear on the other side, but she let Emma do it. That was one thing she definitely looked forward to; once the vampire granted her magic, she could go back to using her own without fear of being found out.

"I'll tell you once we're safe inside," she said, glancing

over her shoulder towards the end of the corridor they'd gone down.

Emma pushed open the door, and they entered a large room packed with shelves. The place was colossal, and her heart sped when she realized there were multiple sections separated by alcoves.

"This is going to take too long," Namika said through her teeth, every second ticking by bringing them closer to potentially failing. They were supposed to be in and out of what she'd assumed was a small storage room with the item they needed, not searching for hours through millions of things placed on thousands of shelves. Most reached the ceiling and were filled.

"Less complaining, more searching." Emma glanced at the paper one last time before storing it. "What we're looking for is something called the Garnet Orb." She used her hands to measure the invisible thing, showing it fit in her palm. "It's red, if that wasn't obvious already, and it has a white glow to it. Three golden chains connect to the center orb." She dropped her arms, staring intently at Namika. "And in an emergency, or once we're ready to go," she pulled out a glass cylinder that shined gleamed similar to quartz, "we use this." Emma put the Lochust gem back into one of the front pockets of her uniform.

Relief flooded Namika at the sight of the artifact; they were difficult to come by and were life-savers in certain situations. Like this one.

Namika nodded and set out to look for the mysterious object. Clocks and various devices ticked and dinged, the only sound in the heavy silence around her. Namika wondered what this Garnet Orb did and why a vampire was desperate enough to send people into one of the prime locations where the Sanguis leader resided.

I didn't know this is where he is, too, and we were supposed to have this type of intel.

Glancing from top to bottom on the shelves as she walked by, she went deeper through the never-ending room. A few items caught her attention, some from curiosity while with others, she recognized the description she'd read in old tomes. She pushed past them and allowed her limited magic to spread around her, lowering her defenses on her emotions. Instead, she used it to help her locate the object she imagined in her mind.

A smaller section held rows of filing cabinets, and Namika froze. She didn't know why, but something about the room sent terror through her blood as though it wasn't supposed to be there. Spiderwebs, long abandoned by their residents, blew in a non-existent breeze.

Namika took a few steps back. This part wasn't really...here. She couldn't explain, but with her magic, she knew for sure this segment was connected to somewhere else. Someplace dangerous. And the very last thing she had any desire to do was enter the area.

Writing pulled her attention to one drawer, and she frowned as she stared at her full name. Documents about her. In a place like this. It didn't sit right with her, yet the thought of stepping through the archway sent alarms ringing in the recesses of her mind, and she trembled. She turned her back to the section and resumed her search for the Garnet Orb; if she found it quickly enough, maybe she'd come back and grab whatever was in her file to keep it away from whoever kept it.

Shivers danced along her skin, and she mentally cursed Linda for the Halloween costume. Once they'd finished down here, what she wanted was to change into something decent. With her luck, Emma would bring her to meet the vampire first.

"Ugh..." Namika muttered.

The loud ticking sound suddenly stopped, and Namika froze as power rippled along the storage room walls. It was familiar—definitely demon—but much stronger, and laced with fury. She ran back towards where she'd last seen Emma, her pulse throbbing in her extremities.

He's here.

4

DEADLY MISTAKES

Red symbols slithered across the stone walls, the glowing light pulsating as though alive. Namika turned to Emma and grasped her arm.

"We need to go. Now."

The room creaked under the pressure of an invisible force. "Did you find the Garnet Orb? We can't leave without it," Emma said in a hurry.

"We have to or we'll get killed." Namika shook her friend as her heart hammered against her chest. She didn't wait for Emma to react, though, and instead, slipped her hand into her friend's pocket, grabbing the crystal.

It looked different from what Namika remembered, so she held it up and arched an eyebrow in a silent question. The ground rattled beneath them, and Emma grabbed the device from Namika.

"It can be used twice," she whispered, gripping her fingers around the metal cylinder at one end.

The door slammed open, the wooden panels breaking against the stone, and Namika let out a gasp. With the dust and debris surrounding the way out, only a figure stood against the low lighting of the dungeon behind them. But she already knew who it was; she recognized the energy pulsating around them.

Mr. Ashton.

"Fuck," Emma whispered.

Namika tightened her grip on her friend. "Now!"

Emma twisted the metallic part, and a flash surrounded them for a split second before their surroundings blurred. Multiple colors flowed along the edges of Namika's vision, and she focused on the white light ahead of her; she'd traveled this way a few times, but her stomach still lurched at the motion.

Her feet hit solid ground, and she stumbled forward, catching herself quick enough to grab hold of Emma as well. Cold air struck Namika as she took several deep breaths, and a small shudder escaped her; it was the first time since being brought to the nightclub she'd been outside. Months locked away, and the sudden realization of her newfound freedom sank in, latching on. She couldn't go back. Not after escaping. But Adam knew where they'd been, and how they'd made their getaway; it wouldn't be long before he'd trace them to their location.

Namika looked around, wondering where, in fact, they were. Wind blew between tall cement pillars, and in the dim lighting of the street lamps beyond the structure, she guessed they were in a parking garage, one with multiple stories, and they stood on the first floor of it.

Emma wiped the sweat from her forehead before slipping the crystal back into her jacket's pocket, a tiny grin spreading across her lips. "That was... close."

"Close?" Namika repeated in a harsh whisper. "He saw us. It won't be long before he tracks us down."

"Don't worry. I'll send him a text to let him know we've

arrived." Emma pulled out a smartphone and tapped the screen to select the contact 'Rickie'.

Namika frowned, wondering why the regional code for the phone number was in Manitoba, but decided to ask more questions later. She still didn't trust this whole business with a vampire, but she counted on Emma.

Emma surveyed the vacant parking spaces. "He should arrive any second."

Namika was about to suggest they hide out somewhere while waiting, but a buzzing sound caught her attention, and she turned. Electricity sparked in the air, encircling an orb that flashed green. Slowly, it expanded until it transformed into an alcove, and a figure strode through it.

The verdant hue created an eerie effect around the man, but it was more than the lighting; something felt... wrong about him. Namika nearly scoffed out loud at her own thought.

Of course I'm getting bad vibes; he's a vamp.

Emma approached, and Namika followed, although keeping a cautious pace. Powers or no, vampires were dangerous in their own rights.

"Emma," the man gave a curt nod, then turned his gaze on Namika. "I notice you have brought one of the two things I requested."

Namika tightened her muscles to keep from backing away from him; trusting him was insane, and she couldn't understand why Emma didn't see it. He'd called her a thing, like she was an object to snatch from the storage room. He chose not to see them as equals or allies.

"Hi to you, too, Rickie," she said with a smile.

Namika wanted to grab her friend and escape from the situation. But the best she could do was keep a close eye on the vamp and hopefully have time to react fast enough before he struck.

The man's jaw clenched as his eyes narrowed. "I told you not to call me that."

"Yeah, yeah. Sorry." Emma glanced over her shoulder at Namika and shot her a curious look. "This is Namika Strang. One of our best hunters." She turned back towards the vamp. "Well, before her magic was stolen."

"Indeed?" He cocked his head as though trying to measure Namika's entire personality based on looks alone. "And what of the secondary item I asked you to get?"

Referring to her as an object again did more than grate on her nerves; it made her unbearably nervous. Still, she did her best to stay focused on his movements. Luckily, the portal behind him hadn't closed, which created good lighting. Something vampires didn't need, and put humans at a disadvantage.

Emma slipped her hands into her pockets. "About that..."

His irises flashed white for a few seconds, and Namika took a few steps towards her friend. "We were interrupted. The leader of the Sanguis demons found us. We had to leave before we located the orb." She was relieved her voice didn't shake like she thought it might.

"I suppose one out of two is better than nothing." His tone had softened, but behind his black irises, cruelty filled his gaze. "No matter. There will be other opportunities to retrieve it."

Emma slumped in what appeared to be relief. "Definitely, yes."

"Just not by either of you." His words cut through the air like a knife, and everything around them seemed to freeze for a few seconds.

Namika hoped she'd been wrong. That she misheard. That her mistrust of the vampire stemmed from years of bias.

Emma let out a nervous laugh. "Look, Rickie. I know I fucked up. He was supposed to be going to a meeting with higher demons tonight, but I guess he came back early. But please give me another chance. I think, next time——"

"You're right," he breathed with a nod. He took a few steps forward, and Emma's smile faltered. "You did fuck up."

The portal behind him sparked, and Namika squinted at the flashes of light as more figures darted out. Before she made sense of what she saw, one beast lunged at Emma, tackling her to the ground. Namika didn't think as she rushed to her friend.

The creature reared back its head, a chunk of flesh and muscle hanging from its needle-sharp teeth. It let out a screech, and Namika covered her ears, the sound piercing through her thoughts. She stared down at where Emma lay, the blackened hole in her neck squirting blood as her figure twitched. Emma's eyes were wide; her mouth opened in a silent scream, but even at a distance, Namika knew her friend was gone.

A force rammed into her, and she fell forward, hitting her skull against a cement column. She gasped, her body aching as she spun. Her stomach churned as the creature leaned nose to nose with Namika, black eyes staring at her as its mouth opened wide.

Another figure appeared next to the monster, but its face was so peeled, Namika couldn't tell if it was the same thing as the one that killed Emma. It looked more human than the other. Like a corpse. It whispered something, each word cracking.

It grabbed Namika's neck, lifting her off the ground. Namika kicked and parted her lips to scream, but the monster tightened its grip. It cut Namika's air off as she gripped the creature's wrists, trying to escape.

It leaned closer, the stench of its breath churning Namika's stomach. Its mouth widened, muffling Namika's screams as it continued squeezing her throat. The creature bit into Namika's shoulder, and Namika shrieked, kicking harder than before. Pain blurred her vision, but she squirmed and twisted, desperate to get away.

It felt like both a second and an eternity before the monster staggered to the side, releasing Namika. She fell to her knees, choking as she screamed and cried. Searing agony shot from her wound to the rest of her body. Her palms scraped against the pavement, and she trembled violently, staring up.

The vampire stared down at her, his dark hair partially hiding his eyes. "You've served your purpose." He crouched in front of her, and she winced, ready for him to strike. "And so has your friend."

Her gaze darted to Emma's body, lying close by. Something gleamed from inside the jacket's pocket, and Namika's pulse quickened.

The creature that had attacked Namika scuffled forward and stood next to the vampire, head twitching.

"Go back." He waved his hand, and it staggered away towards the portal. His irises turned white as he stared at Namika, and she swallowed hard; he was definitely a vampire, and not a nightshade.

"Please—"

"You'll make a lovely meal for my ghoul here," he cooed. "One is not enough. They're greedy."

Before she said anything, the creature who'd killed Emma rushed toward her, digging its hooked claws into her arms and pinning her to the ground. She screamed, trying to kick at it, her heart pounding against her ribs as movement caught her eye.

The vampire walked towards the portal. He was leaving her to suffer a fatal end.

Pavement rubbed against her back and open wound, and she hissed through her teeth, focusing on not passing out. If she did, it was over.

The greenish light vanished, plunging her into near darkness, the occasional street lamp flickering in the distance.

This is it. I'm going to die.

Energy rippled through the air, and before she made sense of anything, the ghoul staggered, releasing her. She rolled to the side, panting. Her palms scraped against the rough surface, and she trembled violently, staring up.

Adam stared down at her, fury dancing behind his red eyes. Without a word, he turned his attention back to the ghoul, flexing his bloodied hand as it backed away from him.

She took the momentary distraction, lunging towards Emma's body. Namika grabbed the crystal from the pocket and twisted the metal cylinder.

IT BARELY TOOK a second before her feet touched solid ground once more, and she frowned at her blurred surroundings. It seemed she'd thought of the underground sewer systems leading to an old safe house protected by magic they'd used years ago. Kept demons and vampires out, and it was her best chance at escape. If Adam caught her, she knew he wouldn't kill her; it would be much worse. The ghoul would've been quicker.

Pushing her palm against the wound, she whimpered at the pain. But she'd have to deal with it later. Her feet splashed into the tunnels; Lumen had built these ages ago.

She shook her head, hoping to clear her vision, and picked up her pace; she had to get to the safe house before Adam tracked her down. Rust covered the metal door at the end of the tunnel, and Namika bit her lower lip as she approached it. Clenching her jaw tight, she dabbed her fingers into her wound until they dripped wet, then got to work on the entrance. She traced the symbols they'd taught her without hesitation, even with her trembling hand. The markings glowed for a second, and she smiled when a loud click resonated through the emptiness, and the door swung open. Her own magic worked for this, too, then.

"Good to know," she muttered as she stepped inside the room and locked the door behind her.

An old tube TV sat atop a dresser that had seen better days, but at least most of the beds looked clean. A shooting ache throbbed from her shoulder, down her back, and she hissed through her teeth. She held her left arm to her side, trying her best not to move anything too close to the wound, and searched around the room for a first aid kit.

As she rummaged, she found discarded clothes, some of which looked like they might fit her. Her top was shredded so badly, she was surprised it hadn't fallen off yet. She grabbed a pair of jeans and a zip-up hoodie as another pang seemed to electrocute her. Leaning against a shelf, she did her best to focus on anything but the agony. But that was all she felt.

She glanced to the side and spotted a medium-sized first aid kit. One more breath out through the sharp pain radiating through her. Something was wrong. This wasn't a normal wound, and she realized she might be in bigger trouble than she originally thought. Her heart raced in her chest as she grabbed the kit and stumbled towards the bathroom.

The door closed with a loud click, and she braced

against the sink. Her hands trembled as she opened the steel box, her vision blurring with each passing second. The vampire had mentioned one of those things was a ghoul—something she wasn't familiar with—but what was the other thing that had bitten and ripped at Namika?

"Okay..." she whispered as she maneuvered, trying to take her top off. The zipper was easy enough to pull down, but tugging on the sleeves felt like she peeled more flesh off with each inch. By the end, she wasn't sure how she hadn't passed out yet.

The thought of losing consciousness while demons were likely hunting her kept her focused. Once her garment fell to the floor with a wet slosh, Namika turned to the side, trying to assess the damage reflected in the mirror.

It was worse than she imagined. That thing had done quite a number on her.

She swallowed through the bile as she stared at the hanging skin from her shoulder, down to her mid-back on her left. Deep gashes bled the flesh red and angry. She'd need medical attention, but not at the usual hospitals; the Venatores used to have people take care of strange-looking wounds, but after what had happened to Emma, Namika wasn't sure who she trusted. The vampire thought she was dead, and Namika intended to keep it that way for as long as possible.

Part of her wanted to unlock her natural magic to heal herself, but with how weak she felt, she was fairly certain she'd end up passing out even quicker.

The towels and washcloths stacked on an open shelf had a yellowish tint to them, but she couldn't be picky. She grabbed one of each, laying the towel atop the toilet cover, then busied herself with the washcloth, running it under warm water. Between taking her time and using a small dose of her magic to numb some discomfort, she was able to clean the injury.

She clenched her jaw, doing her best not to scream. It was like liquid fire ran along the wound. Her body trembled from the pain, but she focused on trying to take her pants off to keep herself distracted. She barely registered getting them off, and by the time she'd finished cleaning herself up, she functioned on an autopilot of sorts.

"Bandage... I need..." she mumbled, listening to her voice to hold herself together. "Don't pass out."

She grabbed the gauze from the kit and angled herself into the reflection of the mirror. Her heart pounded at the sight; the surrounding veins were an angry red and nothing like she'd ever seen before.

Taking a deep breath, she applied the bandages as best she could. The white material turned dark instantly, and she let out a sob when she saw it. If she kept bleeding at this rate, she wouldn't pass out from the pain, but from blood loss.

Darkness edged along her vision as she slipped the hoodie on and zipped it up. It was tighter than she was used to, but she'd figured it would keep the bandages in place since taping it correctly was nearly impossible. The jeans took longer as every time she tried bending down, it felt like something sliced through her skin, sending fresh waves of agony throughout her body. She glanced at the first aid kit and grabbed a scalpel; having any type of weapon could help, even if only a little. She tucked it into the front pocket of her sweatshirt, then stepped out.

Once out of the bathroom, she was grateful for the cooler air against her skin. She slowed her steps, listening for any noises nearby, but everything was silent. Her eyelids drooped, and the exhaustion of the night caught up to her like a truck slamming into her. She eyed the bed, unsure if she could take the chance and rest or if she should keep moving. This place was protected against demons and vampires, but with enough of them attempting to enter, she wasn't certain they couldn't gain access.

Her stomach growled, and she clutched her abdomen, hissing through her teeth. She scurried to the pantry, quickly looking for something—anything—to eat. Her wound still caused her immense pain, but something about her craving felt... unnatural.

Between the hunger pangs and her throbbing wound, she was sure she'd throw up; all she wanted was to crawl out of her body to escape the pain.

Another shockwave of anguish burned through her, and she cried out, landing hard on her knees. She focused on the carpet, counting the patterned lines. Everything caused more pain to radiate through her entire being.

She blinked a few times, trying to unblur her vision; a few seconds passed, and her breath hitched when she noticed a pair of dress shoes in front of her.

Adam crouched, his irises glowing the brightest red she'd ever seen. Fury gazed back at her. She trembled so hard she thought her bones would shatter.

"Now, now," he grasped her chin. "Not time to die yet."

5

LESSER OF TWO EVILS

The room spun faster, and although Namika tried to get to her feet, her limbs refused to obey her. Adam straightened and moved behind her; she closed her eyes, waiting for whatever would come next. She was in no state to fight against him.

His hand slipped to her back, beneath her sweater, and her hands turned into fists when his fingertips glided near her wound. Her nerves lit up in a wave of pain. He pulled off the gauze, and she whimpered, feeling as though she was about to catch fire. Sweat trickled down the side of her face, the room cold against her clammy skin. She counted back from ten, desperate not to vomit.

After a few seconds, the pain subsided, and she released a trembling breath. He helped her up to her feet, and although she felt better, her knees nearly buckled beneath her. She took a few steps back before he held on to her any longer and averted her gaze.

She knew he'd only healed her because he likely wanted answers, but she appreciated it nonetheless. "Thank you," she muttered.

"From what I've gathered," he said in a low voice, "you destroyed one of my children, tried unsuccessfully to steal something from me, got yourself mortally wounded, and your accomplice died." He scoffed when she swallowed hard. "I'd read in your file that you were one of the Venatores' strongest hunters. I suppose it makes a lot more sense why your little group failed now."

Her jaw clenched to stop from hurling any reply; that's what he wanted, to get a rise out of her. And she wouldn't give him the satisfaction. She stared back at him, silent, and he arched an eyebrow.

"Nothing to say?"

"Why? So you can continue commenting on things you know nothing about?" she shot back. Part of her wanted to kick herself for letting him rile her up, but another part took great pleasure in speaking her mind. "You're comparing me now to when I had Venatore magic? Of course I failed."

He took a step closer. "From what I saw in the hidden security cameras, your friend had her powers. Care to explain why?"

"Cameras?" she repeated, pulse speeding. "Since when are there——?"

"That's why they're called *hidden* cameras, Miss Strang." He grinned as she gaped at him. "Where did she get her magic from?"

Namika debated whether to tell him everything she knew or to keep it a secret. If Adam told the demon king that Venatores were gaining their powers back, he'd definitely exterminate them all this time. Not to mention, she wasn't even sure Adam would believe a vampire was the one behind this.

"You can tell me, or I can use other methods to get it out of you."

"We're trained on how to get out of those types of situations." Her heart pounded as she slid her hand into the front pocket of her hoodie, clutching the scalpel.

His gaze shot down as he grabbed her wrist and pulled her hand out, still holding her measly weapon. "Always so quick to give up your life for a cult that never cared about you." His voice came out in a growl, and anger replaced the fear that had enveloped her for the past few minutes.

"You're one to talk," she shot back, wincing as his grip on her tightened. "You gave up your humanity to become a monster. For what? Power?" She tried pulling away, but it was like trying to break free of a metal vice. "You're the coward here."

His pupils turned to slits, and he smiled in a way that sent fear trickling down her spine. "It's cute how hard you try to instigate me."

Her shoulder and back throbbed again, and something warm dripped along her skin. She frowned, but before she made sense of it, Adam stiffened, then turned to the door.

Namika's pulse quickened when she realized someone else stood in the doorframe, arms crossed and looking at them like it was the most amusing scene ever.

"Am I interrupting?" the man asked in amusement.

Adam let go of Namika. "You still can't read a room after all these years?" He let out a sigh, but bowed his head low.

If he's bowing, it means this newcomer is a higher demon.

The demon stepped inside, and she flinched as the door slammed on its own behind him. "You're grumpy," he said, arching an eyebrow.

There was something familiar about the newcomer, but Namika couldn't quite place him. She guessed he was a demon as well, but she didn't remember seeing him at the club.

"I'm perfectly calm." Adam glanced over his shoulder at Namika, and she was glad his stare alone couldn't set her on fire.

"Is that why you haven't noticed that she's bleeding to death?" the demon asked, pointing at her.

Adam scoffed. "I healed her a few..." he frowned, turning towards her, "minutes ago. How are you wounded again?"

The stranger materialized in front of Namika, and she stumbled back, leaning against a table. He smiled as gray smoke enveloped him, energy blasting into the area, and she trembled at how powerful it was. A second later, Namika realized why he looked familiar.

Shiriki. The demon king's second in command.

The same cold silver irises stared back at her as on that day. His white hair fell to his shoulders, but he looked no older than Adam.

"I recognize you." His voice was soft, but there was nothing soothing about it; in fact, she was certain it was the same tone he used right before he tortured people for fun. He tilted his head to the side as though trying to decipher something about her. "You were standing next to Celina during the attack on headquarters, correct?" When she nodded slowly, his smile widened. "Then, you are the friend she requested be protected."

"This is Namika Strang," Adam spoke quietly, as though dreading something. "She's also the one who got Celina help when she was in labor."

Namika wondered why Adam would say anything positive about her. Maybe he didn't want Shiriki to get involved?

Shiriki eyed her with a sudden interest she never wanted to see from him. "And who or what caused a wound you cannot heal, Adam?"

"It looked like a ghoul," he answered quietly, sending another glare towards Namika.

The smell of copper filled the air, and dark spots edged along her vision. "It... wasn't the creature you saw... that attacked... me," Namika said through gritted teeth, trying not to scream from the pain radiating through her.

The room spun again, and she squeezed her eyelids shut, desperate to keep from throwing up. Something was definitely wrong, and it was really serious if Adam couldn't heal it. Was she poisoned?

"Restrain her." Shiriki's voice brought her out of her spiral of panic.

Adam materialized in front of her in the blink of an eye and grabbed her wrists, holding her in place. She stared up at him, fear coursing through her veins.

"What—"

Her sweater ripped in the back, and she yelped, tugging against Adam's hold, trying to get away, her instincts pushing her to fight for her life.

His jaw clenched, and he leaned towards her ear. "Stop resisting."

He wrapped an arm around her waist and pressed her body against his as her pulse sped. She gripped his dress shirt. The material was soft, and she winced at the idea of wrinkling anything of his.

She shivered as Shiriki's energy approached until he was behind her. "This is not a regular wound."

Adam glanced over her shoulder, and after a silent message between the two demons, he held her tighter against him. Shiriki's energy rolled against her in waves, lulling her into a strange sense of numbness. She tightened her grip on Adam's top, her ability to speak vanishing. Shiriki's hand pressed against her wound, and she screamed, burning pain throbbing across her body. Adam had healed her, but not only did it reopen, it was like it had never closed in the first place.

Sweat beaded on her forehead as her legs shook, the numbness vanishing, replaced instead by burning.

Before she gathered the rest of her thoughts, Adam released her as Shiriki spun her around. She backed away from him until she bumped into Adam's chest, and she winced as more pain filled her. She clenched her jaw to keep from screaming, tears rolling down her cheeks as she turned to the Viscus.

Shiriki wiped a tear from her cheek, his silver irises glowing in the cheap lights of the room, staring at her as though searching for answers. "What did it look like?"

She didn't need to ask for clarification. "Like a ghoul, but... more human and less... like a creature." Her breathing grew heavier with each passing second. As though something slithered around her lungs and squeezed them.

Shiriki glanced behind her to where Adam stood, the usual amusement in his expression fading. "Brand her."

Her heart appeared to miss several beats, and she dashed towards the bathroom, needing some sort of escape. Even if only temporary. Shiriki grabbed her by the arm and threw her across the room so she toppled onto the table, smashing it. She whimpered, unable to stand as she kneeled on the floor, trying to catch her breath.

"I won't do it." Adam's tone was final, but something in his expression held a note of fear.

Silence hung heavy in the air for what felt like an eternity. Shiriki approached Adam, the energy radiating from him enough to send a clear signal who had the upper hand.

"I do not remember asking."

Adam clenched his jaw. "You swore you'd never force me——"

"You are responsible for her protection," he hissed, taking a step closer to Adam as more power encircled him. "What do you think happens when Celina finds out her little friend here was cursed, died, and is sentenced to burn for eternity in the Inferno under your watch?"

His words jumbled inside her mind, and she tried making sense of them through the pain and fear. The only thing that seemed to stick was his mention of the Inferno. The place humans called Hell. But that didn't make sense; only people who'd made deals with demons went there. And how would being branded by Adam change any of that?

Her confusion slowly dissipated, and she got to her feet. "I... I don't understand," she said in a trembling voice.

He turned his haughty stare on her, and she flinched. "You will die before I can explain everything. There is little time left for you now."

Adam stared around as though a solution hid somewhere inside the room. "I'm certain Mekaisto can fix this——"

Shiriki grabbed Adam by the throat. "If he finds out about this, he will have you tortured for failing an order. And I will not make it pleasant for you, Adam," he hissed his name between his pointed teeth. "All I need to do is chain you to a wall and repeat history over and over again for you to watch until you wish you had chosen death all those years ago." He yanked Adam closer, so they were almost nose to nose. "And only then will I begin to truly show you the meaning of torture."

He let him go, and Adam staggered back, rubbing at his neck. Namika had never seen Adam pale before, but he looked more terrified than she felt. Adam glanced between

Namika and Shiriki, then settled on the demon, an unasked question hanging in the air.

Shiriki stayed quiet for a few seconds, then focused on Namika. "You are just about out of time."

Something in Adam's gaze seemed to shift, as though he'd made his choice and accepted the fate it came with.

"Wait." She grasped her arm as pain throbbed across. "How is branding me... going to help? I'll end up... in the Inferno either... way," she hissed through her teeth, bile burning in the pit of her stomach.

"No. Branding is not a contract for a soul," he breathed. With a quick side-glance at Shiriki, he strode towards Namika, but she stumbled back.

"Stay back." She raised her hand. "No. Please. No. No. No."

Her pulse quickened. She wanted to ask more questions, the conditions, what it would mean to be branded by him, but a choking sensation grew inside her, and she grabbed at her neck. At the first slice, she cried out, confusion taking hold of her as she stared down at her hands. The left one had turned a dark shade of gray, black veins trailing from her fingers, along her arm, and towards her wound. The claws at the end of her fingers were hooked like talons, bloodied from the inflicted cuts she'd caused along her neck.

Was it already happening? Was it too late?

She pressed her arms against her chest, her mouth open in a silent scream. Her vision darkened, and amid her panic, warmth surrounded her as someone held her close. A familiar scent.

Adam.

"Marking you will slow the curse's progress. It'll give us more time." He leaned forward, his lips brushing against her ear. "It's time to decide now, Namika. Hell or me."

"You."

As soon as the word left her mouth, a powerful energy erupted around them, and she gasped as it nearly crushed her to the floor. His free hand slid along her lower back.

"Surrender yourself," he whispered, his fingers stopping below her wound. "It'll be over soon."

And before she said anything, a burning pain seared through her clammy skin, and she passed out.

6

CONSEQUENCES

S hrieks grew louder. Closer.

Namika searched for the source, but she couldn't open her eyes. Darkness surrounded her; she sensed it even though she couldn't see it. Someone cried, pleading for help. Begging for death.

Light flickered in the distance. Stone walls. Rattling chains. Agony. She clutched at her chest, unsure if she even had a body or limbs. It hurt so much, and it wouldn't stop. She ran towards the figure, needing to help them. Something wrapped around her, keeping her from going far. Twisting along her waist, pulling her back and...

Namika screamed as she sat up, backing away with kicks until her back hit the wall. Gasping for air, she stared down at the blanket around her legs.

Her heart hammered against her ribs as she looked around; stone walls. The sound of dripping water sent shivers down her spine, but she pushed away at the fear creeping inside her.

This was definitely a dungeon, and she had the feeling it was the one beneath the CrowBar. She grabbed at the side of the cot where she'd slept, then back at the gate in front of her.

Why am I here?

Adam walked into view on the other side of the iron doors, and she froze. "Finally awake," he said, glowering at her. "If you're done sleeping what's left of your life away, I suggest you get up."

Her chest squeezed at the way he spoke to her, but before she thought of a reply, another demon appeared next to Adam.

Haku was one of the demons who often kept guard on her while she was a prisoner here. He was always playful and never seemed to take anything too seriously, but he looked angry this time.

The gate swung open, and Adam approached Namika; she stiffened to keep from backing farther into the cot. Instead, she focused on the small silver chain hanging from his vest pocket and tried imagining what it held.

"You stink of old blood and sweat. Go get cleaned up."

His words felt like a slap, and she clutched at the collar of her loose sweater again, pressing her fist into her chest to distract herself. Why did his words make her want to cry? She never cared what people thought of her before—especially not demons. Was this because of the branding?

"Haku." His voice pulled her back to reality, and she wished she could escape into her mind again.

The demon quickly stood next to Namika and bowed. "Yes, Master?"

"Take her to her room so she can wash and change her clothes," he ordered in an icy tone. "I'll meet you there shortly." And without another word, he vanished.

Silence hung heavy in the air between her and Haku, and she swallowed hard. "Have... have I been here long?"

"A day." He turned and walked away without any of his usual quips.

She pushed the blankets off of her, then slowly got to her feet, nervous that her wound would cause her pain again. Her sweater hung forward, having been torn in the back, and so she grabbed at the collar, keeping it up. Fire crackled somewhere nearby, and she swallowed hard as she left the cell. Haku leaned against a stone wall farther ahead, his bright fire-red hair contrasting against the dark stone and the feel of the place. Once he noticed her, he continued walking. She followed in silence; he was definitely mad about something, but she wasn't about to pry.

As they moved down the narrow corridors, she kept glancing at her hand, stretching her fingers out; every little shadow caused her pulse to speed, terrified it would turn ashen again. How long did she have before she was fully cursed after the branding? She had so many questions, and she was scared of getting the answer to any of them.

They finally left the dungeon area and returned to the familiar corridors Namika had gotten to know in the last few months. It somehow felt like another lifetime ago that she'd attempted her grand escape plan, and at the thought, her stomach churned.

Up ahead, Linda rounded the corner and stopped in her tracks when she laid eyes on Namika and Haku. Namika slowed her steps but froze when Linda marched towards her, eyes glowing red and jaw clenched tight.

"You," she spat. "You little bitch."

Haku placed himself in front of the demon, hands raised up. "Don't—"

"Do you have any idea what you've done?" She tried to push past him, but he grabbed her arms, doing his best to hold her back. "You're such a selfish piece of shit."

Heat rose throughout Namika, and her usual inner

calm seemed to burn away as she stared at Linda. Her blonde hair was disheveled, and her usually pristine makeup was smudged, as though she'd been...crying.

Linda shoved Haku to the side, the wall cracking as he slammed into it. She marched up to Namika, but she stood her ground, anger replacing her logic and fear. The instincts and training as a Venatore seemed to evaporate beneath her burning hatred of the demon in front of her.

"You've got nothing to say?" she bellowed. "You're responsible for this mess, you—"

"You're right," Namika said softly. "I should apologize."

Linda grabbed a fistful of Namika's hair and yanked her head back. "You think sorry is going to fix the fuckup you created?"

"No." Namika's eyes watered at the pressure on her skull. "I mean apologize because I got the better of you and escaped despite being powerless."

Linda's face contorted as she snarled. "I'm going to skin you alive, you—"

"Taking it out on me won't change the fact that partying was more important to you than the orders given to you by your master." Hatred heated from within, and for a second, Namika was tempted to lunge forward and sink her teeth into the demon's neck. Why did it look so inviting?

A force crashed down the corridor, and Namika fell to the floor under the pressure. Both demons stayed upright but leaned against the walls to keep on their feet. Adam walked into view, hands in his pockets as if he were taking a leisurely stroll. The hard lines of his jaw and flaming gaze said otherwise.

"That's enough." He didn't raise his voice, but power laced each word.

Namika got back to her feet, blinking back at her confusion; what had happened to her? She knew instigating Linda was the stupidest idea; she'd made the situation worse. And that sudden urge to bite sent an unpleasant sensation in the pit of her stomach.

Linda bowed. "Master, I—"

"I thought I'd made myself clear," his voice sliced through the air like a knife. "I want you out there, assisting in the search, and out of my sight."

Even though he wasn't addressing Namika, she felt a twinge of pain at his words. Linda approached him. "Please. I didn't mean... I—"

Haku placed his hand on her shoulder, trying to pull her back. "Linda, stop."

Linda glanced at Namika, her teeth clenched tight. "I'm worried about you. Because of her, you—"

"One more word," Adam hissed, his pupils thinning into slits, "and your stay at Shiriki's will be twice as lengthy."

The air seemed to freeze around them, and although Linda opened her mouth, as though to say something, she decided against it and vanished.

Namika stared at him, but he averted his gaze and walked away down the corridor. Why did he refuse to look at her? And more importantly, why did it hurt so much?

Namika turned off the water and stepped out of the shower; she'd used up almost all the shampoo and body soap that was left to scrub herself clean, but it still felt like some part of her was... filthy.

She angled her body and stared at her back in the long mirror. Five long claw marks ran from her shoulder to mid-back. Running her fingers along the protruding pink scars, she winced as they were still sensitive to the touch. Her hand stopped near her lower back, where she stared at the brand left behind. A drop of blood within a circle with spikes pointing inward.

Adam's mark.

The magic pulsing through it kept the curse at bay temporarily, but for how long, she had no idea.

She glanced away and moved to the closet within the bathroom, pushing at the clothes on the hangers, needing to find something to wear. Nothing seemed right. She felt too exposed after everything that had happened. The vampire's face flashed in her mind as he watched the creature kill Emma. Her lifeless body staring at nothing as she lay on the pavement, discarded like she didn't matter. What happened to her body?

Namika shut her eyes tight, trying to get the image out of her head. Did Emma die because Namika had insisted they leave without the artifact she was supposed to bring him?

A black turtleneck caught her attention, and she grabbed the top, then slipped it on. It didn't have sleeves, but at least it covered her neck.

The vampire's mocking voice resonated over and over, and she scrubbed her hand over her face. She quickly pulled it back, staring at her arm like it might suddenly turn against her. If she hadn't escaped with Emma, none of this would've happened. Emma would likely still be alive, and Namika would be reading in her bed after cursing out Linda for making her wear such a revealing Halloween costume. Because of Namika's choice, she had nearly died—and with a one-way ticket to Hell. She recalled reading details in a book at the Venatore's headquarters about the Inferno, and a shiver ran down her spine at the memory.

She pulled on a pair of jeans and grabbed a sweater from the pile of clothes discarded on a chair. Adam was right; it was a prison here, but it was a beautiful one that she'd thrown away. Nothing had gone right, and she'd made a mess of everything.

With a sigh, she walked out of the bathroom, pulling her hair up in a messy bun. She still had hundreds of questions, but her most crucial one was whether she was heading to the Inferno any time soon.

Hushed voices caught her attention, and she swallowed hard when she recognized the language: *demos*. Every word slithered into her mind and body as though trying to creep inside permanently, trying to find access to her soul. Demons were such vile creatures that even their language corrupted.

She stepped out into the living space. Adam and Haku stopped mid-conversation, both looking away from her. Another wave of pain shot through her, but it wasn't from the wound anymore.

Adam jutted out his chin towards the door, and Haku left, giving a last glare to Namika before leaving without a word to her.

"I'm not used to him being so serious," Namika said quietly. "He's usually always making jokes. I guess he must be really mad at me."

Adam adjusted the cufflinks on his dress shirt. "We're leaving. Shiriki has some questions for you."

Her stomach churned at the thought of being interrogated by the demon king's second in command, but Adam's dismissal annoyed her more than anything.

"I guess you're mad at me, too." She tried keeping her tone neutral, but frustration laced every word.

He looked at her, and part of her suddenly wished he'd kept ignoring her instead; his irises flashed red. "Try furious."

"I never planned on being attacked by that... thing. That wasn't part of the plan——"

"You took a risk, and others paid the price," he growled, his pointed teeth clenched tight.

She tightened her grip on her arms to keep her focus. "Don't act like this wasn't your fault, too. You're the one who kept me prisoner in the first place."

"You shouldn't have run away." Energy rippled from him as he advanced a few steps closer to her.

She pointed at him, burning anger coursing through her. "You practically dared me to try. Remember? *Make each attempt count.*"

His eyes turned back to the brown she'd gotten used to seeing, but fire still seemed to dance behind his intense gaze. "I suppose the one good thing that came of it is that there's one less Venatore the king will have to destroy."

She gaped at him, her hands dropping to her sides. Tears blurred her vision, the memory of Emma's lifeless body again floating in her mind. She quickly averted her gaze, blinking fast to keep the tears from falling. His cruelty was yet another reminder of what he was.

"One less demon, too," she said, her voice cracking at the memory of how Emma had destroyed Marc.

The satisfaction she felt only lasted a few seconds. Adam appeared before her, and she jumped back, but he grabbed the back of her neck, holding her still.

"Your little friend died because of you," he breathed, and although he wasn't in his demon form anymore, the power seeping from him surrounded her in darkness. "How many is that for you now? Your father, your boyfriend, and the members of that cult you called a family... gone." His grip on her neck tightened, and she winced. "And all I'm hearing is how *you* didn't have a choice. How *you* were kept in a prison and had to escape." He leaned in closer. "You really are alone now, and it's because you're selfish."

He let her go, and she staggered back, rubbing the back of her neck. Tears rolled down her cheeks, and she didn't bother wiping them away; it was what he wanted. To make her feel horrible, make her cry.

Guilt weighed heavily inside, nauseated by her thoughts. He was right. But she was also right about him. They were on opposite ends of an everlasting war, demons and hunters. Predator and prey.

She let out a small laugh, and he arched an eyebrow. "Well, not completely alone. I still have that brand you marked me with, so I suppose you're stuck with me."

7

ASHES TO ASHES

*N*amika gawked as a limo pulled up in front of the CrowBar. It looked so out of place in this area. They'd remodeled the inside of the club, but the outer architecture had remained in the same style as the rest of the old buildings in the Byward Market.

The surroundings looked so different in daylight; early morning, the streets were bustling with people setting up their stalls for the farmers' market along the small streets. A few places allowed vehicles, but most were for pedestrians.

The chauffeur opened the door, and Namika slid inside, relieved to get away from the frosty temperature. It was roomier than she thought, but she still sat as close as possible to the opposing door.

Adam sat at the other end, looking like the limo didn't match the level of luxury he exuded. She glanced down at herself with a frown; she felt so frumpy in comparison.

The vehicle moved forward, and she glanced towards Adam. He scrolled on his smartphone, occasionally typing something. The words from their fight lingered in her mind. Finally, she'd had enough of the silent treatment.

"What *does* it mean to have your brand?"

For a second, she wasn't sure if she'd actually spoken or if he hadn't heard her. Slowly, he slipped his phone into the front pocket of his jacket and turned his attention to her.

"It's different for each person, and for each time," he said in a low voice, as though talking about the subject might cause disastrous effects.

She recalled how she'd felt hurt when he'd ignored and dismissed her after she'd woken up in the dungeon. "Can... can it do anything to... manipulate emotions or something?"

"Why do you ask?" Something in his tone caused her to look up at him; he suddenly looked... hungry.

She shook her head, wishing her cheeks didn't burn. "Just wondering, since you're not really giving any examples."

The limo turned, and she dug her feet into the floor, scared she'd fall on him. Her heartbeat quickened at the thought, and she gritted her teeth. What was wrong with her? It had to be the brand making her feel crazy like this.

The vehicle slowed, and Namika glanced out of the window as they pulled up next to a building. A seven-story high-rise loomed over the street, a strange energy emitting from the place. The driver opened the door on her side, and she swallowed hard, stepping out. Was this really where Shiriki lived?

It explains why it feels unsettling even from the outside.

Adam joined her on the sidewalk and glanced up at the building before turning his attention forward. Without a word, he marched forward, and she followed quickly, trying to keep up with his long strides.

Security guards each opened a door, bowing their heads as Namika and Adam walked past. Namika froze, taking in a deep breath to keep from drowning in the energy pressing against her. She allowed her magic to heighten her senses, but immediately slammed it shut when whispers echoed around.

Victorian-style decoration seemed too proper for a monster——she had expected a medieval dungeon or an abandoned insane asylum. The red and blue colors clashed together, contrasting against the dark wooden furniture. A grandfather clock ticked nearby, each second syncing with her pulse.

A woman limped into the lobby, and Namika frowned. She was human and looked frail. What was she doing in a place like this?

"Hilda." Adam stepped forward and smiled. "You're still here?"

She raised her head higher. "And what is that supposed to mean?"

Namika's eyebrows shot up, but she kept quiet.

Adam chuckled. "Last I'd heard, Shiriki was forced to release you from your contract."

"He did," she said with a nod, gray hair falling from her bun in wisps. "But I've lived here for so long. I don't see the point in finishing my days in some retirement home. This is the place I always knew I'd die, and it's here I'll stay."

Namika took a step forward. "Aren't you scared of dying here with him?"

Hilda's gaze swept along Namika, and a smile curled her lips, bringing a renewed fire to her eyes. "Oh no. If anything, he's the one who's scared."

Namika had no idea what that demon could be afraid

of, but she didn't ask. Hilda pointed a shaky hand towards the staircase. "He's on the fourth floor."

Adam gave the woman a curt nod before starting up the stairs. Namika's stomach roiled with unease at the thought of going up where the Viscus demon waited, but she had the feeling he had some of the answers she wanted.

But at what price?

They reached the fourth floor, and she eyed the long corridor ahead with trepidation. Shadows danced along the walls, vanishing in and out of existence as the low lights flickered above.

Adam glanced over his shoulder at her. "If you don't come willingly, you'll be dragged in."

Namika curled her hands into fists and marched forward. Despite how heavy her legs felt, she pushed on, every step closer to the door at the end of the hallway more painful.

The door swung open, and she flinched back, expecting Shiriki to suddenly pounce out. But no one waited for them at the opening. Not that it made her feel any better; the sounds coming from inside were less than inviting.

She didn't wait for Adam to threaten her again and stepped inside first; she wanted to show him she wasn't always too scared to act. The occasional hissing from machinery kept her on edge, and she slowed her steps, unsure where to go.

Ticking and spinning sounds echoed throughout the room, but a separator stood to one side, hiding most of the place beyond where they stood. She rubbed her arms at the occasional sound of creaking footsteps, not taking her eyes off where they were coming from.

Shiriki walked around the separator, blood dribbling

down his chin, and Namika backed away at the sight. She froze when Adam's hand settled on her lower back, more surprised at her reaction to his touch. Why did it feel comforting?

It has to be the brand.

The Viscus demon smiled as he wiped away at the red liquid. "You arrived faster than I anticipated." He licked at his bloodstained fingers and motioned for them to follow.

A hole in the wall appeared as he approached, and he stepped inside, darkness swallowing him. Namika glanced up at Adam, her pulse speeding so fast, black spots edged along her vision.

His gaze softened as he stared at her, but he glanced away and gave her a little push. She was terrified of going up ahead, but she recalled what the Venatores had taught her; if she acted first, she could better prepare for whatever waited on the other side.

Approaching the hole in the brick wall, she eyed the edges as dust fell to the floor. She couldn't see inside the room as it was pitch black, and she wondered if it wasn't a one-way ticket to an endless void. Although she doubted Adam would let her die after going through the trouble of branding her. The consequence of her dying seemed as grave for him as for herself.

She crossed the threshold and blinked several times, trying to make sense of her surroundings. The room was familiar, but she couldn't place where she'd seen it. She reminded herself it was probably her imagination since she'd never been here before.

Shiriki moved from a corner of the room, and she jumped; she hadn't even noticed him. He took a seat at the large wooden table. "I tracked down a small group of ex-Venatores from your dead friend's corpse."

Bile rose in the back of her throat as she imagined

Shiriki near Emma. She gripped the back of a chair. "What did you do? You didn't... You better not have touched her," she said louder than she expected.

Shiriki arched an eyebrow, but his smile didn't vanish. "Tell me. Are you usually this aggressive, or did you wake with this anger coursing through your veins?"

She frowned, then looked at Adam. "Was that... why I was in a cell when I woke up?"

"We don't know what the effects of the curse are. Usually, a person will turn or die within an hour or so. I didn't want to risk you being a danger to others." Adam pulled a chair and motioned for her to sit.

She ignored his obvious signal to sit and turned her attention back to Shiriki. "You mentioned you found a small group. What did you do? Are they okay?"

He cocked his head. "They are dead."

A mixture of panic and hatred sent heat through her body. Adam grabbed her arm, keeping her still. "Is there any reason you chose to share irrelevant information just to get her worked up?" he asked in an annoyed tone.

"I want her to confirm some information for me." He laced his fingers together, the pointed claws on the ends reflecting the ceiling light above. "You see, the other ex-Venatores I located also regained magic thanks to a mysterious vampire." He sounded amused, but something in his icy gaze told her he wasn't pleased with the situation.

Emma hadn't mentioned how many others had gotten power again, but with the way they were dispersed and most having gone into hiding, she guessed there weren't many. And Shiriki had murdered them.

She slumped down on the chair Adam had pulled out for her. Adam took a seat next to her and shot a stony look towards Shiriki. "I imagine you haven't told the king about them yet, since that would mean mentioning what happened to Miss Strang."

"Indeed." He drummed his fingernails against the table. "The magic they had was not something of ours. It is not from nightshades, and since vampires do not possess natural powers, it is not from this mystery leader of theirs, either."

They continued speaking, but Namika's mind was elsewhere, stuck on the vampire who'd killed Emma and tried to get rid of Namika as well. This "Rickie" hadn't returned to the other members and disposed of them; did they know Emma was dead and how he was responsible? And the curse. How long did she have until she'd burn for eternity?

The door opened, and the woman who'd greeted them in the lobby stepped inside carrying a tray. "Apologies for the intrusion," she said with a small bow.

"What is it, Hilda?" Shiriki asked in an amused tone, as though curious why she was here.

"I brought refreshments for the young lady." She motioned to Namika with a gentle smile.

Namika's eyebrows shot up at the sudden kindness in a place like this, but she smiled back. Hilda placed the wooden tray in front of Namika, and her mouth watered at the sight of food.

"Thank you," Namika said as she scooted closer to the table, her stomach growling. It was as though her body had suddenly realized it was starving because it had noticed something to eat.

Hilda clasped her hands together. "I'm afraid the pantry is a bit bare since we haven't had any visitors who require sustenance for some time." She narrowed her eyes at Shiriki. "If someone had told me ahead of time, I would've ensured we had provisions."

Namika wondered who this woman really was; she

didn't seem scared of Shiriki, so she was either extremely powerful or wasn't quite right in the head.

Or maybe not everyone is terrified of everything like you.

Shiriki shrugged. "The events of last night were short notice for all of us."

Namika stared at the spread in front of her; if this resulted from a bare pantry, she couldn't imagine what it looked like when it was full. There were a multitude of bowls with nuts, crackers, and pretzels, and on a few plates lay a variety of cheeses. A glass of water with a lemon floating inside sat in the corner, and she tried remembering the last time she'd eaten or drunk anything.

"This is...amazing." She beamed up at Hilda. "Thank you so much."

Hilda gave her a small pat on the shoulder and left the room.

Namika grabbed a pretzel and put it in her mouth; it was salty, and she exhaled as she chewed. The texture transformed, and her mouth burned with the taste of something thick and dry. She spat it out, her hand covered in sticky remnants of the black substance. She got to her feet, nearly stumbling, but Adam caught her before she fell back.

"What's... happening?" she asked through bits of food still lingering in her mouth.

She ran her fingers across her tongue, trying to figure out what was going on, and she gagged at what looked like... ashes.

She stared inside the bowl, but didn't see any sign that it had tainted food.

Adam frowned as he picked up another pretzel and sniffed it before licking the surface. "It wasn't tampered with."

"Of course not," Shiriki said with a grin. "It is part of the curse's progress."

He dropped the food back into the bowl and glowered at the Viscus.

She placed her hand over her mouth, desperate not to throw up.

"Is there... a washroom?" she asked in a small voice.

Adam led her away, and she barely paid attention to where they were going as sweat covered her. She just needed to focus on not puking everywhere.

He opened the door to what looked like a large utility room, then leaned against the wall, waiting.

"I can't... I can't relax knowing you're standing out here," she said, trying to catch her breath; it felt like she'd run a marathon.

He crossed his arms. "Pretend I'm not here."

"Where would I run to in this place?" She motioned at her surroundings. "Besides, I have questions, and I'm not leaving until at least *some* of them are answered."

For a few seconds, it seemed like he wouldn't budge, but then he straightened and gave her a curt nod before walking away.

8

INFORMATION

*N*amika was sure she'd set a world record for needing to wipe away bodily fluids from herself in such a short amount of time.

She scrubbed more than once at the sink, and only once her hands were cleaned did she do it again. Her stomach felt emptier than ever, and she hoped she could finally stop heaving.

She cursed Shiriki; he wasn't surprised when her food turned to ashes when she ate it. Had this been some sort of test? She wouldn't put it past him with how cold and calculating he was. The way he'd tracked down the other Venatores using Emma's dead body.

Tears filled her eyes at the thought of the other members of her group. If Namika hadn't run away, would they still be alive? Once again, people had died because of her. Adam's words repeated in her head. Because of her selfishness.

She stared around the small utility room, trying to distract herself. A large sink stood near a water heater, and on the other side of the wall, a box hung with a warning sign on it. Two electric meters slowly turned behind the glass. A small smile tugged at the corner of her mouth as she imagined someone from Hydro Ottawa coming in here to check the meters.

I'm losing it.

A noise outside the room caught her attention, and she left, deciding she'd stalled long enough. As she stepped back into the room, her focus fell on rows of filing cabinets. Her breathing came faster as she realized why she recognized the room they were in. It was the strange one that she was unsettled by in the storage room beneath the CrowBar.

How was it here?

The abandoned spiderwebs hung thick from the ceiling, the same name tags she'd seen on the drawers calling to her. Some names she recognized, but it was seeing her own name that unsettled her the most.

She frowned as she glanced around the room; she was alone; both demons were nowhere to be seen. Although, if they didn't want to be seen, that was an easy trick for any demon to accomplish.

She allowed her magic to move across the room, but when she couldn't find anything dangerous, she closed herself back up and darted to the cabinets. Pulling the drawer open, her shoulders tensed as she grabbed the folder inside. Had this been the one Adam had read in front of her? Her whole life was in those few pages. She grabbed it and flipped it open, her pulse speeding.

It wasn't all there, no.

Father dead, but not how or why. Mother estranged, but no reasons behind her choice. No siblings, and the friends she had were gone. Celina was the only person left, and she lived in the dark realm with her husband and son.

They stapled a picture of Yasuo to a paper with information about his death. She skimmed it, and her chest squeezed. Her boyfriend wasn't killed during the attack on demons. Adam had lied. They'd captured Yasuo and tortured him to find out where the Venatore headquarter was. He killed himself during the interrogation. They'd driven him to death, so he could protect their group.

Tears rolled down as she stared at her boyfriend. "I'm sorry," she whispered, tracing her finger along his face.

They'd known one another for so many years. She couldn't even remember a time when he wasn't in her life. Yet the last time they'd spoken was a blur. What were her last words to him? What were his to her? She knew their lives were always in danger and that death could separate them at any second, but another part of her believed he'd always be there. At one point, she forgot to make every memory of him count and appreciate the time they had together.

He was gone.

She'd known that for a while, but it hadn't sunk in. Not really. Imagining him dying in battle amongst so many others felt more like a casualty of war instead of each individual person she'd lost that day.

She swallowed against the tightness in her throat. Why had Adam lied about how he died? Had he given the order to torture Yasuo? Her group had done the same to demons and vampires countless times.

A hand grabbed her wrist, and she gasped as she dropped the folder, the pages and photos inside scattering across the floor.

Shiriki's vertical pupils thinned as he pulled her closer. "Tell me," he grasped her face, the sharp fingernail of his thumb resting below her eye. "Did you read anything captivating?"

She trembled, but stayed quiet; nothing she said would help her in this situation. He glanced down at the floor before looking back at her. "Lucky you found your own file. If it had been someone else's..." He left the rest of the sentence unsaid, but she knew what he meant in that silence.

Lucky? My name is written right there...

Her eyes darted back to the cabinets, and she cursed herself inwardly; the names weren't written in the Roman alphabet. They were in arcane runes. A language her grandmother had taught her to read, thanks to her natural magic. As far as everyone knew, she wasn't supposed to have any powers after the war. Had he realized it wasn't a coincidence she'd found her own file, or would he leave it at that?

He pressed the tip of his fingernail harder, and she winced as his icy glare seemed to look straight into her mind. "You are even more interesting than I thought," he hissed.

He dragged her two steps and stopped. She looked up through tears at Adam, standing near the doorway.

"You understand that, now that I've branded her, she is mine." He took a few steps closer, sliding his hands into his pants pockets. "I don't share."

Her heart raced, but she was never so relieved to be called his.

As soon as Shiriki released her, she dashed to Adam, stopping a few inches away. She craned her neck and swallowed hard at his glower. Still, she preferred whatever Adam would do to the Viscus behind her.

"I understand this is your first pet," Shiriki said, motioning his hand dismissively, "but I suggest you train her so you can avoid future problems."

She opened and closed her mouth at being called a pet, but clenched her jaw tight, knowing she was already in enough trouble. This was on her, and she was sure Adam wouldn't let it slide without consequences.

Shiriki gave Adam a wink before walking back into the room where they'd been sitting, leaving Namika alone with Adam once again.

"Let's be clear, Miss Strang. Strike one, I'm lenient. Anything after, and my mercy vanishes." His tone darkened. "Do you understand?"

She swallowed hard. "Yes. I'm sorry. It won't happen again."

"I'm pleased to hear."

"AS YOU ARE AWARE, you are still cursed." Shriki's words repeated inside Namika's mind over and over.

She already knew the curse wasn't broken, but to hear it out loud made it too real.

Her grip on the edge of the table tightened. "How do I break it?"

Shiriki chuckled. "I am touched you think I have knowledge of everything. My interests do not lie with curses... especially not the ones that fall beyond powers I do not trifle with."

She arched an eyebrow, glancing from Adam to Shiriki. "What do you mean?"

"Ghouls fall under the realm of reapers, and therefore, the gods," Adam said, leaning his elbows against the table.

Reapers.

She was familiar with the race. They were, after all, the two sides of the same coin. The only ones who would know what she was if they looked into her soul.

They'd know she was a mystic.

Namika's pulse grew erratic; she had to calm down, or even her cloaking spell wouldn't hide her emotions. Focusing, she followed the techniques her grandmother had taught her. A tiny amount of magic cooled the tip of her fingers, and she placed her hand against her chest, concealing her pulse. It was easy enough to seem like she was just worried, but Shiriki gave her a curious look.

"You do not seem surprised to hear about reapers or gods. I was not aware Venatores were taught about them."

"A few of us were," she mumbled, not explaining further. "So, I need to find a reaper to tell me what the curse is, and hopefully, they can also explain how to break it?" She really hoped changing the subject would keep Shiriki from asking for more information.

Adam frowned. "Not just you, Miss Strang. You'll need help, since reapers are not a pleasant bunch to deal with."

"As opposed to demons?" The words left her mouth before she thought them through.

"Just different."

Her shoulders relaxed at not being told off, and she reminded herself to think before she spoke. "But the creature that attacked me wasn't a ghoul. Are you sure it also falls under their realm?"

Adam nodded. "During the ordeal with your little group, the Inferno was infiltrated. Obviously, someone took advantage of the distraction. A few souls escaped into the human world." His phone buzzed, and he took it out, staring at the screen. Scrolling on the device, he continued, "Reapers created ghouls for their armies using lost souls. An exchange Mekaisto allowed a long time ago, on the condition that those souls were returned afterward."

"The creature that attacked me...that cursed me is a

lost soul?" she repeated, then turned to Shiriki. "I thought you said you didn't know what the curse was."

"Did I?" Shiriki leaned back in his seat. "I said I do not know how to break it."

She muttered about demons being too cryptic, but neither of them commented. "Okay, so how does it work? How long do I have? Will I turn into one of those things, or will I just die?" The questions came pouring out of her without stopping to take a single breath, and by the time she fell silent, she was nearly hyperventilating.

Adam let out an annoyed sigh. "I see why you and Celina are friends. You both ask an unnecessary number of questions."

She wanted to snap back that it was normal she'd have so many questions when her life and soul were on the line, but she kept quiet.

Shiriki got up and moved towards a painting of a decapitated man hanging on the wall, his back turned to them. "The curse can cause one of two things. One, it turns you into a ghoul. However, I do not think that is the case since it usually happens within minutes, and by the time Adam located you, you were still whole."

"And the second thing?" she asked in a trembling voice.

"If it was a planned attack on you specifically, and the lost soul is related to you by blood, then the curse is draining your life force and transferring it to the one who attacked you. If not stopped, the lost soul will turn human while you take its place."

Panic filled her mind in a whirlwind. "Emma... my friend said the vampire knew I was alive and where I was. He knew my name."

"You didn't know who this vampire was or what he wanted with you, but the promise of power was enough to make you follow your accomplice blindly?" Adam's tone grew darker, his irises flashing red for a split second.

She bolted to her feet. "I followed a friend I've known for years to get my freedom back."

"And where did that get you?" He stood, towering over her. "More dead friends, cursed... was it worth acting so immaturely?"

The lump in her throat threatened to choke her, but she didn't back down. "Stop treating me like I'm a child."

"If you act like one, I'll treat you as such."

"So how should I treat you since you're acting like a jerk?" she snapped.

The table flew across the floor with a screeching sound as Adam blasted energy. She gasped, falling back onto the chair as he leaned forward, both hands on the armrests.

"You created the mess we're both in. And it's because you act before you think." His eyes glowed redder with each word. "I've branded you. This now gives me certain privileges, so don't test me."

She gulped forcefully, attempting to get her throat to function. "What does that mean?"

"It means tread carefully with me, Miss Strang." He took a few steps back, then straightened his tie.

Her hands curled into fists, but she stayed sitting. More than anything, she wanted to fight it out with him, but with the way he continued staring at her, she didn't dare.

She hated being so afraid.

Shiriki lifted his hand in front of him, and the table moved back to its proper place. "The transformation into a lost soul is delayed because of the brand, but you are, nonetheless, still turning." He smiled at Adam. "Certain actions will accelerate the process, such as consuming *human* flesh specifically. I suggest you find other ways to keep her sated."

Her cheeks heated at the way he'd said that, and she wished she could disappear.

Adam made his way towards the door, and Namika got up, unsure if she should follow; not that she wanted to stay alone with Shiriki.

"Thank you for your assistance with this," he said to Shiriki with a bow. "We'll be taking our leave." He stared towards Namika, and she quickly joined him.

Shiriki clasped his hands behind his back. "Keep me informed, or I will come looking for you."

Namika and Adam left the room and started down the stairs.

"I know of one reaper who's in the business world here. He'll be our best chance for answers."

She glanced at the hand that had turned ashen. "What's the plan, then?"

"Last I heard, he mostly does business in Toronto. We'll head to my office there to try scheduling a meeting. God knows it won't be easy since it's no secret our two races don't get along."

She frowned. "You have an office in Toronto?"

"One in each major city across Canada, the United States, and the United Kingdom." He grinned when she gawked at him. "And nightclubs throughout those countries."

Suddenly, his wealth made more sense; Adam looked like the richest businessman to walk the earth. Everything from his combed hair to the expensive accessories he wore brought attention to his class in a sophisticated way.

He opened the door for her, and she stepped outside, back into the cool air of the end of fall. She'd never been so happy to leave a place, and vowed she'd avoid anywhere Shiriki was for the foreseeable future.

They waited in silence for the limo, and she glanced back towards the building behind them.

"That meeting could've been an email," she muttered.

He burst out laughing, and a strange feeling fluttered inside her chest as she grinned at him; she'd never seen him smile like that before.

9

FIRST CLASS HELL

Namika hovered in the aisle, clutching her ticket with sweaty hands. They built the seats like small sofas, giving each person their own seat, but with no actual separation. Some were individual, and for the life of her, she couldn't figure out why he'd picked one they had to share.

She glanced at the ticket and frowned. "I don't want to be next to the window." She didn't mind the window seat, but it would mean being boxed in between the wall and Adam.

"And I will not stand here and argue." He leaned towards her ear. "Sit. Down." He bit out both words as energy pressed against her.

She rushed into the compartment and sat, pressing herself against the wall as she focused on the screen in front of her. Adam loomed over her as he stepped inside.

Her hands shook as she looked at the ticket. He sat next to her, and she glanced at him. His elbow leaned against the small table on his side, giving her more room, but she didn't budge.

"You smell of so much fear. It's overwhelming," he hissed, his eyes turning red. "You need to calm down."

Her grip on the ticket tightened. "Easier said than done. I can't just turn off my emotions like you."

A Steward waved his hands for attention and began going over the safety instructions, but Namika only half-listened. This would be a long trip, even if it was only an hour.

Her hands clutched at the cushioned seat, digging her fingers into the soft material. Adam arched an eyebrow as the scenery flew by the window.

"Are you scared of flying?"

"No," she said, shaking her head.

"You're lying."

"I know."

She pushed her head against the chair, gritting her teeth as memories flashed through her mind. Sitting next to her father and asking where they were going. She'd been so young and excited about taking the plane like a big girl. But the rest was foggy. It was the following plane trip that was the worst. She'd sat next to a social worker, crying. And no matter how much she sobbed, no one would explain why she had to go live with her estranged mother. Her family had been murdered, and she was left with more questions than answers. Questions her mother refused to answer, and always got defensive about when brought up.

"So tell me, when you're not hunting down and killing my kind, what do you enjoy doing?" he asked, sounding almost bored, like he didn't actually care.

She frowned at him, trying to think of a snappy come-back, but nothing came to mind, so she just told him the truth. "I like to garden... take care of plants."

"Is that right?" He slid his hand along the seat's headrest, leaning so close he caught her between his body and the wall of the plane.

"What are you doing?" she hissed, pressing into the cabin interior of the plane so hard, her muscles throbbed.

He arched an eyebrow at her and grinned. "Afraid I'll bite?"

"It's not like you don't," she snapped back, placing her hands against his chest as he moved closer.

The plane lurched forward.

Her heart seemed to skip a couple of beats as his gaze pierced through her. "You never told me why you have a tattoo of a buttercup on your shoulder."

The tension between them sparked as though there was electricity in the air. "I guess I'm lucky it was the other shoulder that was maimed or I'd have to get it remade."

"Lucky, indeed." He grinned. "Tell me why you have that tattoo."

"No."

"I'm not asking."

She frowned. "You can't make me if I don't want to." Why was he acting like this?

The plane picked up speed and tilted, getting it in the air. Her breath quickened as it straightened, and soon enough, her stomach stopped lurching. Minutes passed in silence as the plane reached altitude.

He retreated into his seat and took out his smartphone.

She gawked at him. "You... were distracting me."

His eyes held a twinkle of mischief. "I don't know what you're talking about."

A ding sounded, advising the passengers they could unbuckle their seatbelts.

She swallowed hard a few times, willing her ears to pop. "Well... thanks."

"I didn't want you causing a scene and getting us

kicked off the plane," he said, with a hint of iciness in his tone. "There's no way I'd travel six hours by car like some sort of *peasant*," he finished with a grin.

Her chest squeezed at his words, but she narrowed her eyes at him. "I'm going to the washroom." She needed space away from him to gather her thoughts.

He gave a curt nod, and she strode past him. The flight attendant walked to Namika, smiling ear to ear. "Is there anything I can assist you with?"

"Just going to use the washroom," Namika said, glancing over the woman's shoulder towards the sign marking the place.

"Let us know if there's anything you need."

Namika locked the door behind her, and the light switched on automatically. From the second she'd stepped inside, she knew it was bigger than the usual closet-sized washrooms, but this was ridiculous. It was built to be narrow, but lengthy; a toilet stood at the far end with a built-in table on the side where magazines were left for people to read. A small puff caused Namika to jump, but when she spotted the automatic spray of perfume, she burst into a giggle.

"I'm such an idiot."

For a few seconds, she'd actually thought Adam had distracted her because he cared. After finding out Celina was half demon turned full, she'd put it in her mind that maybe they weren't pure evil, but none were actually good. Although she'd had no issues with leaving Namika at the CrowBar and never checking back on her.

Maybe Namika couldn't trust anyone after all.

After she used the toilet, she washed her hands, staring at herself in the mirror, lost in thought. Something sliced at her palm, and she gasped, looking down into the sink. Her hand had turned ashen again, the hooked claws black and horrifying; it looked like her arm belonged to a monster.

"No, no, no," she muttered, stretching the twisted limb out as far as she could in front of her.

Cracks splintered the glass, and an uncontrollable shudder swept through her body as she followed the breaks, her face twisting into different pieces. The left side paled, black veins snaking beneath her flesh. One eye went fully black, and a cry left her lips.

The door opened, and she jumped, backing away as Adam stepped inside. He frowned as he stared from her arm to her face, his expression unreadable. She wanted to beg for help, but her throat didn't work.

Heat burned her skin, and she screamed, trying to get away, but there was no escape. A red vine crashed through the wall and impaled her chest, sending debris everywhere, and she raised her arms, trying to protect her face from the agony. Flames melted her flesh, and her heart seemed to have stopped from the shock. But she was still alive, and the pain didn't stop.

She sobbed as her skin and muscles turned to liquid, dropping to the ground. The smell and sounds of sizzling meat caused her stomach to heave. Why wouldn't she die? Her bones turned to ashes, dissipating away while she sobbed. People screamed and shrieked, an endless torment as her body shattered.

"Namika!"

Adam cupped her face between his hands, and she tried to move, to push him away; he'd burn too if he touched her.

Her surroundings flashed, and she blinked several times.

The washroom.

The airplane.

It wasn't destroyed.

Adam held her arms, staring at her with concern etched in his features. A few employees muttered to one another but didn't seem ready to intervene yet.

She remembered how she'd looked a few seconds ago, and quickly pushed her body against Adam, trying to shield herself from view. How would they explain this to them? They'd think she was infected with something terrible. And then what? Would they quarantine her? Send her to get tested somewhere as time ticked away on the curse.

Her body trembled as she pressed her hand against her chest. Her heart was still beating. What the hell had happened?

Adam tried to pull her away, but she gripped his jacket tighter, shaking her head.

"Sir," a woman's voice broke through the urgent whispers surrounding them, "you need to let us handle this——"

"She suffers from an anxiety disorder, but it's passed now." He rubbed her back, and she closed her eyes, letting Adam's energy wrap around her. It was comforting.

"Should we call for a doctor once we land?" the woman asked, not sounding too convinced about the situation.

"No, but thank you for the concern. She'll be fine." He grasped her arms, helping Namika to her feet. "I'll need anti-nausea medication, ginger ale, a blanket, and a cold washcloth."

"But——"

Someone else cut the woman off, and Namika caught something along the lines of Mr. Ashton being a VIP and not to be bothered.

He stood, bringing Namika up with him, and pulled her away enough to look at her.

"My... my face is..."

"It's back to normal. I promise." He slid his finger along her arm, and she realized it had gone back to normal again.

Adam walked them to their compartment, and Namika stared at the aisle floor as a few passengers shot them dirty stares.

The woman who'd asked Namika if she needed help stopped near them, holding the requested items in her hands. Adam got to his feet, grabbed the blanket, and covered Namika with it. A sudden lightness filled her at the warmth, her muscles relaxing as she stopped trembling so hard.

He held a lime-green pill and a glass filled with the ginger ale he'd requested. "Take this."

She shook her head, pushing out a shaky hand to push him away. "It'll turn to ash." Her voice cracked at how much she'd screamed.

He looked like he wanted to argue, so she grabbed the cold washcloth and placed it against her forehead.

"What... what happened? Why...?" She stopped, lost for words about how to explain what she'd gone through when she herself didn't know.

The intensity in his gaze rooted her to the spot. "Describe it to me."

She froze, her mind flashing to what had to have been a nightmare. It obviously wasn't real since the place was intact and she was still alive. But it had felt so real.

Her mouth went dry, and she swallowed a few times. "I don't know. One second, I was washing my hands and the next..."

He took the washcloth from her and pushed a few strands of her hair from her forehead. "And?"

She sighed but told him everything. How she was being burned alive. The red vine.

"Was that... it was because of the curse, wasn't it?" she asked.

"You're losing your life force a bit more as time passes. It leaves you open and vulnerable," he breathed.

She lifted the blanket higher, trying to shield herself from her surroundings. From everything.

"So what I saw was... the Inferno. What it's like to..." She left the rest unsaid, already knowing she'd guessed right by the way he looked at her. She frowned. "Wait. You came in before... how did you know I was in trouble?"

He hung the washcloth along the small table in front of him. "I felt your pain and terror before you started screaming." His gaze darted towards her seat. "You asked me before what my mark did exactly. One thing's for sure," he looked at her, his pupils turning red, "it's allowing us to feel one another's emotions when they're heightened.

"Oh." The idea of him knowing how she felt sent her pulse racing. She tried recalling the last few times she'd sensed a wave of emotion that didn't quite feel like her own, but gave up as her mind didn't cooperate; the nightmare of the Inferno had exhausted her mentally more than she'd realized.

10

PERSONAL

amika craned her neck to stare at the skyscraper. The tinted glass reflected its surroundings in eerie darkness, making it look like a glimpse into another world. She swallowed hard at the golden numbers and letters at the front, announcing the company.

Ashton Real Estate.

Adam placed his hand on her back, and goosebumps ran along her skin despite the coat he'd given her when a private car picked them up at the airport.

He led her to the doors and opened one, so she stepped inside. They waited for one of the many elevators to ding open. Adam pushed on the number sixty-five, the top number, and Namika's heart lurched into her throat as the metal box rose.

This had to be the tallest building she'd ever been in.

The dark wooden walls and golden ramp gave a cozy feel to the sizeable space, but she couldn't relax. Each second since they'd gotten off the plane was an emotional rollercoaster. Part of her still felt trapped in the Inferno, drowning in agony. Not knowing when that kind of vision could happen again kept her on edge.

The elevator halted on the top floor, and they strode out.

The woman at the reception desk fumbled with her phone when she noticed Adam. Her device fell onto the surface with a loud clang, and she quickly got to her feet, pink staining her cheeks.

"Mr. Ashton." She grabbed a notebook and flipped through the pages. "Your next appointment here isn't until next week——"

"I'm in town for business." He rested an elbow against the elevated side of the desk. "Call every client I have scheduled for the next... three weeks, and have them reschedule for today or tomorrow. If they can't make it, cancel and let them know we'll reschedule next month."

Her mouth hung open, and she glanced from her boss to the calendar. "But sir, you have a dozen clients. We can't fit them all within two days, and on such short notice."

"Then they'll wait until next month." Adam's tone held indifference, but he smiled. "If any of them give you a hard time about this, transfer them to me, and I'll deal with their issues."

At his words, her shoulders relaxed a bit, and she nodded. "Thank you, sir."

"I'll remain in the penthouse suite for the next few days. You can reach me there or on my cellphone." He motioned over his shoulder as he took his phone out. "This is my guest, Miss Namika Strang. She'll stay here with me for the duration of my stay."

The woman pursed her lips as she stared Namika up and down, as though resenting that she was forced to acknowledge her presence. "A pleasure to meet you."

Adam typed something on the screen, then slid the

device back into his pocket. "This is Cindy Beaton, my administrative assistant."

Namika did her best not to glare at the woman, but she didn't make it easy; she really hated snobs. Cindy pushed her short blonde hair behind her ear, showing off jewelry on her fingers and arm. The kind Namika was willing to bet cost more than her monthly rent when she had one. Everything about the woman screamed wealth, but in a way that irked Namika. In the way that flaunted it to everyone for attention. Her hair was without a single strand out of place, as though she'd gone to the salon that very morning. And her perfect manicure just grated on Namika's nerves.

Adam glanced towards Namika and grinned as he quirked an eyebrow curiously. She crossed her arms, recalling how they could read one another's emotions.

Stupid brand.

Cindy's hazel eyes shot daggers at Namika before she leaned towards Adam and smiled. "Sir, if you plan on going out, let me know and I'll order some better-suited clothes for her to wear." She closed the notebook and placed it back on her desk. "It wouldn't do well to have you turned away from a respectable restaurant, Mr. Ashton. People would talk."

"Oh, no worries." Namika waved her hand dismissively. "I'll get my own. Don't trouble yourself. I can see you're busy with..." She glanced from the phone on the desk back to Cindy. "*Work.*"

Cindy placed a hand on her chest, as though taken aback by Namika's unfriendliness. "I was only trying to offer my assistance," she said, still only addressing Adam. "I meant no disrespect."

"Yes, you did." He glowered, and she paled. "I pay you

to do your job. Not for your opinions on my private affairs."

"I... I apologize, Mr. Ashton," she stammered, averting her gaze.

He glanced towards the frosted double doors beyond the reception desk. "I expect those calls to be made within the next few hours." His tone had softened, but Namika still felt the fury seeping from him.

Cindy nodded and quickly pulled out a folder, busying herself. Namika wanted to feel bad for the woman, knowing what it felt like to be on the other end of Adam's anger, but she decided against it when Cindy shot a last glare at her.

Adam led Namika to the end of the hallway and swiped a key card against a black box. A private elevator opened, and they stepped inside, going up one more flight to stop on the penthouse floor, sixty-six stories up.

Namika rubbed her arms but froze when she stepped into the small lobby where red doors stood. A large golden number six hung above, and she glanced from it to Adam.

She raised a hand. "Hang on. Six, six, six? Are you kidding me?"

He shrugged, but the corner of his mouth curled. "Why not have fun when I can?"

"I had no idea you had a sense of humor," she muttered, grinning at how ridiculous the joke was.

"It happens on occasion." He scanned the card against another black box, and the doors unlocked.

She stared at the sunken living room, blinking a few times to ensure her eyes weren't playing tricks on her. The windows provided an incredible view of the downtown area, the sun high in the sky glinting against the tall buildings.

Adam tugged on her coat, and she flinched. "What—?"

He arched an eyebrow, giving the collar a small tug. She gave a quick nod, allowing him to help her out of it, her heart racing. His proximity reminded her of the times his warmth had reassured her, and she pushed the thought from her mind.

A fountain took up most of the wall to one side, and she peered at the bottom where the water flowed and gaped. Fish swam inside, avoiding the tiny waterfall falling into their pond.

The dark red sofas matched the large rug taking up most of the living room. Patterns of darker reds and browns created similar warmth from the elevator despite the skyscraper's black and gray exterior. An electric fireplace stood in the heart of the place, flames dancing and creating shadows and lights everywhere.

"You live here?"

"It's one of my many homes, yes."

She walked farther into the sunken living room. "How many do you have?"

She wasn't sure why she was curious about his living situation, or if she just wanted to break the heavy silence between them.

"I have several."

She stared outside the window with her back turned to him, but kept an eye on his reflection. What was it like to live in different places constantly? Did he have a favorite place? Was he ever lonely? The silence continued, and she rubbed her arms despite the heat coming from the fireplace.

"How do you decide which personal items to keep where?" She forced her mouth into a smile, but her mind didn't register his answer. Why was she so lost in thought?

He grasped her chin, and she yelped; how had she not heard or seen him approach? He dropped his hand, his brown eyes boring into her. "You lived in an apartment, and you also had accommodations in the Venatores' headquarters. How did *you* decide what to keep where?"

"I had two of every necessity," she said with a shrug. "I guess you do the same, but I imagine it's more than two."

"Apart from the clothes you were wearing when you arrived at the CrowBar with Celina, you had nothing else on you. Both locations you called home had no personal items either. Unless the ones we assumed belonged to your boyfriend, Yasuo, were, in fact, yours? You did share that apartment, correct?"

She narrowed her eyes, recalling what the folder had said about her deceased boyfriend. She backed away from him, despite his gaze darkening. "You searched my room and apartment?"

"We did." He crossed his arms. "I'd forgotten you looked through your file at Shiriki's place. I suppose it means you know what really happened to your lover boy."

"Don't call him that," she shot. "He was more than that. He was also a great friend for years. And one of your demons tortured him until he killed himself. Yasuo didn't deserve that."

"When you go up against my kind, casualties are expected. Thinking otherwise makes you a fool."

"I'm not stupid," she said through her teeth. "I knew people would die. Even I could've been murdered." She shook her head. "I guess I had always hoped the people closest to me would make it."

"Dying in battle amongst others was a merciful lie."

Her hands curled into fists. "I don't need you to bend the truth."

They stared at each other, her emotions jumping from

one to the next, unsure which were her own and which belonged to Adam.

Finally, Adam broke the silence. "*Did* you have a personal item we forgot?"

She wondered why he wouldn't drop the subject. "No. I left pretty much everything years ago when I moved from my mother's house." She glanced around. "Doesn't matter though, since they were just things."

"True, but some can hold memories that are at least a slight comfort," he said, his tone cooling.

He's been hurt too.

The sound of ringing caught her by surprise, but she welcomed the distraction.

Adam moved into the open kitchen and grabbed a cordless phone. "Yes?"

Her stomach clenched, and she pushed against it, hoping the pressure would help ease the pain. She hadn't eaten since... the pretzels had turned to ashes. When was the last time before then? She couldn't recall, but it didn't matter; it wasn't like she could eat anything. Another wave, and this time, nausea seemed to burn the inside of her chest. She closed her eyes to focus on anything else.

"In the meantime," Adam's voice brought her back to the present, "you should get some rest."

"I'd rather not... I don't want to take the chance of ending up in that nightmare again." She poked her hand out of her sleeve, staring at it with trepidation. "Besides, I don't have much time, and I don't plan on wasting what I do have sleeping."

"You weren't sleeping when you had that vision of the Inferno." He motioned for her to follow as he strode down a hallway.

She caught up to him, still holding her stomach as something seemed to gnaw at her insides. "Okay, but I still need to be doing something. I'm still at square one with this curse."

He opened the door to a beautiful room with a king-sized bed. "Haku texted me. He set up a meeting with a reaper by the name of Sebastian Ecter. He'll be here at six o'clock this evening to meet with us."

"Really?" Her body felt like it was tingling. "Why didn't you tell me sooner?" She didn't bother hiding the frustration in her voice.

"I got the notification while I was introducing you to Cindy." A slow grin curled his lips. "You seemed distracted with other... things."

Heat filled her cheeks, and she walked into the room, hoping to hide it from him. "You'll wake me up before the meeting?"

"Of course." He leaned against the doorframe and crossed his arms. "In the meantime, I'll be in my office to deal with business of my own. If you need anything, come down one floor and ask Cindy for assistance."

She let out a sigh. "I'm sure she'll be thrilled to hear that."

His smile widened, but he didn't comment as he held out a keycard. "This is for the private elevator. I'll leave it by the front door in case you need it."

"Okay. Thanks." She winced as pain twisted her insides again. "What happens... if I get too hungry? Will that kill me? What if I end up attacking a human to... eat them because I'm starved?" The thought caused the back of her throat to burn, and she swallowed hard.

"If that happens, I'll be there to hold you back." He straightened, something burning deep within his gaze. "And if it comes to it, I have an emergency solution for your hunger."

She eyed him. "Oh?"

"Get some rest, Miss Strang." And without another word, he closed the door behind him.

11

──────

CONSIDERATION

For the few minutes Namika got to sleep, her dreams were hazy, but one involving Adam made her give up trying to rest. She kicked the blankets off and let out a groan, frustrated at being denied a proper nap. The digital clock next to her showed she'd slept a little over thirty minutes.

Good enough.

The meeting with the reaper would take place soon, and she looked forward to making some progress with regard to breaking the curse. The threat of spending eternity in the Inferno loomed over her, and she let out a shaky breath.

Running her tongue along her teeth, she grimaced. She refused to meet with the reaper while having fuzzy teeth. With a sigh, she stood, then went into the bathroom attached to the guest room. Her eyes went round at how huge it was, and she shook her head.

She searched for a few seconds through the multitude of cupboards, then gave up. No toothbrush or deodorant.

She made her way to the entrance and stopped near

the small table by the door. The keycard lay on the wooden surface next to a flip phone with a sticky note on it.

For emergencies. - Adam

A small laugh escaped her throat as she picked up the device and flipped it open; of course, it wouldn't be a smartphone with internet access. She selected contacts, not surprised to see only Adam's name saved.

She slipped her boots back on and stepped out. She wasn't looking forward to asking Cindy for anything, but the urge to brush her teeth was so overwhelming it drove her nuts.

The elevator dinged, and Namika walked over to the reception desk, trying her best to stay polite.

Cindy raised her head, then returned her focus to her notebook. "Yes?" she asked in a cool voice, biting out the word.

"Is there a place nearby where I can get a toothbrush and deodorant?"

She exhaled, but her expression switched to a grin as she stood. "In the storage room." She opened a door leading into a small walk-in closet. "Mr. Ashton prefers to have these kinds of products here for the women he brings upstairs. Doesn't like it cluttering his personal space."

Namika stiffened. Why was she jealous? She forced a grin, refusing to take the bait. "An excellent idea. Keep everything that would clutter his home down here."

Cindy's gaze turned icier, but her smile didn't falter. The woman was good at keeping her mask, but so was Namika. She'd had so much practice throughout the years.

Cindy returned, items in hand.

"Here you are," she said, giving her a toothbrush and deodorant. "Let me know if you need anything else. Mr. Ashton keeps plenty as he brings a different person every visit."

Another twist in her gut, but before Namika replied, the main elevator doors opened, and Linda stepped out.

Namika's eyebrows shot up at seeing the demon again, recalling how, during their last interaction, they'd both nearly gotten into a physical altercation.

Linda held a garment bag in one hand and a small duffle in the other. She appeared incredibly misplaced in this fancy lobby, wearing maroon pleather pants, hugging her curves, and a halter top barely covering her breasts.

Cindy seemed even more displeased to see Linda than when she had greeted Namika. "Miss Boulet. What brings you here?"

Linda waved the items she held. "Apparently, playing errand-girl."

"Is that not what Mr. Ashton pays you for?" Cindy asked in an overly sweet tone. "I can't imagine what else he could possibly employ someone like you for."

"Shut it, you old raggedy bitch," Linda snapped back.

Namika's eyebrows shot up, and she pressed her lips together to keep from smiling. She didn't care about swearing at people, but the woman had it coming.

Cindy rested her hand on her chest as though Linda had stabbed her there. "I will not tolerate this kind of abuse in the workplace. I haven't attacked you in any way—"

"Oh, please," Linda said with a snort. "Just because you're passive-aggressive about it doesn't make it any less abusive. Don't dish it out if you can't take it, lady."

Tears shone in Cindy's eyes as she turned her attention to Namika. "You're a witness. Now did I say anything offensive?"

"What?" Namika held up the toothbrush and deodorant. "Oh, sorry. I was so busy reading the instructions that

I wasn't paying attention." This time, she didn't bother trying to hide her grin.

Cindy's face contorted as she grimaced, sitting back down at her desk. She muttered something about commoners and people of low breeding, but Linda just walked over to Namika.

Namika frowned, wondering why Linda was here in the first place. Did Adam know? Namika glanced towards the frosted doors to his office and guessed he likely was the one to send for Linda.

"So you break the rules and get treats?"

Namika pointed at the bags Linda held. "Those are for me?"

"Yeah. Lucky you," Linda said through gritted teeth.

Namika rolled her eyes. "I'm here trying to survive and save my soul. None of this is fun," she said in a whisper, hoping Cindy wasn't listening in; she had the feeling this employee didn't know what her boss really was.

Linda scoffed as she walked over to the private elevator. Namika caught up to her, but didn't scan the keycard; no way she'd get into an enclosed space with a demon who'd threatened to skin her alive not long ago.

"I don't have all day," Linda snapped.

"In a hurry to finish what you started last time?" Namika scowled. "I'm not going anywhere with you until I know for sure your master knows you're here."

She took out her new flip phone and selected Adam's name, then brought the device to her ear.

It rang once, and he picked up. "Is this an emergency, Miss Strang?" he asked in an annoyed tone.

"It might be, depending on your answer." Why did her heart beat faster at the sound of his voice? "Did you really send Linda here to bring me stuff?"

"I did. As you know, her punishment for allowing you

to escape was originally supposed to be being sent to Shiriki, but I've thought of an even better way of making her suffer."

A shiver shot down Namika's spine. "Is that so?"

"Yes. Being forced to serve you is a much better consequence, don't you think?" he asked in amusement.

Namika's eyebrows shot up as she stared at Linda. "You've got to be kidding me. She already wants to murder me. Are you trying to make her hate me even more?"

Linda sneered. "I don't think that's possible."

"Miss Strang. I assure you that she will not harm you in any way."

Namika opened her mouth to argue but let out a sigh instead. "Okay, fine."

"I'm pleased to hear your enthusiasm at having your own personal servant. Try to keep the arguing to a minimum, though; I don't want the police coming here because of a noise complaint." And without a goodbye, he hung up.

Namika put the phone away, eyeing Linda like she was a bomb ready to explode. Stalling wouldn't make anything better, though, so Namika swiped the keycard, and they both stepped into the elevator in silence.

Once back in the guest room of the penthouse, Linda hung the garment bag on the hook anchored into the wall near the door and put the other on the floor.

Namika crossed her arms. "Look. I'm sorry you got in trouble because I ran away. It was never my intention for anyone to get hurt."

"That's bullshit." She pushed her blonde hair over her shoulder. "You destroyed Marc, didn't you?" Although her tone was neutral, anger burned behind her gaze.

"I... I'm not the one who killed him, no. But I also

won't pretend that I wasn't an accomplice by bringing my friend down there to begin with."

"And after?" Linda materialized inches from Namika, and she yelped. "If you'd gone back to your dying group and gotten your power as planned, you would've started hunting us again. Don't pretend you care what happens to my kind."

Namika narrowed her eyes. "The Venatores wanted to kill you, but my goal was always to lock demons into the Dark Realm to protect people from you."

"So you spend months trying to escape from the Crow-Bar, but then have the audacity to stand here and say you want to imprison every single demon in the Dark Realm?" She leaned closer. "You're such a hypocrite."

"Imprison? That's where you belong," Namika shot back, but even to her own ears, she didn't sound as certain anymore.

"Viscus and higher demons, yes." Linda stared at the flames of the electrical fireplace. "But we're Sanguis. We were once human... We don't belong here or in the Dark Realm for too long."

Linda's words circled in Namika's mind a few times; they were still a threat to humans, regardless. But maybe it was more complicated than Namika was led to believe.

"Well, either way, I never meant for Adam... for Mr. Ashton to be dragged into this. If I could go back in time, I definitely wouldn't have escaped the way I did." Namika stared at the floor. "There are a lot of things I'd change from that night."

Linda scoffed as she grabbed the bags again and shoved them into Namika's arms. "I would've definitely made sure to lock you in a cage that night. And the only reason I'm not doing that now is because my master gave strict orders not to harm you in any way."

"Is being stuck as my servant really worse than spending time with the king's second in command?" Namika asked as she went to the guest bedroom.

"Just different." But the small shiver that went through Linda told Namika otherwise. Still, Namika was glad the demon wouldn't be sent to Shiriki; she didn't wish that on anyone.

Namika pointed at the garment bag. "I'm guessing these are clothes for the upcoming meeting?"

"They are. My master gave me a list of things to bring to you." Linda leaned against the wall, eyes narrowed. "Why does he like you so much?"

"Adam?" Namika burst out laughing, pressing her palm against her mouth to muffle it. "Sorry... it's... He... Mr. Ashton doesn't like me at all. He hates me."

She unzipped the garment bag. "Are all humans stupid, or is it just you?"

"Look, if you're jealous or something, you can stop worrying. Seriously. He's mentioned it more than once how your king should've exterminated me and my group."

Linda pulled clothes out of the bag. "Well, mister-apparently-doesn't-care-about-you requested I buy these on his credit card. He would prefer that you wear more appropriate clothing for the meeting you two have."

"That doesn't mean anything," Namika said in an aggravated tone. "It would be embarrassing for him to hold a meeting while I looked like I had crawled out from the streets." Her eyebrows shot up when she grabbed the jeans on the hanger; they were clean and made of a light-blue material. A white t-shirt was hung with a dark gray suit jacket, giving it a relaxed style.

Linda's grin was triumphant. "I tried talking him into getting you an expensive dress suit instead, but he insisted you'd be more comfortable with what you usually prefer to wear." She crouched and unzipped the duffle bag, taking out a striped black and blue purse. "He rarely notices details like that about people, but I guess it's because he hates you so much, right?"

"It's—"

"And even if this does involve you, he usually pushes people away and takes care of things on his own. I don't recall a single time he's allowed someone to attend a business meeting with him."

Namika pressed her lips together, not having any smart replies this time. Adam seemed like the type of person who'd be private and keep everyone at arm's length, but she hadn't even needed to plead with him to be involved in everything. And he could've had Linda bring clothes from Namika's room in the CrowBar if it was a matter of wearing something clean. Why bother buying her a new outfit? And in the style she loved to wear.

Linda pulled out black heel boots. "Get changed." And without another word, left Namika's room.

It only took a few minutes, and by the time she stared at herself in the floor-to-ceiling mirror, she smiled. She looked great; the outfit fit her like a glove. She grabbed the toothbrush she'd left on the nightstand and made her way to the private bathroom. She grinned, wondering what Linda had said to Cindy on her way out.

Yet, her smile faded as she recalled what Cindy had said about having a stock of hygiene products for the women Adam apparently brought back here. The words repeated inside Namika's mind, and her hold on the toothbrush tightened.

The thought of Adam bringing other women here flashed in her mind, and she gritted her teeth. Namika despised herself for the jealousy overwhelming her.

He can sense your emotions.

She cursed and leaned against the marble counter, counting backwards from ten. Linda hadn't helped by insinuating that he liked her. Not that Namika believed the demon, but why did a part of her wish for it to be true? Nothing good would come of that. Not even if Namika wasn't cursed at the moment.

Unlike what most people thought, demons loved, but it differed from what humans were used to. They possessed, claimed, and eventually destroyed those cared for. If that person were human, they didn't always survive the intensity.

Namika brushed her teeth, pressing a bit too hard a few times as her emotions jumped around. She hoped Adam wouldn't comment about her jealousy.

12

COMPLICATIONS

An imposing desk stood near the windows, looking out into the city. The large chair, with its back to the view outside, gave it a look of authority. Two armchairs sat in front of it for guests.

Namika glanced at the bar at the far end of the room; bottles of expensive liquor stood in perfect rows along with glasses. Adam certainly knew how to make a good impression.

A few filing cabinets stood against the opposite wall, and she was reminded of what happened with Shiriki. A tiny chill coursed through her body, still anxious he'd realize it wasn't a coincidence that she'd come across her own file.

The phone on the desk rang, and Adam picked up. "Yes?" A pause, and he frowned. "Fine. You can go home now, Miss Beaton."

Namika's eyebrows rose, wondering why he sounded annoyed. A few seconds later, she realized why.

A woman walked into the office, a tablet in her hand.

She stood near one of the chairs, but didn't sit, glancing from Namika to Adam.

"My name is Estelle Manning. I'm one of Mr. Sebastian Ecter's assistants." Her black dress suit gave her an air of professionalism, while her black-rimmed glasses made her look stricter.

Adam laced his fingers together. "And where is Mr. Ecter?"

"I'm afraid he won't be attending this meeting. He has no interest in involving himself in the matters of demons, so he's sent me here instead."

Namika stared at the woman; from what she sensed, Estelle was a normal human. However, her knowledge of demons made this strange. "Wouldn't it have been better to decline the meeting? Why agree if he was going to send you?" Namika asked, not hiding her frustration.

"My employer was curious enough to send someone to find out what you wanted to see him about." Estelle slid her palm along the side of her black hair as though making sure no strands were sticking out; it was braided in the back so tight, it didn't look possible for a single frizz to exist.

"And what makes him think I'd tell you anything after being insulted?" Adam snapped. "You may know about things beyond regular human knowledge, but that's likely where your skills end."

She shrugged. "Mr. Ecter didn't expect you to release that information to me, but he instructed me to ask, nonetheless." She turned the tablet in her hand and typed something on the screen. "As for my presence insulting you, I apologize for that."

Adam materialized inches away from her, and she flinched, but didn't back away.

"If you know who and what I am, why come here?" he asked quietly. "What's stopping me from snapping your neck for wasting my time?"

Namika clenched her jaw, debating whether to tell him to stop threatening the woman or not. She didn't want to undermine him in case he had a plan in mind, but she also didn't want to stand by as he terrorized her, either. Though, by the look on Estelle's face, she didn't look frightened.

The woman stared at Adam, brown eyes unblinking. "I am but one of many assistants, Mr. Ashton. The job description is high risk, high reward." She glanced towards Namika for a second. "Kill me if you want. It's not like I can stop you."

Namika quickly moved closer to the two. "No one is killing anyone," she said, shooting a glare at Adam. "It's... I really need to speak to Mr. Ecter. It's regarding a curse."

"Let me see," Estelle muttered as she typed a few more things on the tablet. After a few seconds, she shook her head. "No. He's not interested. I'm sorry." She pressed the device against her chest. "And before you ask, he won't meet with just you, either." She stared at Namika. "You're involved with demons, and while my employer is not opposed to all of them, anyone with a direct link to the demon king or his second in command is not on the list of approval for any kind of transaction."

Namika's shoulders slumped. Would this be the case with all reapers? Would none of them have anything to do with her because of Adam?

Silence hung heavy in the room, but Adam broke it first. "The only reason you get to leave here alive today is because I'm in no mood to argue with Miss Strang about killing you." His irises glowed bright red, and this time,

Estelle looked nervous. "Now leave before I change my mind and decide it's worth the argument."

Estelle gave a curt nod and left quickly. The door shut with a click, and Namika crossed her arms over her chest. They'd already hit a dead end. Adam had tasked his demons to research in the meantime, but from what she'd heard growing up, reapers kept their secrets close. Most of the information regarding them was kept within their city, a world away from this one.

Was working with the first Sanguis demon an appropriate plan? Would she be better off on her own? The thought of leaving him behind didn't sit right with her, though.

"You're not getting away from me that easily, Miss Strang," Adam said in a silky tone. When Namika opened her mouth to lie about what she thought, he pointed towards her lower back. "I can sense your emotions, remember?"

She averted her gaze. "Did your brand have to come with this weird side-effect?"

"Count yourself lucky it wasn't something worse." He walked to the door and opened it, waiting. "Come on."

She followed him out of the office. "Where are we going? What's the plan now? Are——"

He grabbed her shoulders. "One more question. I dare you."

Her stomach hardened; she made a mental note to only ask one question at a time.

The lobby was empty, and Namika relaxed a bit at the thought of not having to deal with Cindy again; the last person Namika wanted to see in that moment was that nasty woman.

Adam pulled out his phone. "I need to go see Shiriki since I told him I'd give him an update after the meeting."

Her stomach clenched; on second thought, the last person she wanted to see was actually the demon king's second in command.

He seemed to follow her train of thought and chuckled. "I'm not looking forward to telling him about what happened, but if I don't go to him, he'll come for me instead."

"We're flying back to Ottawa already?" Her eyebrows shot up at the thought of the cost. "Isn't that really expensive? Even for you?"

"It would barely make a dent in my accounts. Besides, I'll be going on my own and using Dark Realm magic to get there almost instantly."

She crossed her arms. "Wait, so if you can fast-travel without needing vehicles, why did you pay for tickets? I don't know how much time there's left before this curse finishes me off. Why not teleport us both here?"

"Traveling through the king's realm isn't safe for a human." A glimmer of mischief shone behind his gaze. "And as to the reason we used transportation, I'm leaving a trail to see if that mystery vampire of yours tracks us."

Anger burned its way through her body as she clenched her fists tightly.

"First of all, he's not *my* vampire. He murdered my friend and tried to kill me," she said through gritted teeth. "Secondly, you're using me as bait? And now you're leaving me here alone? What, now that the first plan fell through with the reaper, you've given up? You're going to run away and leave me to die and end up in the depths of the Inferno?"

His irises flashed crimson, his pupils thinning into vertical slits. "You'll do well to remember my fate is tied to yours because of your decisions the night *you* escaped." He approached, only stopping once he was a few inches away from her. "If you die, I won't end up in Hell alongside you, but with what Shiriki plans on doing to me, I may as well be," he hissed through his pointed teeth.

Her pulse sped, the edges of her vision darkening. Tears blurred her vision as the past days seemed to crash down all at once.

"I never meant..." she scoffed while wiping away at her cheeks. "It doesn't matter what I meant. This is my fault." She met his burning red gaze. "I *will* fix this."

A slow smile curled his lips, his irises changing to their usual brown, warm and gentle. "*We* will fix this. You're not alone in this."

"Thank you," she said, and although she smiled, more tears rolled down until her breath came out in a sob.

He pulled her close, and she stiffened at first, but eventually relaxed in his arms, allowing herself a moment to let her emotions out.

"While I'm away, stay inside the penthouse," he said as he rubbed her back, the warmth of his hand grounding her. "It has magic that protects it, and the brand I marked you with will alert me if anything happens." He traced a finger along her lower back.

When Namika nodded, he kissed the top of her head. She pulled away quickly, her heart hammering against her chest as she stared up at him. He seemed as surprised as she felt.

Before he said anything, she pulled the keycard out of her pocket. "I'll stay inside. Don't worry."

She walked away, and as soon as she stepped into the private elevator, she leaned against the wall. The kiss was an accident; a subconscious move on his part to reassure her. That was it.

She kicked off her boots and put on the slippers he'd left by the door for her. Linda's words about Adam liking her circled her mind, and Namika slumped on the sofa. She wasn't even sure how she felt about the man.

"Not a man. A demon," she muttered.

With a groan, she jumped to her feet and paced the living room. It was impossible to calm down. Everything had fallen apart at the first step of their plan. The curse was already complicated enough to deal with. She didn't need Adam adding to it by being... affectionate.

Heat rose through her, and she slipped off her jacket. She needed to keep her mind busy while she waited for Adam to return, or she'd go crazy. Deciding to explore the penthouse, she strode through the hallways. Paintings hung on the walls. No photos. She recognized the generic decorations. For a while, she'd kept the few items she brought with her from her home in Nanaimo, but it became too painful. She tore away at her possessions in a rage, ripping things to shreds.

All but a small teddy bear her grandmother had sewn for her in the color of Namika's birthstone. But she left it behind at her mother's house when she'd moved out at eighteen.

She glided her finger along the tan-colored wall, slowing as the hairs on the back of her neck rose. A tiny prickle of energy brushed up against her bare arms, and she frowned, staring down the corridor. Nothing was out of the ordinary, and yet, something was. She swallowed hard, but pushed it out of her mind. It was likely the stress, lack of sleep, and food. With a sigh, she rubbed her face; she'd at least lie down and try resting.

She walked into the guest bedroom and switched on the overhead light; the sun was already set at this hour, so close to winter.

The door creaked, and her heart skipped several beats when a figure moved in the window's reflection. She spun, her skin becoming clammy as it closed from the inside, and the vampire who'd caused this whole mess walked forward from the corner.

"Hello again, Namika," he said in a sly tone.

13

———

MESSAGE

*N*amika's heart raced when the vampire spoke her name.

Last time she'd seen him, it was dark save for the street lights a few feet away. This time, she saw him more clearly for what he was: a monster. His dark brown eyes were cold and void of any pleasant emotions.

"Why are you here?" Her real question was *how* he was here, since Adam had said the place was protected by magic. Even if he wasn't normal as far as vampires went, his own powers shouldn't bypass the Sanguis demon's magic.

He cocked his head, his black hair falling to the side. "I'm here for you, of course."

"And what is it that you want with me?" she asked.

"Well," he clapped his hands together, "imagine my surprise when the Venatore I was waiting for to die just...didn't die," he said with a laugh. "And because she was branded by the Sanguis leader himself, of all people."

Her stomach churned; he knew Adam had branded

her. But why hadn't he shown up to help? He would've felt her terror by now.

The vampire stepped to the side and tapped the side of the wall where a symbol was carved into the plaster. "Stops any demon from sensing anything within the vicinity."

Her pulse throbbed in her ears. Some higher beings could read minds, and she hoped that he'd guessed what she was thinking.

"So who are you, exactly?" she asked, trying to keep him talking while she planned her escape.

The elevator would be too slow, and he could sabotage it into falling without a problem. She'd noticed a fire alarm near the door to the suite. If she pulled it, others would be alerted.

Plan after plan ran through her mind, but as he stalked towards her, the only thing she thought of was running away as quickly as possible. Anywhere but here.

"I have to say, I never thought Adam would brand someone." He pulled out a knife from his jacket. "But I've always enjoyed killing two birds with one stone, so this works out nicely." He materialized inches from her and grasped her arm. "For me."

His smile widened, and before she could beg for her life, he plunged the blade into her abdomen. Burning agony sliced through her body, and she screamed. Her hands trembled as she fought for any release from the unbearable pain, but it wouldn't stop. Her vision swayed, but all she saw were the white eyes of the vampire in front of her.

He smiled. "Does it hurt?"

The tears rolling down her cheeks were warm against her clammy skin, and every gasp seemed to rip through her. He wrenched the knife out, and she shrieked, falling to her knees as she pushed against her wound. The smell of copper burned her throat as she stared at her hands. Blood seeped between her fingers, and no matter how hard she tried, she couldn't get her magic to heal the wound fast enough.

He spun the bloody knife between his fingers. "You've pushed the limits of my patience already. First, stopping Emma from getting that artifact I needed, and then having the audacity not to die. Try to make it quick, won't you?"

He lifted his sleeve and checked his watch; she took the momentary distraction to dash into the bathroom.

"No, no, no," he called out in a sing-song tone from the other side of the door. "I need to make sure you're dead this time."

She pressed her hand harder against the wound; she needed to find a weapon. Something. Anything.

She staggered back with a scream.

A woman lay in the tub, so pale, it took a second for Namika to recognize it was a person once. Blood covered most of her maimed body; two distinct bite marks on her neck told the story of what likely happened. Her eyes were wide, as though still living through the terror.

Her heart pounded as she blinked back tears and focused her magic on the woman. No signs of life; not even a weak pulse.

It wasn't the first dead body she dealt with. Unfortunately, she'd grown numb to it after a while. Especially after Venatores had declared war on Mekaisto. Members wounded and killed became commonplace.

But this...

A message written in what looked like blood was left on the wall above the tub.

Didn't I leave you to die?

The doorknob wiggled, and Namika's pulse sped. With

her hands already so bloody, she traced a symbol on the floor, muttering a spell her grandmother had taught her.

The door burst open as she traced the last part of the symbol and pressed her fingers against it. "Banish."

The vampire howled in fury and pain as his body exploded, and he vanished without a trace. She knew the vampire wasn't destroyed, but healing would take at least a day, no matter how powerful he was.

Namika slumped forward, her energy draining out of her. Using that much magic at once always caused her exhaustion, but having to heal herself at the same time was the limit. She lifted her top and watched as the last few inches of her flesh mended together.

Her vision darkened, and she fell on her side, wincing as something hard pressed against her hip. She pulled out the flip phone and selected Adam's contact information.

As the line rang, she used her sleeve to wipe the symbol she'd drawn. She didn't have the energy to explain anything, and was scared she would let it slip about her natural-born magic.

"Yes?" Adam's voice warmed her as she shivered on the bathroom floor.

"...help," she whispered.

She closed her eyes for a second, and when she opened them again, Adam was crouched in front of her.

"Namika? Look at me." He sat her up, his expression unreadable. Yet the fear and anger filling her chest didn't feel like her own. "What happened?"

"The vampire," she muttered, staring at the tub. "He tried to kill me again, and——"

"Let me see." He grasped the hem of her shirt, but she clutched his hands.

She shook her head. "I...need to get out of here. Please."

He grasped her arms and helped her up, his gaze intense like he was trying to see if she hid something.

Once inside the bedroom, she pulled away from him, wrapping her arms around her waist.

"You're soaked in blood," he said in a quiet voice.

"I'm fine. He barely grazed me." When he frowned, she added, "Maybe it's your brand that healed me?"

He didn't look like he believed her even for a second, but he dropped the subject. "I'll show you to the main bathroom where you can get cleaned up."

"Would it be okay if I slept on the sofa in the living area tonight?" Returning to the guest bedroom, knowing that the attached bathroom held a mutilated woman wasn't the best thing for her nerves; that screaming expression wouldn't leave her mind.

His gaze lingered on her for a few more seconds, his stony expression impossible to decipher. "Don't worry about sleeping arrangements. Take what you need from this room and come with me."

She nodded and moved past him. Not wanting to linger any longer than necessary, she grabbed a robe and stepped out. As she followed him, she fidgeted with her sleeves, her mind replaying what had happened a few minutes ago.

The door clicked behind her, and she leaned against the wall for a few seconds, trying to regain her composure.

The attack altered nothing. She still needed to find a way to break the curse to save herself and Adam. Having the vampire hunting her added another minor complication.

She scoffed as she slipped out of her blood-stained clothes; next time Adam bought her anything, she'd request it in red. How many items of clothing had she been forced to throw out in the past couple of days?

Running a washcloth under the tap, she stared at herself in the mirror. Black veins spread from her shoulder to the base of her neck, the skin graying around them.

Did using her magic accelerate the curse?

She gritted her teeth and washed away the blood on her abdomen. Her skin was raw from all the scrubbing, but the pinkish hue reminded her of blood, and she let out a sigh that bordered on a growl. Why was everything going so wrong?

Someone cleared their throat, and she yelped, spinning. Adam's gaze slid along her body, and she was suddenly very aware she was in her underwear.

"What the hell are you doing here?"

His eyebrows shot up. "I've rarely heard you use such foul language."

"H-e-double hockey sticks is hardly foul language," she shot back. "Now, why are you here?"

A small smile touched his lips. "I'm here because I wanted to make sure you're actually alright."

The air was chilly against her bare skin. It was embarrassing, but she couldn't seem to move under his gaze. Soft, yet so dangerous. Her breath came faster, and she swallowed hard. She met his gaze, his brown irises intense as he waited. For what? She had no idea.

"Can you please leave?"

He slid his hands into his pockets. "I have questions about the attack. Meet me in the fourth room to the right once you're finished." And without saying anything else, he disappeared.

She quickly slipped on the robe she'd brought from the guest bedroom and strode down the corridor, counting the doors as she went.

The master bedroom. She froze at the threshold,

staring at Adam; he was sitting on the end of the king-size bed, his suit jacket discarded.

She crossed her arms. "Can your questions wait until tomorrow? I'm really tired."

"It's better now, while it's still fresh in your mind." He pulled his tie off, his gaze not once leaving her.

She eyed him, unsure what to say or do. He patted the mattress next to him with a playful grin, and her cheeks warmed.

"So, what exactly do you want to know about the attack?" she asked as she took a seat as far away from him as possible.

He pulled out his phone and handed it to her. She stared at the photo he'd taken of the arcane symbol etched into the wall, and swallowed hard.

"Did the vampire mention what this was?" he asked.

"He said it made it impossible for demons to sense the surroundings." She handed him back the device. "He knew you branded me."

Adam ran his fingers through his hair, leaving them slightly disheveled. "Interesting. Well, I've sent the image to Shiriki. See if he knows anything about it."

"Speaking of him," Namika leaned her elbows against her knees, "did he say anything about the whole meeting thing? Did he have any other ideas or suggestions?" She pressed her lips together, stopping the flow of questions she had.

"No other suggestions at the moment."

"Great." She bit out the word, then let out a sigh. "Are there any other reapers who would talk to us? Or any way to get Sebastian Ecter to change his mind?"

"Let's deal with that after I make sense of what happened during your latest attack." He slid closer. "If the vampire was here to kill you, how are you still alive?"

"Disappointed?" she shot back, forcing a laugh.

His eyes narrowed. "Is there a reason you're avoiding my questions about this?"

"Look, I don't know. He showed up to taunt me and said he wanted to finish the job, but then left." She shrugged. "Maybe he's playing a game of cat and mouse or something."

"Explain why your shirt was bloody, then." He glanced at her abdomen for a second. "You're not wounded. Not even a graze. But that was *your* blood on your clothes."

She clenched her jaw. "So that's why you snuck into the washroom when you did. You wanted to check me yourself to make sure I wasn't lying to you."

"It's no secret you prefer keeping things to yourself. But yes, I wanted to make sure you weren't actually wounded."

She swallowed against the lump in her throat and averted her gaze. "That woman... did you know her?" She hoped she could divert the topic.

"I don't recognize her, but I'll have Haku look into who she was. Perhaps it'll lead us to where we can find this vampire." He got to his feet and pulled back the bedcovers. "For now, there's nothing we can do, so get some sleep."

She wanted to argue, but he was right; what could she do right at that moment besides brainstorm ideas? And with how exhausted she felt, it was impossible to think straight.

He grabbed her arm and leaned in. "I don't usually tolerate when people lie to me, but I'll let it slide for now."

"I have no idea what you're referring to." But she did; she was hiding her magic from him.

He took her hand, staring at it as though it were the most captivating thing in the world. "You're a convincing liar, but keep in mind I can feel your emotions because of the brand, remember?"

She wasn't ready to tell him about her magic, too scared of the consequences once he'd reported it to his king.

When she stayed silent, he let her go, and she slipped beneath the covers. She pushed her face against the pillow and closed her eyes, inhaling deeply; Adam's scent seemed to wrap around her like a cocoon, protecting her in that moment.

Why did he make her feel safe despite everything?

14

CLOSER

*N*amika wrapped the covers around her, squinting at the light from the window. She was still lying in Adam's bed, safe.

With a sigh, she got out of bed. While she was relieved she'd finally gotten some sleep, another part of her urged her to hurry and take action. No one told her how long she had until the curse took hold and took her life, and taking naps could wait until after.

She glanced around the room for a few seconds as she tightened the cord around her robe, then stepped out.

Adam sat at a rounded table in the kitchen area, an open laptop in front of him.

"Well?" he snapped, and she flinched at his tone. She opened her mouth to snap back, but he held his finger up and motioned at the Bluetooth in his ear. "Perfect. You've done a good job." He tapped against the device, then turned his attention to Namika.

"Good morning."

She leaned against the counter. "Good news?"

"Linda found out Sebastian Ecter will be conducting a

business meeting in Winnipeg." He closed the laptop. "I've rented a private jet to get us there in a few hours."

The words private jet lingered in her mind for a few more seconds, as it seemed so out of this world. "If he didn't want to meet with us before, ambushing him likely won't make him happy. Or make him want to help us."

He gave her a playful grin. "You think this is the first time I've had to *persuade* someone to do something they don't want to do?"

"Okay, so what exactly is the plan?"

"Apparently, our reaper has an appetite for anonymous sexual encounters."

Heat burned from her chest to her face, and she swallowed hard, unsure what to say about that tidbit of information.

He got up from his chair. "With that information in mind, Linda will lure him into a secluded area with the promise of fun, and once he's where I want him to be..." He left the rest unsaid, but she knew where he was going with the whole thing.

It didn't quite sit well with her, though; she was still convinced Sebastian wouldn't help them if he was forced to. He could easily give them false information or withhold essential details that could get her killed. However, for the moment, it was the only plan they had, so she kept quiet.

She glanced down at herself. "Any extra clothes in that closet of necessities you keep downstairs for the women you bring here?" Her tone came out colder than planned, and she wished she could take it back.

He arched an eyebrow. "Basic things, but not entire outfits, no."

She tugged at the sleeves of the robe. "I guess it's better that way since we wouldn't want to bother Cindy. She was angry at me for bothering her about personal items. Not sure if she invented everything to get a rise out of me or something."

Stop. Talking.

"I take it those feelings of jealousy I felt beforehand were from you?" he asked with a chuckle.

She narrowed her eyes. "What do I care how many women you've brought here? It's none of my concern."

"Indeed," he said, smiling as if enjoying her squirm. "I suppose that means it wouldn't bother you to know the people I bring here are mostly to take my pleasure from."

With the amount of heat radiating off her, she was sure he felt it despite the distance between them. She was both jealous and aroused.

She swallowed hard, wishing she could get her legs to work and walk her out of the situation. He materialized in front of her, leaning his hands against the counter and trapping her.

A lewd smile curled his lips. "Curious you'd become aroused at my words." He moved a strand of loose hair behind her ear. "I smell the stench of jealousy, but the lust is so much stronger."

"My body's reactions are none of your concern. Now please get out of my personal space," she said in a less-than-convincing command.

"You're the one instigating this topic of conversation, Miss Strang." His tone was laced with hunger, but he still took a few steps back.

"I..." She swallowed hard, thinking up an excuse. "I was asking about how I need clothing before we go out."

"Linda is bringing you some new clothes. And as a heads up, she's pretty pissed off at having to buy you some more already," he said with a small smile.

Lovely.

"Okay, well, in that case, I'll get ready..." She stared

down the corridor, an icy shiver running through her. The guest bathroom flashed in her mind, and with it, the dead woman in the tub. "Is she still...?"

"I moved her body to the cold room."

"Cold room?" she asked in a whisper.

"To keep bodies from decomposing too quickly before the cleaning company can dispose of them."

She gaped at him. Some part of her had forgotten what he was. What he was capable of. Yet, it didn't revolt her like it used to.

"And do you need to use that place... often?"

"I rarely kill, but it does occasionally happen." He cocked his head. "Does that frighten you?"

She narrowed her eyes. "You kill to feed."

He chuckled. "You know that's not true. I've ripped people apart and hurt them for no other reason than fun."

"I know what you are. Demons cause pain. I get that. But so do other beings." Her pulse sped. "Why are you trying to scare me? Don't you think I've been freaked out enough to last me a lifetime?"

He grasped her chin, so she had to look at him. "You've lowered your guard around me. And not because you've accepted what I am, but because you're pretending I'm not a monster."

She wanted to deny it, but he was right; she'd allowed herself to be vulnerable around him. A dangerous mistake she wouldn't have made only a few days ago. But there were several things that had changed in that time.

She pulled away from him. "Look, can we... I need to stay focused on the next steps of this new plan. We don't have time for"—she motioned her hand between them —"this."

His gaze changed; he looked as if he was fighting inwardly about something. Without another word, he returned to the table and busied himself with the laptop again.

"One thing I can't quite figure out is the message the vampire left behind over the tub."

"What's there not to get? He left me behind to die," she said, crossing her arms.

"You said he attacked you in the guest bedroom. His plan was to kill you then and there, so it was likely you never would've made it into the bathroom. So why bother leaving a body and a message for you?"

She glanced towards the guest bedroom. The vampire attack played in her mind again, and she wrapped her arms around her waist. It was like he was still here, taunting her. Telling her not to take too long to die.

She recalled something else and straightened. "I don't know about the message part, but I remembered he... The vampire said something last night that reminded me of something."

Adam arched an eyebrow. "Oh?"

"The night I... escaped with Emma. You found us in your storage room in the dungeons." She tried her best to ignore the icy glare he gave her. "She said he wanted an artifact called the Garnet Orb. When we met up with him, everything seemed okay until Emma said we weren't able to get it, and that's when he..."

"There are no artifacts I'm aware of with that name," he said in an indifferent tone.

Anger rose inside at how bored he sounded at the information, but she pushed the uneasy feeling to the side. Instead, she described what Emma had told her the artifact looked like, hoping he'd know of something similar.

Adam drummed his fingers against the table's surface. "That sounds like the Arunis Orb, but it's not something

I've ever had in my possession. I don't even think Shiriki has ever found it."

"Really?" It seemed impossible for that demon not to get whatever he wanted. "Do you know what it's for?"

"I don't know that it even really exists, but if it does, and I'm remembering correctly, it has something to do with the Inferno." He glanced at his watch. "Linda should arrive any minute."

She took that as her cue to leave and headed to the bathroom, her steps slow. Time ticked by, though, and she didn't have the luxury of being squeamish about murdered people.

Eventually, she'd end up with a fate worse than death if she didn't focus.

Namika stepped onto the private jet, gawking at the inside. Never in a thousand years did she ever imagine she'd be flying in one of these. The gallery alone looked more expensive than the places she'd lived.

They'd installed an entire kitchen, complete with refrigerator, microwave, oven, and coffeemaker. Marble counters surrounded a sink, above which champagne and wine glasses were displayed in a cabinet.

"This place is... amazing," she said as Adam joined her.

He nodded. "When I fly private, the Direct World jet is definitely my go-to. Not too expensive, either."

"I have the feeling my definition of expensive is very different from yours," she said with a grin.

Without the rows of seats, it left room for white leather sofas and recliners. The look of sophistication definitely matched how Adam looked. He wore a dark blue suit with a white dress shirt; it fitted him perfectly, accentuating his muscles.

He placed his hand on her lower back and led her towards the sofa that took up a large portion of one side. She tried to ignore her speeding pulse at his touch and quickly took a seat.

Fresh flowers stood in a vase on a table next to her, and she breathed in the wonderful scent.

The wide-screen television in front of them switched on, showing the plane's trajectory from Ottawa, Ontario, to Winnipeg, Manitoba, and she gripped the armrest tightly. For a second, she'd forgotten this wasn't just some beautiful place, but a jet that would be in the air in a few minutes.

She leaned her head back and closed her eyes, trying to relax. The leather seat was soft, but not so much that she sank into it.

"Here." Adam's voice snapped her back to reality.

He held his smartphone out towards her, and she arched an eyebrow, but took it anyway. The screen showed a bunch of different settings for things like the temperature, ambient lighting, window shades, and even what played on the television.

"You're kidding," she muttered. "There's an app for the inside of a plane?"

"Of course." He slid closer to her and motioned towards the buttons. "Modify anything you'd like to make it more bearable for take-off and the flight itself."

She stared at him. "You're putting me in charge?" She mentally kicked herself for sounding flirtatious.

"For now," he breathed. He was the definition of handsome, but darkness always lingered behind his gaze. And she surmised it wasn't just the fact that he was a demon.

The pilot strode into view and smiled. "Mr. Ashton. Good of you to fly with us again."

"I scheduled the plane to leave three minutes ago. Is there a reason for the delay?" Adam's voice was suddenly icy, and Namika nearly had whiplash from the difference in his tone from a few seconds ago.

The man paled. "My most sincere apologies, sir. There was news of a potential snowstorm rolling in towards the prairies, and we were waiting for confirmation that it was safe to take off."

Adam glanced at Namika. "I appreciate your due diligence in keeping us both safe."

"Of course, sir," he blurted. "We'll depart right away." And he walked away so fast, she wondered if he was maybe a demon who'd used super-speed.

"It's not his fault the weather isn't cooperating, you know," she said in a reproachful voice. "They don't call it *Winterpeg, Manisnowba* for nothing."

He chuckled, then pointed at the smartphone she still held. "Not changing any settings?"

"Oh, right." She stared at the screen and tapped a few buttons, glancing up every time she did in case she'd caused the place to blow up somehow.

The lights switched from white to a soft orange, and most of the window blinds nearby were closed. With a final tap, the temperature lowered, and she relaxed a bit; keeping cool usually helped her with the nausea.

Adam took the device back as the plane door locked behind a whooshing noise.

As soon as the vehicle moved, she pressed her back into the seat, trying to keep her trembling under control. Her stomach churned, and she breathed in deep through her nose.

Adam leaned in close. "Would you like me to distract you again?"

She recalled how he'd flirted with her during their last flight, and her body seemed to instantly combust.

"That's not necessary," she said quickly, turning away, and instead, focusing on the flowers next to her.

The engines were so quiet, she flinched when the plane lifted and straightened within seconds. A few minutes ticked by in silence as she continued focusing on her breathing.

Her stomach growled, and she pushed her hand against her abdomen. "It figures the one time I'm on a fancy plane, I can't eat anything," she said with a forced laugh.

"Then, once you're cured, I'll take you on another flight, and I'll make sure you can enjoy fine dining," he said in a soft voice.

His expression was so gentle, she almost felt like crying, but she pushed the emotion away. "Maybe we can skip the flying part?"

A loud grinding noise caused her to turn towards the front of the plane, heart racing. "What was that?" she nearly screamed the words, despite there being nothing out of the ordinary.

When he didn't answer, she glanced back.

He was gone.

She bolted to her feet, looking around. "Adam?" she called out. It wasn't unusual for him to disappear, but something felt wrong this time. It was as though everything around her had stopped.

Slowly, she allowed her magic to scan her surroundings, but there was nothing. Her extremities tingled as she began hyperventilating. What was happening? She rushed to the window and pushed the blinds open. Flames roared on the other side, and she staggered back with a gasp.

The plane creaked, a few parts caving inward. The metal glowed red from the heat, and the leather seats melted. She backed away, but nearly tripped when her boots stuck to the floor. Smoke rose, and she looked around, trying to find something to grab to pull away. But everything burned. She coughed, trying to call out for help, but her throat didn't seem to work. Her surroundings shook violently, and she fell back.

Her whole body felt like it was on fire as the floor pulled her down, melting around her. She shrieked, the smell of burning flesh and clothing filling her nostrils. The ceiling collapsed, and she lifted her arms to protect herself, but cried out when her flesh tore from the hot metal.

The familiar bloody vines from the Inferno shot down from above, impaling her. She tasted blood in her mouth, her pulse speeding; she only hoped her heart would stop so the agony would end, too. But this was Hell; it was eternity.

Her eyelids flew open as she gasped. She grabbed the nearest thing, her grip tightening against the soft material. She focused on Adam's suit jacket.

"Try to slow your breathing." Adam's voice was gentle but commanding.

Despite her shaking hands, she didn't relax her grasp. Too scared he'd vanish again. She couldn't go back. She'd lose her mind before the curse ever finished taking hold of her.

She burst into tears, her sobs making it impossible to catch her breath. Words stumbled out of her mouth, but they didn't make sense even to her. But nothing made sense, and nothing was fair. She cried, half-screaming about the Inferno and what had happened.

He took her in his arms, and she barely registered her surroundings as he took a few steps and sat, cradling her in his arms. Someone else spoke, and a few seconds later, he wrapped a blanket around her, not letting go once.

"You're here with me. You're safe." He repeated those words every so often, his fingers gliding through her hair.

Her throat burned as though the smoke was real, but she reminded herself it wasn't; it was all the screaming. "Those... vines. They're always there. They hurt so much every time," she mumbled in a cracking voice.

She drifted in and out of consciousness, not sure if she had fallen asleep or passed out. What felt like an eternity drifted by, but as time passed, she relaxed, gaining a grip on her mind once again.

The sound of the intercom's static brought her back. "We'll be landing in Winnipeg in approximately fifteen minutes."

She straightened, but groaned, her body feeling like she had the flu. How had two and a half hours gone by already? She tried to slide off his lap, but his arm wrapped around her tighter, keeping her in place.

Adam looked at her, his expression unreadable. "Are you alright?"

The last time anyone had held her like this was when she was a child; it was so embarrassing. She didn't want to imagine what he thought of her. That she was weak.

"I'm okay." Her trembling voice didn't match her statement.

He wiped away her tears. "No, you're not. This can't be good for your mental health. Or your soul's health," he said quietly, concern lacing his tone.

If she'd learned one thing in life as a Venatore, it was that dependence was a burden to others.

"I can take care of myself like a big girl." She tried her

best to force a laugh and smile, but it came out as a half-sob.

He traced her bottom lip. "I'm here with you, remember? To lean on. To ask for help when you need it."

"I'm not usually this weak," she said, trying hard to swallow against the lump in her throat.

He chuckled. "You're strong, but you *are* human. Fragile. So easy to break." His irises turned red, vertical pupils thinning. "And you're also mine to protect, Namika."

Her heartbeat sped at his words. They should've terrified her, but instead, she felt warmth encircle her. She cupped his cheek, her breathing coming quicker. A hungry smile curled his mouth. He looked ready to devour her. But when his lips touched hers, his kiss was gentle. As though he was teasing her with what he could do.

The static sound of the intercom echoed in the plane again, and she jumped like an electric shock had zapped through her. She slid off his lap, averting her gaze.

What was she thinking?

"Apologies for the second interruption. There will be turbulence because of a snowstorm. Please stay seated."

Namika glanced at Adam, who scowled at the ceiling as though ready to murder the pilot for interrupting. She took the seat across from him, wrapping the blanket tighter around her shoulders. She slid the window blind open, ever so slowly, part of her still expecting to see flames on the other side. Instead, large snowflakes fell from the sky.

She wondered how fast they could talk to the reaper. And how willing he'd be after being coerced to help.

Her shoulders slumped; not like she had a choice. The Inferno felt like it crept closer to her every day. She silently cursed the vampire who'd done this to her. Part of her was angry at Emma, too, for dragging her into this.

But it was Namika's choice to follow her old friend. To

break into the storage room. To escape the CrowBar. And to meet with the vampire.

She frowned and turned to look at Adam as her pulse sped. "Emma... when she called the vampire to meet us, it was the regional code for Manitoba."

"I doubt that's a coincidence." His smile didn't match the dark look in his gaze. "I bet Sebastian Ecter is there to look into this mystery vampire and his ghouls," he said before he pulled out his smartphone and tapped the screen a few times.

She stared back out at the city, lost in thought. The memory of his kiss crossed her thoughts, and she touched a finger to her lips.

15

AMBUSH

By the time they left the airport, it was nearly three o'clock in the afternoon. A car was already there to pick them up, and Namika was relieved to be on their way. She desperately needed to make progress at this point.

The ride was silent, but it wasn't uncomfortable; if anything, there was a quiet understanding between them both about needing a bit of time to make sense of everything. As the car pulled into a parking area, Namika surveyed her surroundings, attempting to determine their destination.

From this angle, one of the few skyscrapers in the city was visible; she'd gotten so used to living in Ottawa that it was strange not to see more. She stepped outside, the wind blowing against her like a tidal wave. And so cold. Not the same humidity as the eastern side had, but it was still enough to nip at her exposed skin.

A warmer coat was definitely necessary here.

Adam opened a dark brown metal door at the back of a building made of what looked like beige stone, and she darted inside. Heat surrounded her, and within seconds, she was warm again.

But she wasn't sure if it was the indoor heating or the sights making her feel so hot under the collar.

From where she stood, purple and pink lights shone on the grungy stone walls. A small stage held a few poles, the metal shining in a blue color from the lightbulbs above. This wasn't at all like the CrowBar.

"Er... is this place a... nightclub too?" she asked, her voice suddenly feeling small.

He grinned. "It is. Just a bit niche in its type."

She opened her mouth to ask for more information but decided against it. The leather whips and wooden paddles on display gave her a pretty good idea of who this place catered to. And she was glad the place didn't seem open at this hour, or she might have burst into flames.

"And you own it?" she asked as they descended into the basement. A few nights ago, she would've dreaded going below, especially while following the first Sanguis demon. It felt so strange how everything had changed so fast.

"I own it, yes. This club is called the Dragon's Lair." There was a note of teasing in his voice, and she rolled her eyes, forgetting once again that he sensed her emotions through the brand.

Double doors at the end of the corridor opened on their own as they approached, and Namika grinned.

"Do you have something against using doorknobs or something?" she asked playfully.

He arched an eyebrow as he slipped out of his coat. "No, I just prefer to save time." He helped her out of hers but stayed close. "Although some things I definitely prefer using my hands for."

Goosebumps rose along her arms, her pulse speeding.

The place looked like a large studio apartment, everything open concept. Black panels decorated the walls along with many lit candelabras, giving the room a gothic style. All the furniture was black or crimson. She glanced towards the four-poster bed and swallowed hard, wondering what would happen next. What did she want to happen?

A notification alert caused his phone to vibrate, and she let out a breath. He pulled out the device and frowned as he stared at the screen.

"What is it?" she asked, unsure if he'd tell her.

"I had ordered my children in this area to keep a lookout for any suspicious activities around reapers. One of them, Elijah, texted that he has information about something that occurred yesterday." He looked up from his screen at her. "Apparently, witnesses stated there were monsters tearing at someone with glowing red eyes."

She gawked at him. "Wait. Are you saying ghouls attacked a demon, and people saw this?" Most supernatural beings usually stayed out of the public eye; the situation would become even more problematic if this news got around.

"Police haven't commented, but rumors have it that they're saying it was drug users," he said with a scoff. "I'd like to know what kind of substance they'll blame it on."

She glanced at the door. "I know we just got here, but should we go check it out now?"

"I'd prefer going out under the cover of darkness in case there are still police around." He walked over to the large bed. "We've got a couple of hours before then. I want you to get a bit more sleep before we head off."

"I'm not tired." She sounded like a toddler, even to her own ears. Plus, she was lying, but she couldn't stand the thought of still doing nothing.

He drew the silky red sheets back. "You still can't eat or

drink. The least you can do is make sure your body has enough rest."

"I slept on the plane."

"You *passed out* on the plane." He looked at her as though daring her to lie again. "That's not the same thing, and you know it."

"But——"

"Do as you're told," he said in a stern voice that caused a shiver down her spine.

She hated being talked to like she was a child. "No."

"No?" he repeated. "Is that your final answer?" He materialized inches from her.

"Yes..." she said, her tone wavering.

"I'm sure I can change your mind." He slid his hand to her lower back. "Are you resisting because you want me to put you to bed?"

Before she answered, he picked her up in his arms. She yelped, and he sat her on the edge of the mattress, his gaze pinning her to the spot.

Her heart beat so fast, she was sure he'd hear it. "I... I don't want to wrinkle my new clothes." Part of her hated herself for fearing what could happen between them. "Linda will never let me hear the end of it if she has to buy me some more."

He grinned, and her shoulders relaxed. He didn't seem frustrated with her. "I'll find you a t-shirt you can sleep in, then."

She stared up at the black curtains hanging over the wooden structure of the bed. Why couldn't she get their kiss out of her mind? Did she want more than that?

Frustratingly, she rubbed her face. She was being ridiculous; Adam was a demon. And a good-looking one at that. He could have anyone he wanted. The best he'd likely offer her was a one-night stand or friends with benefits.

She scoffed at the thought. Friends? She wasn't sure what they were, but part of her knew it wasn't usually that simple with his kind. The normal steps of relationships—platonic or otherwise—weren't the same as with humans. No matter how much part of her wanted more. If they broke the curse, she'd remain branded to him. The only reason they were spending any time together was to lift the curse and save both of them from an eternity of anguish.

At the thought of not spending every day with him, her chest squeezed.

And by the time he returned with a black t-shirt, her mind was made up. She appreciated his help and the comfort he brought her, but that was as far as she was willing to go. Eventually, they'd part ways, and she couldn't bear the thought of it if she continued getting closer to him.

"Here," he handed her the top, then turned around, giving her privacy.

She quickly stripped down and slipped the loose-fitting t-shirt over her head. His scent seemed to almost hug her, and she clenched her jaw as she slid beneath the covers. The silky material was cool against her skin, and as soon as her head touched the pillow, she relaxed.

He leaned his palms against the mattress, looking at her. "I'll wake you in a few hours."

She nodded, but when he tried to leave, she grabbed the side of his trousers. She was still terrified of being alone. Terrified that the Inferno would come back for her.

"Can you stay close until I fall asleep?" She wanted to kick herself for how needy she sounded.

Didn't I just decide not to get too close to him?

He sat on the edge of the bed, the mattress dipping

under his weight. Something in his gaze gentled despite his red irises almost glowing. "Of course."

"ARE you sure this is the right place?" Namika asked for the hundredth time. "I don't see anyone."

Elijah had pinged his location, leading them to an industrial area of boarded-up factories. Many buildings still stood, but they looked like they'd been there for as long as the province had existed. The sun had already set, but luckily, floodlights illuminated a good portion of where they stood.

"The coordinates lead here." Adam pointed towards the side. "It's close to the motel where witnesses saw the attack."

She let out a breath, a puff of white visible in this cold. "Oh good, we'll have a place we can go in to warm up afterward."

"We're not setting foot in there. It's a dump."

She scoffed. "I'm sorry we can't all afford a penthouse, mister fancy-pants."

"Oh, don't get me wrong. There's something to be said about inexpensive places. They keep their noses out of other people's business and don't ask questions." He leaned closer to her. "They'd never ask about any noises they'd hear... like moaning or screaming."

Her body seemed to combust at once as her pulse throbbed between her legs. The bastard knew how to use his charm.

"And you're sure Elijah didn't say anything about meeting him anywhere else?" she asked quickly, desperate to get her heart rate to slow.

A loud bang echoed from nearby, and she straightened,

looking around, trying to find the source. It sounded like something heavy had fallen, but with the multiple empty buildings surrounding them, it was hard to tell where it came from.

Adam motioned with his head, and they walked forward. As they turned towards a path winding between two large buildings, Namika slowed her steps.

He glanced over his shoulder. "Everything alright?"

"I'm not sure..." She stared around. "I think there's something nearby."

Figures blurred around them, and she froze.

Ghouls.

Beneath their skin, black and red veins pulsed, their soulless stares empty. One snarled, and she took a step back at the needle-like teeth. They were surrounded, and despite being trained to fight demons and vampires, these were beyond her knowledge. What would hurt them? And she'd locked her magic down to protect herself after losing her Venatore powers; how was she supposed to defend herself?

Adam grabbed her arm and pulled her close, not taking his eyes off the monsters. "I'll distract them. You run and hide, understand?"

"I'm not leaving you to fight a dozen——"

His grip tightened, and she flinched. "I can deal with them, but not if I'm worried about your well-being. Now go."

She quickly scanned her surroundings, attempting to determine the direction to take. Depending on how long he kept their attention, she had one of two options. She could run inside one of the nearby factories and have time to find a good hiding spot. But if her time was short, she'd have to hide somewhere else——and fast.

They lunged, and she screamed, ducking as one

jumped at her. They moved quickly, but she had no problem following their movements. Yet, the shadows clinging to them seemed to travel faster and gave the illusion that the ghoul was running when they stood motionless.

He raised his hands, and a glowing string circled around him. With a flick of his wrist, it flew forward, taking hold of a few monsters and lifting them off the ground. They screeched, contorting against their binds until Adam curled his fingers into a fist and it sliced through them. The string continued floating around him, blood drops sliding along the thin lines.

More ghouls attacked, and she ran in the opposite direction. Adam was right; he needed to focus on killing them, and she was in the way. But leaving him alone to deal with so many felt wrong.

She glanced over her shoulder, checking to make sure she wasn't being chased. None followed; they attacked him all at once. He was buried underneath ghouls, slashing at his body with their claws, ripping through him. She quickly dashed behind a large garbage container. She wouldn't let him die.

Sliding her hand across her forearm, she muttered the words she'd learned as a child. The spell her grandmother had taught her to lock down her magic. It was only to be used to heal herself, and nothing more; those were the rules she was taught. The sigil lit up beneath her skin, and she paused, her pulse beating in her ears until it felt like she was underwater.

She frowned. No. Everything had fallen into a deep silence.

As fast as she could muster, she returned to the place of the attack. Tears blurred her vision at the scene; not at the ghouls' bodies scattered around in pieces, but at the lone figure lying face down on the pavement.

"Adam," she screamed, running to him.

Please don't let him be dead. Please.

The thought of him gone sent bile in the back of her throat, but she ignored it.

A force rammed into her, knocking the air out of her lungs as it threw her backward. Her vision darkened after her head hit the hard surface, and everything spun around her. She was sure the ghouls were destroyed. So what had attacked her?

With a groan, she rolled to the side, wincing with every inch as she staggered to her feet. Her breath caught in her throat as Adam stood.

He locked gazes with her. His irises glowed red, but it was what lingered behind that caused her fear. It was deeper than the usual darkness she glimpsed; this was evil. Her instincts warned this wasn't the demon she knew.

Something was wrong.

16

POISONED

Crimson smoke billowed, surrounding them. Namika took a step back, but flinched when something sliced into her side. The fog turned to glass, the edges as sharp as razor blades.

"Adam?" Her voice sounded so loud in the heavy silence.

He appeared suddenly before her, and she gasped. Black liquid dripped from his mouth; it looked like the same stuff that ghouls bled out.

"Poor little Namika," he hissed through pointed teeth. "You've gone through so many hardships in your brief life. And for what? Cursed by your own kin and sentenced to burn in Hell for eternity."

"I know it's not you talking," she said, trying to keep the fear from her voice. "You need to snap out of it."

He wrenched her closer. "Maybe once I'm done with you, I'll bring what remains to one of my cells. Keep you there for myself." He slid his hand on the side of her neck, his thumb tracing along her throat. "I want to shatter you beyond repair."

"Please——"

"Save your begging. I've heard it all."

He threw her back, and she flew across the way, hitting a nearby wall. Every part of her felt bruised, but she quickly got up, despite nearly toppling over from how much everything spun. She didn't linger and dashed into the nearest building, hoping to find somewhere to hide.

At least long enough to call for help. The only other person on her contact list was Linda. Namika wasn't sure if the demon could stop her master, but maybe she'd call reinforcements.

The inside of the building was mostly empty, save for debris left behind. It looked like a fire had taken this place years ago. She looked around, trying to make out where to go, but with how dark it was, she was having trouble. The last thing she needed was to take a misstep and end up plummeting into a hole.

She followed the large pipes on the wall, hoping they would lead to somewhere she could hide. Every step crunched loudly, and she tensed. He definitely knew where she was and toyed with her at this point.

A light up ahead flickered, and she rushed over as she pulled out her flip phone. The floor beneath her feet gave out, and she shrieked, trying to grab hold of anything on her way down.

She hit a metal grate, and she held her breath, the pain in her ribs sending a wave of nausea through her. Dust fell around, and she moved her hand in front of her, trying to locate her phone.

Instead, her fingers curled around a cylindrical object, and when she brought it closer, she realized it was a flathead screwdriver.

Adam approached, and she slid the tool to her side, out of view.

"I was thinking of what happens after we break this little curse." He crouched in front of her, his eyes glowing so brightly it was hard to meet his gaze. "I enjoy the moments we share together and want to continue enjoying them. You're branded. Mine forever. No one could stop me from keeping you." He grabbed her ankle and yanked her beneath him.

She clutched the screwdriver. "Adam, please. You're not thinking straight."

"It's funny, isn't it?" He leaned closer until they were almost nose-to-nose. "You got us into this whole mess because you wanted to escape me so much. And in the end? You'll never really get away from me, will you?" He licked his lips, and she shivered.

His mouth moved to her neck, and she froze as his pointed teeth grazed across her skin.

"Stop!" she tried pushing him away.

"I can smell you," he whispered in her ear. "I just need a bit of you. Your blood, your life. You."

She plunged the screwdriver into his shoulder and kicked with all the strength she had. He fell to the side, and she crawled away, still trying to find her phone to call for help. She had to get hold of Linda.

He seized a clump of her hair and yanked her head back. She gasped, her scalp burning as he pulled her up to her feet.

He gripped the screwdriver and yanked it out before throwing it to the floor. It fell with a clank, and her pulse sped at the fury burning in his gaze.

"Ah, ah," he cooed, grasping her chin and forcing her to look at him. "That wasn't very nice." He tightened his hold, and she winced. "I'll admit I'm impressed, though. More resourceful than I thought."

"Thanks," she snapped in the driest tone she could

muster. He wouldn't kill her, and she counted on that to hopefully get help later.

He laughed, but it had the same twisted amusement as Shiriki. "I'm going to make you pay for stabbing me." He let go of her and traced his finger along her neck. "Biting you? Or maybe tying you to a post and whipping you? Tell me which you want. Pick one."

She placed her hand against his chest, allowing some of her healing magic to flow to her fingertips. "You... said you'd protect me." She spoke so low, she wasn't sure he'd heard.

A pained stare changed his features, as though he woke from a nightmare. Slowly, he released her and took several steps back, pressing his hands against his head. He coughed, and more black liquid poured out of his mouth.

She rushed to him, but he shook his head. "Stay back."

"Are you...you again?" she asked, but from the look in his eyes, she already knew the answer. "Give me your phone. I'll call for help—"

"No." He bit the word out, then collapsed on the floor. "No. I don't know if I'm still... I don't want to hurt any of my children."

She took a few tentative steps towards him. "What do you need me to do?"

"Leave me. Go somewhere where there are other people. Stay away from here until I know for sure I'm safe to be around." He sat on the floor, leaning back against the wall. "I'm... I'm so sorry, Namika."

Part of her was still terrified of him after what happened, but she cared more than she feared him. "I'm not leaving you."

She slid her fingers along her arm again and finished muttering the words. Her magic swelled up inside her, and she focused on the warmth floating within her core. She pulled it forward, allowing it to flow around her until it felt like it enveloped her like a cocoon. The room glowed in a white light. Adam's eyes were wide as he stared up at her.

Not waiting for him to say anything, she crouched in front of him and reached out, but he grabbed her wrist, holding her back.

"You said only your friend accepted the vampire's powers." He didn't hide the anger in his voice. "But this whole time——"

"I was born with this magic, but kept it locked away my whole life." She wrenched her hand away, her jaw clenched. "And now, I've unlocked it despite being told never to do that to save your ungrateful ass, and this is how you thank me? By calling me a liar?" She shouted the last words and then placed her hands against his chest to heal him. "Well, joke's on you because I'm not leaving you here alone, and I *will* heal you whether you like it or not."

He stared at her with an unreadable expression. She'd never used this much magic before, and she was careful about how much she used in case it could hurt demons. After a few seconds, he coughed again, gasping as he sputtered out more of the black liquid. She stopped only when there was nothing left.

She grabbed his wrist and tugged.

"Namika——"

"Right now, you owe me a favor, so you're going to get up and let me finish helping you."

His eyebrows shot up, but he slowly got to his feet. He staggered, so she threw his arm over her shoulder. Blood gushed between his fingers, and her heart hammered.

"I'm sorry I can't heal you completely. I'm not used to using my magic on others." She glanced up at him. "You'll be okay, though, right?" she asked.

"The wounds are starting to mend."

She looked up at him. "Any chances of you going evil again? Should I be worried?"

"No. What happened before was...something else. The ghouls held me down, and one slit his throat and bled out into my mouth. I think it poisoned me," he said quietly.

"Are you still poisoned?"

"I think your magic got rid of it." He pulled away his hand, staring at the blood. "I'm still not fully healed, though. It's why I told you to leave me behind. I'm not safe to be around."

She pulled his phone from his jacket. "Well, let's get you back to that den of debauchery you call home. Maybe I can finish healing you there."

He chuckled as she searched for taxi services in the area and called one up. Once ordered, she looked him over with a frown. There was no way the driver would allow Adam to get into his vehicle; he was hazardous with all the blood splattered on him.

She helped him lean against the wall for support, then slid her coat off. Without a word, she pulled on her sleeve until it covered her hand and began wiping his face.

The way he looked at her sent butterflies fluttering in her stomach.

"The ghoul blood is too thick," she said with a grimace. "I'll go outside and see if I can find a puddle or something."

She went to walk away, but he grasped her wrist. "You'll come back, right?" He seemed so scared for a second.

She nodded. "I promise."

The outside air sent her body into near shock at how cold it had gotten, but she pushed on. She stopped near a gutter and poked the thin ice at the foot of the spout with the tip of her boot. It gave a satisfying crack, and she quickly dipped her sleeve into the freezing water beneath.

By the time she returned to Adam, the wound in his abdomen was closed, and blood had stopped gushing out. She finished cleaning him as best she could, trying her best to ignore how fast her heart was beating.

Her mind raced with one thought. Ghoul blood acted as poison to demons. Not something she wanted a repeat of with others. Had the demon who gave them the location died? Or maybe it was never Elijah who'd texted Adam in the first place; this could easily have been a trap.

"What about the bodies?" The last thing they needed was for the police to find a dozen remains. Especially since they weren't human.

"I'll text the cleaning crew in this metropolis."

She helped him with his phone, texting the words he instructed since his hands still trembled too much; he'd nearly dropped the device twice. Just as she hit send, a horn honked close by, announcing the taxi had pulled up. She helped him button up his coat to hide how shredded and bloody it was, and they walked out together.

At this hour, the Dragon's Lair was filled with people, and Namika was relieved. Adam seemed too tired to tease her about the sounds coming from the main room.

She kept a close eye on him as they walked down the corridors, partly to make sure he wouldn't turn into a monster again and that he kept upright.

He opened the door to his studio-type apartment. "Take the shower in there. I'll take the one for guests down the hall."

For a second, she imagined them showering together,

but she pushed that thought out of her mind as fast as it appeared. "Okay."

Once inside, the noise from the club upstairs vanished, and she was left in deafened silence. She slipped off her coat and boots, glad that she had a bit of time alone to process everything. The electric fireplace heated the area nicely, but she couldn't seem to warm up.

She trudged to the bathroom, the door closing behind her with a soft click. She gawked at the shower; it looked even fancier than the one in the guest bathroom of his penthouse. It was the size of a walk-in closet with so many shower heads and individual jets that she couldn't count them all.

Black vines with red flowers bloomed along the metal frames holding the glass; it was so beautiful.

She stripped and turned the simplest-looking valve, hoping it wouldn't turn on everything at once. Luckily, the two shower heads above poured water down, and she got inside.

Her muscles relaxed beneath the hot water. She ran her hand along her shoulder where the curse was left behind, the scar a constant reminder of what awaited her for eternity if she couldn't break the curse.

After scrubbing off most of the dirt, she slid her arm along her waist until she reached her back, tracing Adam's brand. Even though he'd been out of his mind with poison, his cruel words lingered in her mind. Had he meant any of it? Were they subconscious thoughts?

She dipped her head beneath the running water. If she'd had a shower like this at her old apartment, she never would've left. At the thought of her old place, Yasuo's face flashed in her mind. The memory of her deceased boyfriend sent a pang of guilt through her. After demons had tortured him, caring for one was a betrayal of his memory.

But when she thought Adam was dying, her heart felt like it was crushed. Leaving him behind was impossible, and she knew, in that moment, that she cared more for him than she'd thought.

She wished she could freeze time and stand here forever, but she'd stalled long enough.

As she dried herself off with a fluffy white towel, she eyed her dusty clothing. Thankfully, she had a change of clothes this time and didn't need to wait for Linda to bring her anything. She put on some leggings and a long top, then grabbed the spare slippers before stepping out.

The door opened, and Linda walked in.

"Is my master still in the bathroom?"

Namika's cheeks heated. "Of course not. I was just in there."

Linda shrugged and sat on the sofa, stretching out her legs. "Where is he, then?"

"He's getting cleaned up in the guest shower." Namika took a seat across from the demon. "I'm sure he'll be back soon."

"Got yourselves dirty?" she asked with a wink.

Before Namika responded, Adam walked in, and she swallowed hard. He wore black sweatpants and an open dress shirt, revealing how muscular he was. His hair was still damp and fell above his ears, almost messy. She'd never seen him so laid back before.

"Linda," he gave a curt nod. "Find anything?"

She beamed. "I've got good news, and even better news."

He grabbed a glass from the bar and poured himself an amber liquid. "That'll be nice for a change." He downed the whole thing, then slammed the glass on the surface, cracking it.

Linda glanced at Namika and gave a questioning look with her raised eyebrow, but didn't wait. "Sebastian Ecter is a part-owner of an exclusive restaurant in the city. He's dining there tomorrow night."

Namika's pulse sped. "So we can corner him when he leaves?"

"Even better." Linda grinned as she leaned forward. "We're getting inside. I got an invitation with a plus one."

Adam leaned against the mantelshelf of the fireplace. "Miss Strang here remembered that the vampire has a phone number with the regional code for this province. Meaning, the reaper is likely here investigating things on his end."

Namika's stomach churned at his tone; he sounded like he was angry with her. As though she'd withheld that information. She wanted to retort that she was a bit busy being attacked, but she decided he was in a bad enough mood as it was.

"So he's here checking things out. So what? How does that change our plan?" Linda asked in a sulking tone.

"Meaning, he's likely steering clear of demons since I requested a meeting with him about a curse."

Namika's mind worked a million miles a minute. "Steering clear of demons, but not of me," she breathed.

Adam's glower burned brighter than the flames in the fireplace. "Out of the question."

Linda stared at Namika with a grin. "Little Miss Virgin here flirting with a known womanizer? I'd pay to see that."

She gawked at the demon. "I was a hunter with the Venatores. Of course I'm not a... You know."

Adam cocked his head. "What does being a hunter have anything to do with it?"

A shiver ran across her body, and she blinked a few times as she stared from Adam to Linda. Did they really not know how it worked within the Venatores? Deciding she didn't want to explain that part of her training, she went a different route.

"I've been bait a few times."

Adam sat next to her, the heat of his body feeling like it was engulfing her. "And how do you plan on flirting when you blush at the mere mention of sex?"

Of course, her body proved him right as her cheeks burned. He smiled in satisfaction, but she held her head high.

"Some like the whole shy girl thing." Her words came out in mumbles, and she cursed herself for not being assertive. "Besides, I also have something else up my sleeve." She hoped he knew she meant the connection she had to reapers since she was a mystic.

He smiled, but it didn't reach his eyes. "Linda, you'll take Miss Strang shopping for an appropriate outfit tomorrow."

"Yes, Master," she said, bowing her head.

When Adam said nothing else, Namika turned to Linda. "Getting those exclusive invitations must have been difficult. Thank you."

Linda's eyebrows shot up, but she quickly regained her composure, flicking her long blonde hair over her shoulder. "It was easy. Just need to know the right people."

Adam nodded. "You did well, Linda."

She looked like she was floating on cloud nine as she smiled at him. "Thank you, Master."

And without another word, Linda vanished, as though she didn't want to chance sticking around for anyone to ruin her happy moment.

A second or two ticked by, and Namika decided not to wait.

"Why are you upset with me?" she asked.

He narrowed his eyes at her. "If you had told me you were a mystic from the start, we might have been able to meet with the reaper back in Toronto."

"Maybe. But if he'd still refused, then we wouldn't have this second chance. He doesn't know a mystic is involved, which will make it possible for me to get close to him."

"Looking forward to that, are you?" he snapped.

Jealousy squeezed her chest, and she realized it wasn't her own emotions. "You can't be serious. You said it yourself that I'm obviously uncomfortable with anything related to... intimacy."

"Yet you jumped on the opportunity to take Linda's place pretty quickly."

"Because I don't want to be condemned to the Inferno, and for you to endure eternal torture." She slammed her palms against the seat and bolted to her feet. "Why are you acting like this? Is it because I saved you? Because I emasculated you by having my own powers? Or——"

"You lied to me." His voice seemed to slice through the air, the hurt in his eyes making her heart beat faster.

She sat back down. "It wasn't personal. I've never told anyone. Only my parents and grandparents knew. No one else. Not even the Venatores. Not Celina or Yasuo."

"And now me," he said quietly.

"Yes, and now you." Tears blurred her vision, but she blinked fast to make sure they wouldn't fall. "And I did it despite not knowing how to lock it back."

"Why?"

"It was my turn to save you."

"And I appreciate it." He drew closer. "Someone once

lied to me, and it cost me everything. It's why I don't tolerate being lied to by those I trust."

"I'm sorry you were betrayed like that," she said, and meant it.

"But I also understand that keeping personal secrets isn't the same as lying. I shouldn't have insinuated that you lied to me."

"Are you going to tell your king?" Tears blurred her vision. "I can't lose this part of me——"

He placed his finger on her lips. "I won't say anything unless he asks. Besides, he can't take that magic from you even if he wanted to, since it doesn't fall under his realm."

Her muscles relaxed. "That's good."

His gaze searched hers. "I was born in 1342 as Hayden Wilkes Leverton. Only Mekaisto and Shiriki know this, and now you do, too."

She gaped at him, her heart hammering. He was over six hundred years old. How much he must've seen. Why had he changed his name? So many questions flew through her mind, but she pushed them away; it wasn't the time to ask.

"Thank you for trusting me. I swear I won't ever tell anyone."

He pushed a strand of her hair behind her ear. "I'm sorry about before. I shouldn't have reacted the way I did to you being bait. I... I worry."

She placed her hand over his. "I'll be okay." She smiled. "So, what exactly *is* the plan?"

17

CONFIDENCE

*N*amika pushed the dresses along the rack, occasionally pulling one out to look at it. After a few seconds, she put it back with a sigh.

"What was wrong with that one?" Linda asked in an annoyed voice, crossing her arms.

"You may have forgotten, but I've got a huge scar from my shoulder to mid-back that I need to hide."

Linda scoffed. "Lots of people have scars. Just shows off you won."

"I haven't won yet," Namika muttered.

"Then it's a reminder to keep fighting." Linda approached the clothes rack and searched through it as well. "Besides, we need to find you something sexy. Meaning, your scar will show, and that's fine."

Namika recalled how Adam had reacted to her being bait. "Not too revealing, though."

"Ha!" She pulled out a dress that didn't look like it had enough material. "This one is perfect."

Namika took it from her. "I *just* said not too revealing."

"Try it on." Linda pushed it against Namika, and she

grabbed it to keep it from falling to the floor. She wanted to argue, but Linda put her hands on her hips and arched an eyebrow as though daring Namika to refuse.

As Namika guessed, there wasn't enough material. The back was fully opened, dipping low until it stopped at her lower back. The front had two straps that got wider as it descended, just enough to cover her breasts, then connected above her navel. The material had a shine to it, the dark blue contrasting beautifully with the rose gold chains hanging around her hips and the ones connecting the straps at the front.

It was a gorgeous dress, but her scars were too visible. They looked so ugly. The lump in her throat tightened, and she focused instead on Adam's brand. Even that was partially visible in this dress. But no matter how much she tried focusing on other parts, the scarring kept coming back into view. What would Adam say if he saw her like this? Would he find them disgusting?

She glanced down at herself, and any self-esteem she had flew out the window. She was always comfortable with her body—although having larger breasts than a size A-cup was an occasional wish—she liked herself. But it was difficult to look past the scars.

A knock on the changing room door made Namika jump, and she opened it. Linda grinned as her gaze raked along Namika's body.

"Oh, this is going to make my master lose his mind," she said with a cackle.

Namika's eyebrows shot up. "Any particular reason you think angering him is a good idea?"

Linda pulled Namika out and pushed her in front of a mirror that had better sunlight. "Oh, please. Don't pretend you didn't see how jealous he got last night at the thought of you being bait." She pulled on the chain around Namika's hips and placed it at a better angle. "You wearing this will drive him insane."

Namika caught a few people glancing at her and whispering amongst themselves. Her shoulders slumped, and she hugged herself, feeling too vulnerable. "Look, I get you might still be pissed off at him for the whole personal servant thing, but I don't need him angry at me again."

"This isn't just about him," Linda said, raising her chin. "You need to get out of your comfort zone and do this right. Your role is to be the sultry woman who entices Sebastian Ecter into ignoring the precautions he's taken and invite you to the private area of the restaurant so you can talk to him."

Namika opened her mouth, but closed it again, staring at herself in the mirror. "How am I supposed to do that when I feel like I'm naked?"

"Being naked *is* showing your power. You own your body, and you allow others to see what you decide they can." Linda grasped her shoulders, staring at Namika's reflection. "Have confidence, and everything you wear or don't wear will be sexy."

Namika straightened a bit, doing her best to imagine herself being confident. Being sexy. She giggled and pressed her hand against her mouth, surprised at her own reaction. Linda grinned and led her to the platform in front of mirrors where tailors made adjustments.

Linda had taken them to one of the finest dress shops in Winnipeg. All on Adam's credit card, of course.

Nearly three hours later, Namika stood in what would be the final outfit. Linda had added rose gold bracelets that matched the dress's delicate chains, as well as a short necklace that accentuated her neck. The dress was long, but with the high heels the tailor had recommended, the material didn't touch the floor.

Namika gave herself one last glance in the mirror.

"Not bad," she said as her heart continued hammering against her chest as though trying to escape.

Linda slapped Namika's arm. "You can do better than that."

Namika rubbed the spot, but stared back. "Very... good?" she said tentatively. When Linda raised her hand again, Namika moved to the side to avoid her. "Okay, okay. I look fantastic. And... sexy," she whispered the last word.

Linda nodded with a smile on her lips. "Better. Now, time for hair and makeup. Then we'll head to the restaurant."

NAMIKA TIGHTENED her coat as they stepped out of the taxi. The wind blew hard from two different directions, creating a sort of funnel, and her teeth chattered. Her legs burned from the intense cold, but she focused on Linda walking up ahead.

Apparently, the temperature didn't affect the demon, and for a second, Namika envied her.

They dashed into the side alleyway, and Linda knocked on a metal door as she fished out two black tickets with crimson fonts.

A small slot opened, and Linda handed the tickets without a word. After a few seconds, the door swung open, and they stepped inside. Namika's back ached with how violently she shivered, cursing the weather.

The man at the door stamped the back of their hands, the ink glowing for a second before vanishing. Namika gawked at her skin, but kept silent about it; she wasn't about to question everything in this place. It was a restaurant that catered to the paranormal, so she was bound to see things out of the ordinary.

Linda slipped out of her coat and handed it to the woman behind a counter. Her own dress was dark red and fit her like a glove, falling along her curves below her derriere. The black corset accentuated her chest, while the thigh-high black boots showed off her long legs.

Namika gave herself a mental shake and took her own coat off, following the demon's lead. Still, she couldn't seem to calm down; the stakes were so high, she barely could keep her pulse from racing. What if the reaper had no interest in Namika and didn't invite her to the VIP area? They didn't have a Plan B, and she was already panicked about how much time they'd lost. At least if she knew how much time she had left in the first place... but what if it was a few hours? Or minutes?

"You look terrified," Linda whispered, bringing Namika out of her downward spiral. "I mean, that works for some people, but I suggest going for the whole sexy but shy school girl act."

Namika took a deep breath. "Sorry, sorry. Just... I'm overthinking."

"You? Overthinking?" Linda said in mock shock. "Never."

"Okay. I can do this."

"Fuck yeah, you can," Linda said with a grin as she slid her hand along Namika's arm and led her into the main room.

The place was almost a cliché of supernatural elements, and Namika wondered why they went for that look. Or maybe that was the whole point? Making fun of the stereotypical things associated with them?

A large bar stood against one wall, a pentagram centered between the shelves holding various liquor bottles.

Archways along the sides gave way to painted murals showing what looked like skeletons dancing in flames.

Namika took a seat at the table, and Linda sat across. This seemed so strange, like she'd stepped into another world. Even the menu had a pentagram with a skull in the middle.

Everything was illuminated in candlelight, most of which were candelabra hanging from the walls. Although the massive fireplace at the end of the room definitely contributed to the glow.

"There," Linda whispered, motioning with her head towards the back.

Namika slowly turned and stared towards a staircase leading up to where two men stood on either side. It led up to an overhead balcony hidden from view, but she felt someone there. She had to figure out how to catch the reaper's attention from below, but she wasn't sure how. The confidence she was trying to build up during the day seemed to deflate straight out of her at this point.

She had to act, or she'd end up psyching herself out and being too scared. Without a word, she stood and walked towards the bar; at this angle, the second floor would be visible.

The ceiling overhead in the VIP area was also visible, and Namika's pulse sped. It was painted in the depiction of what most people imagined Hell to look like. This wasn't exactly the reminder she wanted staring down at her. Faces with pointed teeth stared from above, their black horns swirling into shadowy forms. Black cities surrounded by red smoke and lava stood at the bottom.

She focused on her magic, doing her best to keep it as reined in as possible; she still hadn't mastered it since unlocking it. Her powers flowed upward, identifying her as a mystic.

One of the men who stood near the stairs approached. "Mr. Ecter has requested your company."

She nodded, hoping her throat would work when she came face to face with the reaper in question. Linda gave her a quick smile, and Namika reminded herself of the demon's words about confidence. The stairs seemed like they were endless, yet at the same time, she was upstairs too quickly.

Sebastian Ecter waited for her near the railing, and she allowed more of her magic to surround her. He smiled, but there was something deadly about him.

"Well, well," he said in amusement. "I rarely get the treat of meeting with a mystic. Especially one that's had their thread severed."

Namika's breath hitched at how fast he noticed that. Her grandmother had warned her about reapers time and time again, and here she was, walking right into the company of one. It was one reason she had cut that very thread in Namika's soul when she was a kid. Just like she'd done to Namika's father. To keep them safe from reapers.

"Have a seat," he said, motioning to the black loveseat.

"Thank you." She took a seat and did her best to keep calm.

He sat and crossed his legs, leaning back. He wore a black suit with a white dress shirt opened at the top, his brown hair falling above his ears in unruly waves. Drumming his fingers against the armrests, the silver rings clanked against the wood.

"I noticed you came in with a demon. Your date?" He asked nonchalantly, but she picked up the sharp edge in his voice.

"I'm actually here because you refused to meet with me before."

His green irises suddenly seemed brighter as he

straightened. "Ah, so you're the one who was cursed by a lost soul." He eyed her from head to toe. "Branded by the first Sanguis demon. I see why."

"He branded me to slow the curse's progression." She felt the need to defend Adam's actions, not wanting him to seem like he'd made that decision lightly.

"I wasn't aware it was a mystic who was cursed." He leaned closer. "Unless he didn't tell me because he didn't know either?"

"He knows now." She shifted to face him better. "The God of Shadows knows how to break this curse, but I don't know how to summon him. Can you help me?"

He leaned his elbow on the sofa's back. "What do I get?"

"Adam—Mr. Ashton—is prepared to offer you a favor from him."

"At any time, without questions or contestations?" Something sinister lingered behind his words, and she swallowed hard.

But Adam had already agreed to that ahead of time. "Yes."

"Before I agree, I want to see if you're worth saving," he said, his mouth curling into a smile that was all teeth and frightening. They weren't pointed, but he looked ready to rip through flesh.

His irises glowed so green she could barely look at him. Light fell across the room, strange shadows dancing on the walls, and across the reaper's face. She stiffened when black surrounded the skin around his eyes and on the side of his mouth, creating a shadowed skull.

Light seeped from her core, the filaments floating in the air. He reached out to a few gray ones, and she shivered when his fingers brushed against them.

"Sadness, pain, loss," he said. "Lies, deceit, and abandonment from those you needed most. Hatred and fury. Distrust of most." He tugged on several blue filaments, and she gasped, pressing her hand against her chest.

A sudden coldness hit her as she glanced down; the filaments lingered from her body. "What are you doing?" she whispered, staring at the reaper.

"This." He held a white strand, his gaze boring into hers. "This is hope, love, and the need to trust. Friends, lovers, and family. But you only have one, whilst most people have several." He let go, and the light seeped into her body. "You barely have any of it left because it's so damaged."

"Stop," she whispered, hating how deep his words cut.

"Ah, there it is." He touched one that had turned black; it was barely visible in the darkness surrounding them. "The severed thread. The one that once connected you to your fated soulmate. Sliced away, never to be."

The room flashed to normal, and she gasped, feeling as though she had been thrown back. She swallowed, panting like she'd run for miles. Her skin chilled as sweat lingered, the surrounding air colder than before.

She clenched her jaw. "I don't remember agreeing to you looking into my soul like that."

"Didn't think you'd mind considering you're the one who ambushed me here in the first place," he said in a somber tone.

"So in your opinion, am I worth saving, then?" she asked, not counting on it with what he'd said while searching her soul.

"It occurred to me, you know my name, but I don't know yours," he said, resting his chin against his knuckles.

"Namika Strang."

He blinked a few times. "Are you related to Namika Okabe?"

Her heart seemed to skip several beats. "She was my grandmother."

"You're Mimi's granddaughter..." he said, a slow smile curling his lips. "I knew her in her youth. She was part of a rebel group. Quite problematic for my kind. But we got along, despite our differences." He seemed lost in thought for a second, then grinned at her. "Alright then, Mimi's granddaughter. I'll tell you how to summon a god."

18

EXCHANGES

Sebastian got to his feet and walked towards an alcove. Without a word, he raised his hand, and electricity sparked between the two columns until a green light swirled into view.

Namika quickly backed up, putting up her defenses, but when the monster she expected to walk through didn't appear, she retracted her magic.

He arched an eyebrow. "It's just a portal."

"It looks identical to the one the vampire popped out of when he had my friend murdered and cursed me."

He frowned. "That's disconcerting. I mean, each reaper portal is unique, but if it looks similar to this one, it means this vampire is getting help from one of my people..." He looked into the light, his eyes sparking. "It would certainly explain how he's connected to ghouls."

She eyed the portal. "I'd like Adam to come with us, if that's okay?" She wasn't really asking since there was no way she was about to go anywhere alone with a stranger.

"So he can give the location of my private library to his superiors?" he said with a chuckle.

"Please." She took a step closer. "I can't blindly trust you. Especially after seeing you have a similar portal to the vampire who's been trying to finish what he started. You could be taking me anywhere, or leading me into a trap."

"Fair points." He glanced towards the railing, and a few seconds later, Adam appeared at the top of the staircase.

Adam strode forward, glancing from Namika to the reaper as though trying to assess if she was in any danger. He stopped next to her and brought her closer, so she stood right next to him. She suddenly felt like the best protected person in there.

"I'm surprised you allowed me up here," Adam said, staring at the portal. "Were you trying to take her somewhere?"

"Trying? Yes. Failing? Also, yes." Sebastian shrugged. "She wouldn't go without you."

Namika tugged on Adam's jacket sleeve. "Mr. Ecter agreed to tell us how to summon Lokesh."

"And that requires leaving the restaurant?" Adam asked, focusing on the reaper.

"I don't know about you, *Sanguis*," he nearly hissed the word, "but I don't know every method of summoning off the top of my head."

Adam glowered, but remained silent.

Namika let out a sigh. "Can we go?"

Sebastian nodded and walked towards the portal as Namika and Adam followed closely. A flash of green light enveloped them for a few seconds, but the next thing she knew, they were inside what looked like endless darkness. Further ahead, light sparked, and she frowned; it was like they were walking down a corridor of pitch blackness that connected two portals.

"Reapers can create shortcuts of sorts," Adam

explained as they continued. "From point A to point B anywhere in either world, shortening the distance by quite a lot."

She stiffened when they approached the second portal; anything could be on the other side. What if she was trusting blindly again? The last time she had, Emma had died. At the thought of the same thing happening to Adam, her chest tightened.

Before she had time to second-guess herself too much, they stepped through, and she relaxed a bit when they stepped into what looked like an old office. There were no windows, but the stone walls and wooden furniture gave the place a cozy warmth, especially with the multiple candles illuminating the small space. The shelves were filled with books, so much so that some were left on top of others. A table stood in the middle of the room, taking up most of its space, with papers scattered across it.

Both Adam and Sebastian didn't seem like they fit in the décor of the place; it looked like the inside of an old cottage, while both men looked like they belonged in the fanciest hotels.

The reaper walked to one bookshelf, his gaze scanning the spines. As he grabbed a few books, Namika turned to Adam.

"That portal we went through is the same kind as the one the vampire was using when I first met him." She motioned with her head towards Sebastian. "He said each reaper has a unique portal, so if we can somehow get a video or photo of the one the vampire used, maybe we could find out which reaper is helping him."

Adam frowned, but before he could say anything, Sebastian chimed in. "Doubtful. There are millions of us, each with a specific signature. It would be like trying to find a needle in a haystack."

She narrowed her eyes. "Wish you would've said that when you brought up the whole uniqueness part in the first place."

"Some are skilled at identifying them. One of my brothers is actually one of the few people who can." Sebastian shrugged as he approached the table and laid out a few open books. "Besides, I'm here to explain how to summon a god. Nothing more, nothing less."

Leaning her hands against the surface, she focused on what was important: the information. "Okay, so how do we do it?"

Sebastian smiled, but there was nothing kind behind it. "In summary, you'll need a medallion embedded with the power of reapers. The stronger, the better. Once you have it, you offer a sacrifice to call on Lokesh. If he's in an agreeable mood, he might share with you how to break the curse."

"And can you...give me a medallion?" Namika asked tentatively.

Sebastian wiggled his finger as though scolding a child. "For a fee, I can provide you with one of mine."

She clenched her jaw. "Small fee?"

Adam crossed his arms. "I thought you'd already agreed in exchange for a favor—"

"That's for the information on how to summon Lokesh. There are a few more items you'll need, and the words to call him. All of which I'll give you in exchange for that favor."

"But you want something more for the medallion?" Adam asked, not hiding the edge of anger in his voice.

"Yes, but we'll get to that later. First, let's get you the other necessities." He pulled out his cellphone and hovered it over the book. "Smile," he said with a grin, and the flash went off. "This photo has the incantation to summon him, and..." He turned the page and took another picture. "This one has the list of ingredients and instructions."

Namika bit her lower lip. "Is it complicated?"

"Not really," Sebastian said, but the amusement in his gaze didn't reassure her. "It's more that, if you screw up, you'll end up... How should I put this?" He tapped his chin. "Worse off than dead? Or maybe in your case, since you're cursed, automatically sent to the Inferno."

"Oh..." She wasn't sure what else to say, but she was having trouble focusing.

Adam rested his hand on her back. "Don't worry."

Somehow, his words reassured her, and she nodded; she trusted he wouldn't let her down.

Sebastian slid his finger down the list of ingredients and stopped at one. "This isn't something I have in my possession... A sealed vase of Strix's Bone."

Adam waved his hand dismissively. "Shiriki will probably have one. I'll ask him for it."

The reaper's eyes flashed brighter for a second. "Speaking of him, I hope we understand one another when I say I don't want him anywhere near me for any reason."

"You're not the only one," Namika mumbled at the thought of that demon.

Adam grinned. "He won't bother you. We're well aware of the treaty made between our two races centuries ago. We're not about to start another war."

Namika's eyebrows shot up; there had been a war between the two? She'd never heard about that. Not from the Venatores or from her grandmother growing up.

Sebastian gave a curt nod. "Good. I'm glad to hear it."

"You also mentioned needing a sacrifice?" Adam asked as his cellphone pinged with a message. He pulled it out and handed it to Namika. "The list of ingredients," he said in a soft tone.

She looked at the list; Sebastian was right. It wasn't complicated, but some aspects were extremely specific. And the words for the incantation were not in a language she recognized.

Sebastian closed the books and returned them to their shelf. "Any sacrifice will do. All types of humans, demons, vampires..."

She didn't like the idea, but pushed it out of her mind; she was sure Adam knew of some who might deserve death.

Namika was going through the instructions and frowned. "We can only summon the God of Shadows on a new moon."

Adam took his phone back and interacted with the screen a few times. "Three nights from now."

"And what about the medallion you mentioned?" she asked.

"Let's go back," Sebastian said, the ghost of a smile touching his lips.

She had a bad feeling, but followed him back in silence. Once they returned to the loft of the restaurant, she took the same seat as before, and Adam sat next to her. Sebastian took the sofa across from them and leaned back.

What felt like an eternity passed by in painful silence until Adam let out an exasperated growl. "What do you want for your medallion then? Another favor from me? An artifact you've been looking for? A—"

"Nothing from you, Sanguis." His gaze rested on Namika. "I want something rare for such a precious gift."

She stiffened. "What do you want?"

"A small taste of your magic."

Her instincts warned her to refuse, but she didn't really have a choice when it came down to it; she desperately needed the object Sebastian had, and he knew it.

Adam placed his hand over hers, his irises glowing red. "Not a chance."

"I accept." Her voice was calm, despite the terror in her mind. She grasped Adam's hand and squeezed. "We need the medallion."

"I won't allow it," he said through gritted teeth, his pupils thinning into slits.

Normally, she'd hate if a man had said that, speaking as though he owned her and made the decisions for her. But with Adam, she knew it was out of wanting to protect and keep her safe, and she appreciated it.

"Adam, please. It'll be okay," she said with a small smile.

His gaze searched hers, the demonic eyes that once would've horrified her, lulling warmth into her core. With a nod, he let go of her hand, his muscles visibly stiffening as though willing himself not to hold her back.

She got to her feet and approached the reaper, eyeing him.

He patted his thigh like he wanted her to sit. "Hop on."

"Are you trying to make Adam want to murder you?" she asked dryly.

"He knows he has to control himself if he wants to save your soul," he said loudly enough so Adam heard him.

She glanced over her shoulder and swallowed hard as Adam's murderous glower seemed to burn right through the reaper. Still, he didn't stop her or say anything.

"You asked for a taste of my magic. That can be done without having to sit on your lap."

Something in Sebastian's gaze turned dangerous. "So, is your answer no? Isn't that why you got dolled up? To appeal to my deviant nature?"

She wanted to throw him over the railing, but he was right; she'd dressed with the goal of enticing him. And besides, she had the feeling he wouldn't give her the medallion if she didn't play along.

Biting the inside of her cheek, she sat on his lap, heat filling her cheeks. He took her hand and brought it to his mouth, his lips brushing against her palm.

Heat flowed from her core to the tip of her fingertips, and she shivered at the strange sensation. Light glowed beneath her skin, vanishing as it neared his mouth. Her heartbeat seemed to slow, and soon, she was having trouble keeping upright as her muscles grew heavier.

Their surroundings shook, and she stared up as the candelabra chandelier above swung from side to side.

Sebastian's arm tightened around her, and he grinned. "I don't think the owner of that brand on your back is too happy at the moment." He glanced towards the railing, where people's chattering voices rose at the sudden energy spike. "Mind keeping from destroying the place with your jealousy?" he shot at Adam.

Adam's hands curled into fists, but his power vanished as quickly as it appeared, and Namika slumped forward; she hadn't realized the amount of pressure that was building in the last few seconds.

"Are you alright, Miss Strang?" Adam asked in a growl.

She nodded, but it was hard to; like every part of her body was falling asleep on its own. Even her lungs were making it difficult for her to take deep breaths.

Sebastian forced her head to turn, so she'd look at him. "Nothing to worry about. You'll be tired for a few hours, and then you'll be back to your old self." He let go of her chin, then put his hand out in front of them. "As promised."

A medallion spun above his palm for a second before landing. It was about the size of a toonie, but thicker and not as perfectly shaped. A few places curved on the sides as though it was shaped manually, and not with a machine. The center held a skull with a rune below, which she recognized represented the number three.

He handed it to her, and she took it, pulse speeding. "Thank you."

Adam leaned his elbows against his knees, gaze fixed on the reaper like he was trying his best not to kill him. "You can let her go now."

Sebastian chuckled, his hold on her tightening again. "Once you've exited my barriers, yes. Until then, you're not going to try anything with her so close."

"I thought we already established that I'm not about to start a war."

Sebastian leaned back as though not bothered by the whole situation. "Hurting me would hardly start anything."

Her head drooped a bit, and she blinked several times, trying to stay awake. Warmth slowly filled her chest, and she straightened.

Adam got to his feet. "You know how to contact me when you need that favor?"

"I'll find you, don't worry." Sebastian motioned towards the stairs. "I'll let her go as soon as you're downstairs."

Adam clenched his jaw but left without another word.

The reaper stood, and Namika gasped as he put her down. She wavered a bit, still tired, but could stand on her own.

He smiled, and this time, it was filled with kindness. "It

was lovely to meet you, Mimi's granddaughter. I see a lot of her in you."

A lump squeezed in her throat at the memory of her grandmother. "Thank you."

"Oh, and one thing that isn't on the list of ingredients, but that you'll definitely want." He leaned closer. "Bacon cheeseburgers. Two dozen, unwrapped, and in a bowl."

She blinked several times. "Wait, what?"

"Trust me. It'll pretty much guarantee that Lokesh will tell you what you need to know." He grinned as she continued gawking at him. "May I recommend Mrs. Mike's burgers? Best in the city."

"I... Hmm. Okay. Thanks."

She walked away, a sense of unease settling over her as she felt Sebastian's gaze on her. She tightened her hold on the medallion, the edges digging into her palm.

As soon as she reached the bottom of the steps, she locked eyes with Adam. He stood near Linda, where she chatted with a few other patrons, but he was only focused on Namika. She approached, renewed hope burning inside at the information they'd gathered.

He took her hand, holding it out as his gaze raked over her. "By the way, you look absolutely mesmerizing," he said, his voice huskier than usual.

Her heart picked up more speed than she thought possible. She smiled, doing her best to ignore Linda's knowing grin.

"Thank you."

Linda glanced over her shoulder at the crowd surrounding them. "Would it be alright for me to stay behind, Master? The invitations here are difficult to get, and—"

"I want you to find Elijah. Information about where he

was last seen, what he was doing." He checked his watch, the silver standing out against the black sleeves of his suit.

When Linda's shoulders slumped, Namika spoke up. "This place caters to the paranormal. I imagine that, for the subject of your missing demon, Linda might get clues here, right?"

Namika swallowed hard as he narrowed his eyes, as though lost in thought for a moment. After a few seconds, he gave a curt nod. "Perhaps." He turned his attention back to Linda. "Ask around, then. I want to know where he is."

Linda kept a serious expression, but the corners of her mouth twitched as she bowed. "Yes, Master."

Adam turned to Namika. "Did you want to stay as well? I hear there's a beautiful aquarium in a private section of this place."

She swallowed hard and nodded. "I'd like that."

As they walked towards the back of the restaurant, Namika handed him the medallion. "I imagine it might be safer with you."

He took it from her, his gaze boring into hers. "I'll keep it safe."

NAMIKA GAWKED as they entered a section of the restaurant that had a very different theme. The massive aquarium caught her eye right away, taking up most of a wall. It was low enough so they could lean against the edge, and with no top, the massive koi fish were clearly visible. There was a variety of oranges, reds, golds, and whites, all of them at least two to three feet.

She approached, staring at them. "Oh, wow."

Adam stood behind her. His hand slid along her waist until it rested against her abdomen. A sense of anticipation filled her as he pulled her against him.

"I hate that he touched you," he said, a growl vibrating in his chest. "Are you alright?"

She nodded. "Sitting on his lap was embarrassing." She pulled away and turned to face him. "He... knew my grandmother."

"Oh?" He leaned against the side of the aquarium. "I assume she was a mystic as well?"

"Yes. Both my grandparents and my father." She played with the bracelets on her wrist, the occasional clinking sound keeping her from getting lost too deep in her thoughts. "I was raised by the three of them. We lived in Nanaimo, British Columbia, but we visited Japan a lot since most of my extended family still lived there. I was very close to my grandmother, especially after my grandfather passed away when I was six."

"Was it a good childhood?" he asked quietly, as though dreading the answer.

She wondered what to tell him; it was so complicated. "The house I grew up in was wonderful. Surrounded by forests, and a few minutes away, there was a waterfall. I used to love taking walks with her to that area. When we walked near the shore, we sometimes saw orcas."

"That sounds lovely."

He didn't push for more, and she appreciated him giving her time to gather her thoughts. "I was home-schooled. Not just in the government's curriculum, but in the arts of the magic of a mystic. My grandmother always told me it was something I needed to learn about, but had to hide because the world wasn't kind to us. Not by the paranormal or the human world."

"It must've been hard growing up thinking you were disliked for being what you are. It certainly explains why you have trust issues."

Her mind flashed to when Sebastian had looked into her soul, and tears burned her eyes at the thought of what he'd said. Her trust in people, love, and care had vanished throughout the years. "Sebastian looked into my soul," she said, her voice cracking.

"He did *what*?" His voice sliced through the air, and she flinched.

"It made me remember the day my grandmother severed the soulmate thread connection. I hadn't thought about it since it happened, and it's..." She pressed her hands against her face and burst into sobs. The memory of her father holding her down as her grandmother sliced at one filament of her soul flooded her mind. She wished it would stop.

Adam's arms wrapped around her, and he held her close. She trembled, trying to regain her composure, but she couldn't seem to. It felt like she was going through it all over again. The slices as a part of herself were torn away that day.

She struggled to swallow with the lump in her throat. "She did it...to protect me. Told me reapers would come steal me away if it wasn't done. As it was done to my father when he was young. And to everyone in my family tree."

"Nonetheless, you went through a traumatic event, and it was done by people you trusted and loved," he said, rubbing her back.

She pulled away from him. Part of her debated how much more she wanted to tell him, but she'd opened the floodgates; it felt like she couldn't stop even if she wanted to. Walking away from him, she paced at the far end of the room, trying to find the words.

"One night, when I was eleven, people broke into our home." She spun one of the bracelets, focusing on the rose gold gems. "My father held them off while my grandmother got me from my room. She brought me to the trapdoor hidden in her closet and told me to hide beneath the floorboards and not come out."

The gems' texture was rough against her fingertips, and she focused on that feeling. "I heard them scream. They were using some of their magic to fight back, but it...it didn't matter." She looked up at Adam as tears blurred her vision. "There isn't much they could do against that many demons."

His expression remained unreadable, but there was anguish in his gaze as he stared at her. He stayed quiet, allowing her to continue in her own time.

"I heard the demons laugh and spit on them. Fed on them both. I remember my father begging for mercy, but one of them said this was revenge for my mother killing one of theirs. They'd come here to kill her daughter, but settled for my family instead." She let out a harsh laugh. "I remember thinking that it was funny. I didn't even know my mother. What good would it have done to kill me? She didn't care." She wiped at the tears. "It seemed like a really long time, but after a while, I heard them die. And even after it was quiet for a long time, I did as I was told, and I didn't move."

"How long did you stay hidden?" he asked, his voice barely a whisper.

"Two days. The police found me dehydrated and hungry. They rushed me to the hospital, and that's when a social worker came to talk to me. I'd be going into my mother's custody since my father and grandmother were dead now. Police ruled it as a home invasion gone wrong, and because there was so much wildlife around, and the doors and windows were left open... Well, it's how they explained the mangled bodies."

"And so you went to live with your mother?"

"Yes. When we arrived in Ottawa, she tried to console me. She talked about how she hadn't seen me since I was three years old, and how much I'd grown." She clenched her fists. The emotions of that little girl inside were still raw. "But I hated and resented her from the moment I'd heard those demons say they were there because of what she did. In my heart, she was the reason I'd lost my family. My real family. So out of spite, I wanted to make sure she'd always remember who she was responsible for killing, and insisted she call me by my grandmother's name. Namika."

He arched an eyebrow. "It wasn't your name?"

"I was born Eve Strang."

He blinked a few times, as though letting the irony sink in. His lips showed a hint of a smile. "Is that so?"

She let out a small laugh. "I know. It's kind of funny. Especially after you told me your name wasn't always Adam." She frowned. "Why did you choose that as a name instead?"

"When I became a Sanguis demon, it reminded me of the bible story of the first two humans. So from that point on, I went as Adam."

She smiled, and it was as though she could truly smile. Like she could be herself because he'd understand. "Well, I guess that's all to tell, really. I eventually joined the Venatores since it's required for parents to bring in their children. But that's it," she finished with a shrug.

He approached her, and when she didn't move away, he leaned his forehead against her, his gaze boring into her. "I will never break your trust, Namika."

Her heart seemed to skip a few beats as she tried to find the right words. But there were none. None to express how she felt at that moment.

She cupped his cheek and kissed him.

And he kissed her back.

19

———

INTIMACY

Their intimate moment was interrupted by Adam's cellphone ringing. The ringtone differed from what she'd heard before, and he sighed.

"That would be Shiriki," he said as he answered it.

He moved away, speaking in hushed tones, the demos language sending shivers down her spine. The call was quick, and within minutes, he'd returned to her.

"Good news, I hope?" she asked.

"He has a vase of Strix's Bone he's willing to part with. Requested we meet him at the Dragon's Lair."

"That was fast," she said in surprise.

"I called him while you were finishing upstairs with the reaper." He put away his cellphone. "Shall we go?"

They walked to the exit so they could gather their coats before heading out into the freezing cold. All the while, she was lost in thought at Adam's words. Shiriki was willing to part with something to further their goal. He'd been the one to insist Adam brand her in the first place to slow the progression of the curse. But why?

Once inside the taxi, she rubbed her bare legs, trying to

get some circulation back. She wanted to ask why Shiriki wanted to keep her from being sent to the Inferno. Not that she didn't appreciate it, but he was a demon. And an evil one at that. He should've loved the idea of her being sent there despite never having made a deal.

The ride back seemed so different in contrast to when she'd arrived with Linda. Most of Namika's stress had lowered by quite a bit. They'd finally made some progress towards breaking the curse, and even the one ingredient they needed was waiting for them at the nightclub.

As the car pulled into the parking lot, the motion sensor lights buzzed to life. Namika trembled slightly at the sight of Shiriki waiting for them outside. He wore a long black coat that wavered in the wind, his white hair falling on his shoulders; it didn't look like the weather bothered him in the least.

They stepped out of the vehicle, and Namika shivered.

"Shiriki," Adam said with a bow.

He opened the metal door, and she stepped inside, grateful for the warmth. Although it was suddenly too hot as the noises from the club's participants echoed from the front room. Without waiting, she went downstairs, in a hurry to get away from the discomfort she felt.

But apparently, the basement wasn't any safer from the spicy activities taking place. A man wearing leather pants and nothing else walked down the hallway holding a leash. On the other end, a woman with a collar around her neck followed, fully naked.

Namika thought for sure she would burst into flames. She grasped her coat, tightening it around herself as though it would protect her from the immodesty.

A small part of her laughed at the thought, considering what the dress she wore looked like. And if the two people were having fun, why was she so embarrassed by it?

She swallowed hard and forced her legs to continue forward; the heels she wore were suddenly too wobbly for her, and her vision darkened on the edges.

"I have you," Adam whispered in her ear as he wrapped an arm around her. "Are you feeling alright?"

She nodded, sweat trickling along her forehead. "Yeah..."

He helped her to the door of his studio apartment, and once they stepped inside, Adam pulled off her coat. She instantly felt less dizzy, but then remembered that her dress barely covered anything, and Shiriki was there.

The Viscus demon's gaze ran along her body, and he grinned. "You look lovely, little Venatore."

Adam shot him a glare, but before he could say anything, Shiriki put out his hands in front of him, and a vase appeared. It looked like it was made of sandstone and wasn't much bigger than a foot. Shiriki handed it to Adam.

"When you unseal it, make sure you do not breathe in the first bit of dust that will escape," he said with a smirk. "Unless you wish to decompose from the inside out within minutes."

Adam nodded. "I'll keep that in mind."

"As for that symbol you had sent me, I can tell you it is from an old spell that was used by the guardians back before the world split." Shiriki stared at the flames in the fireplace. "The person who used it is highly skilled in controlling that kind of powerful magic."

Namika recalled how the symbol in the guest bedroom at Adam's penthouse had made it impossible for any demon to sense anything in its surroundings. The vampire could use magic, but she was willing to bet it was whoever gave him the powers in the first place that had conjured that symbol.

"Do we know of anyone who has the kind of magic to control a symbol like that?" Adam asked with a frown.

"A few, but no one that comes to mind who would help a vampire and orchestrate all this."

Namika's stomach churned as she debated whether to ask her question. It wasn't necessary for breaking the curse, but her curiosity got the better of her, despite knowing she should keep quiet.

"Why are you helping me? Helping us?" she asked.

Adam stiffened. "Namika——"

Shiriki raised a hand, and Adam fell silent. The second in command watched her for a few seconds, his silver eyes feeling like they were looking into her mind.

"Your fate is tied to that of Adam's. I will not allow years of... *nurture*," he said in a sly tone, "to crumble away because of a human's mistake."

"I don't buy it." She wasn't sure why she wouldn't let it go. Part of her argued to shut up, while another urged her to find out the real reason. "Adam wouldn't have been punished for me being cursed. I'm the one who ran away. Celina wouldn't have blamed him for that. And even if he was, since when do you care about not torturing people? Or any beings, for that matter?"

The usual amusement vanished, and his energy unleashed with such force, Adam held onto Namika to keep her from slamming on the floor. Her knees buckled under the pressure, and she winced as Shiriki stepped closer. Within seconds, Adam was thrown backwards, and Shiriki grabbed her by the neck.

"Did Celina tell you what my sentence was for everything that happened during the war your little group started?" Shiriki asked, as his pointed fingernails sliced into her skin.

"You... were banished from the Dark Realm," she muttered in a shaky voice.

"And what reward do you think my king and his dear wife would give me if I saved her best friend from an eternity of anguish?"

"Shortening your banishment? Or removing it altogether?"

"Exactly." He pulled her closer, and she held her breath. "Now then. Have I answered the question to your satisfaction?"

She had the feeling there was a bit more to the why, but she had pushed her luck too far. Half of her expected him to change his mind and rip her apart then and there. He slammed down against his energy and let her go at the same time. She staggered back, bumping into Adam as she did.

He glared at her as he held the vase against him, his other hand pressed against his abdomen. Blood seeped through his vest, and she fidgeted on the spot. She wanted to heal him, but with Shiriki still with them, she didn't dare.

Shiriki materialized inches from Adam, and Namika gasped.

He cocked his head. "When was the last time you fed?"

"A while," Adam said, as though reluctant to answer.

"And you have been wounded for some time." He glanced at his abdomen. "Any reason you are depriving yourself of healing?"

"No."

Shiriki grinned. "I suggest feeding soon, or you will be too weak to be of use to anyone." And without another word, he vanished.

Namika averted her gaze, ashamed. How had she not noticed Adam was still hurting? She'd instigated the Viscus demon, and because of her, Adam was wounded further. She was sure she'd healed him fully after the last ghoul attack, but maybe it hadn't been enough?

Adam strode to one of the many display shelves, opened a glass door, and placed the vase inside for safe-keeping. She felt like such an idiot; why had she pushed so much to get an answer from Shiriki? And in front of Adam like that, she couldn't blame him for being angry.

He finally broke the silence. "Is there a reason you didn't ask me about Shiriki's motives before deciding to ask him directly?"

"I'm sorry. You're right; I should've asked you about it before saying anything to him."

"In the future, avoid speaking to him directly unless it's answering a question." He placed a hand on her shoulder and gave it a gentle squeeze. "He's an excellent manipulator and can get so much information from just letting people speak."

"I promise. I am really sorry."

He gently kissed her forehead. "I know. It's alright."

She looked up at him. "But why didn't you tell me you weren't fully healed? I could've tried again."

"There's only so much magic can do." An unreadable expression settled on his face. "But Shiriki is right. I need to feed."

She swallowed hard. "Well... you can feed from me if you want. As long as it doesn't kill me, you know," she said with a grin.

"I doubt you're aware of how it is we prefer to consume, or you wouldn't be offering," he said with amuse-ment in his tone.

"What do you mean? Don't you feed on blood and energy?"

He nodded. "To get the most possible without killing

the human, we often do it when their senses overload and their minds are foggy with the after-effects of an orgasm."

Namika averted her gaze as she pictured being in Adam's bed. What he'd do to her while feeding. Her cheeks heated, and she pushed her legs together, trying to get the throbbing to stop.

Adam smirked. "Still offering yourself now?"

She tried to make sense of what she wanted. On the one hand, she imagined him going to the woman who'd walked down the corridor fully naked on a leash. Or would he choose someone else from the club upstairs? The thought of him going out and finding someone else to do that with sent a wave of jealousy she didn't care for. But she was also too scared that he'd be disappointed when he realized her body didn't function the way it was supposed to.

"Jealousy and arousal," he said in an amused tone. "Such a strange mixture of emotions."

She narrowed her eyes despite the heat in her face, and he laughed. He slipped off his jacket and laid it on the back of the sofa. The black vest he wore with his white dress shirt made him look so handsome. It fit him perfectly, yet tight enough to see his muscles beneath. She remembered how he'd looked when he wore an open top, his chest and abs carved from smooth stone. A work of art.

"Indulging in a bit of *apodyopsis*?"

His voice pulled her out of her mind, and she frowned. "*Apo*-what now?"

"The act of mentally undressing someone." He rolled up a sleeve, then the other. "Picturing someone naked."

If it wasn't for ending up in the Inferno, she wanted to die in that moment. Was it that obvious, or was he feeling her emotions again? She had to suppress a groan.

"Well... I mean... Look at you." She motioned up and

down at him, and he arched an eyebrow. "You're hot as *hell*," she whispered the word as though saying it too loudly would allow it to manifest, "and I mean that both seriously and pun intended."

He grinned. "I'm aware of my physical attributes, but thank you for noticing," he said with a wink before making his way to the bathroom.

She stared at the vase sitting inside the cabinet. He needed to feed, but was she willing to let him take from her? What if he got angry with her when he realized it wouldn't work? Her stomach churned at the thought. Having sex with a demon was scary enough, but one who might lose control while furious was beyond terrifying. But the ghouls and that vampire were still out there, and having Adam at full strength was vital.

He returned to the room and sat on the sofa. He'd removed his tie, and the top of his shirt was unbuttoned; he seemed so relaxed. His hair dripped, falling in an unruly manner. She joined him, taking a seat next to him. The dress didn't feel like it offered much coverage compared to what he wore, but she tried her best not to focus on that.

He suddenly pulled her onto his lap, and she yelped in surprise. "What are you doing?"

He nuzzled her neck, his pointed teeth brushing against her skin. "I would enjoy having you spread for me without your cumbersome clothing." He pulled away and glided his fingers along her bare chest. "Not that there is much to remove."

She squirmed a bit, trying to slide off him.

"Are you taunting me, buttercup?" His voice turned husky.

Goosebumps crawled along her skin, her pulse speeding. "What makes you say that?"

He scoffed. "Because you're grinding against me."

She froze, slowly realizing the hardness she felt beneath her wasn't his pants bunching up. After a few seconds of silence, she let out a breath. "Look. I don't want you to find another person to feed on. But I also get that you don't have a choice since I... can't... I don't... I mean..."

He grasped her chin and turned her head so she was forced to look at him. "What are you trying not to say?"

"You said the person has to..." She swallowed through the dryness in her mouth. "And I... I've never..."

"You've never orgasmed with another person?"

She grabbed his wrist, trying to get him to let go of her face so she could look away from his burning red gaze. "No." When he didn't let go, her shoulders slumped. "No, because... It's... I don't...like it. So I never... You know." When he inquisitively raised his eyebrow, silently questioning her, she sighed. "I don't get... I mean, I... It's...dry."

When he let go of his grasp, she quickly averted her gaze, wishing she could vanish like demons did. This was beyond mortifying. Why couldn't she have kept her mouth shut and told him to go feed on someone?

He slid his hand along her upper thigh, sending goosebumps across her skin. "Do you touch yourself?"

Why couldn't she disappear? Turn back time and erase this conversation? When he stayed quiet, she nodded, shame filling her from head to toe.

"And you orgasm then?"

Maybe the Inferno won't be so bad if I died right now...

She nodded, but quickly added, "but I don't... in. You know? I just..." She cleared her throat. "Touch."

"Ah, so you climax from clit stimulation and not from penetration."

His words seemed too loud inside the small room, and she twisted on his lap and pushed her hands against his mouth. Her eyes were wide, and she was having trouble catching her breath. "Don't say it so... *openly*!" she nearly shouted.

He pulled her hands away. "You're cute when you're blushing that deep."

"You're the worst."

He chuckled. "Alright, so I take from what you didn't say that penetration is painful because you don't get wet." His fingers slid a little higher up her thigh. "That's when lube is your friend."

Her breath hitched, and she grabbed his wrist. "It should be natural." She didn't mean for the words to sound so disappointed, but she was having trouble controlling her emotions.

He pulled his hand away and instead brushed his lips along her neck near her scars. "There are a lot of things the human body *should* do, but it doesn't always. For various reasons. There's no shame in that."

"But what if... it doesn't help to use that? And then it... hurts?"

"Then we don't have *that* kind of sex. I can go down on you, and the only thing I'll be using is my mouth and tongue."

She covered her face with her hands; she was sure that if she stepped outside into the freezing temperature, she'd be able to melt the surrounding frost.

He pushed her hair behind her ear and nipped at her earlobe. "Are you still offering that I feed from you?"

"Yes." This time, she didn't take a single second to think about her answer.

He kissed her cheek. "If you don't like something I do, you tell me at any point. Understand?"

"During?" she said, eyes wide. The thought of talking or even looking at each other during something so... lewd nearly made her heart stop.

He slid her off his lap, and before she could catch her breath, he kneeled in front of her. A slow smile curled his lips, and a shiver shot down her spine. He slid his hands along her legs, his thumbs tracing her inner thighs. This was too intimate.

"Wait. Can we turn off the lights?"

"You're aware I can see just as well in the dark, right?"

She turned her head to the side. "Well, I can't."

All the lights were switched off, leaving only the electric fireplace burning nearby. The orangey glow barely lit the place, but with his glowing red eyes, it somehow felt so... erotic.

His palms traveled along the outer sides of her legs this time, and he hooked his thumbs into her panties. Her chest heaved as her breath came in quicker, and she lifted herself from the sofa so he could slide the underwear down.

Once off, he took her foot and placed it in his lap, slowly undoing the laces of her high heel. He slipped it off, kissing her ankle, then did the same with her other foot. Her pulse was throbbing between her legs with a need she'd never felt before. Like she might explode if he didn't touch her.

He glanced up at her without moving his head and shot her a knowing smile. The bastard was doing it on purpose. He took off her other heel, trailing kisses along her leg, slowing as he reached for her knee. She spread her legs for him and nearly shut them closed when she realized she'd reacted out of instinct. But he'd grasped her knees, keeping her open to him.

"Was that a change of heart or nerves?" he asked quietly.

"Embarrassment at my reaction."

"That shyness of yours is addicting." He pressed his mouth above her knee. "So, so addicting."

He slid his hands beneath her ass and yanked her forward so she was on the edge. She yelped, grabbing hold of the back of the sofa to keep from falling. His irises turned into slits as his gaze focused on her. He pushed her dress to the side and leaned between her legs. He stared between her legs with a hunger she'd never seen, and the tips of her extremities tingled at the thought of him desiring her.

"I'm going to go down on you until you cum so hard, you won't remember what shame feels like."

He lowered his head between her legs. The man had more patience than she thought possible. Just with the tip of his tongue, he licked at her sensitive nub. Up and down, in a steady rhythm that built within her core, sure to send her over the edge in a torturously long time.

"Please," she moaned, unsure what she was begging for. To stop or bring her over the edge so she could cum.

"You want more?" He blew against her wet folds, and she arched towards him, needing more.

He lapped at her opening faster. He covered her pussy with his mouth, fucking her with his tongue until she couldn't breathe. She squirmed, crying out as an intense orgasm ripped through her. She rode the waves crashing against her, setting her nerves on fire. But he was relentless. She tried pulling away from him to get even one second for the intensity to stop, but his grip tightened. His tongue lapped between her folds, and he wrapped his lips on her clit and sucked.

She cried out, moans and screams escaping her throat as she orgasmed, still riding her last one. Her hips rose, bucking against his mouth, but he sucked and licked more until tears ran down her face.

"Adam, please. I can't." She turned her head from side to side, then gripped his hair. "Please."

He gripped her thighs tightly as he slanted his mouth over her pussy. Something like a moan and a scream ripped out of her, her heels digging into his back as she came again. Her nerve endings stirred and tingled as she rode out her pleasure. His lips brushed against her inner thigh, and she shuddered when he licked at a spot that sent her pulse throbbing.

Burning pain sliced through her as he bit down, and she opened her mouth to scream, but nothing came out. A strangled cry left her parted lips. The pain mixed in with the orgasms, lulling her into a strange numbness. Her body tingled as her energy drained out of her. Exhaustion hit her, and her eyelids drooped as he held her close to him. He laid her on the bed, the sheets so soft and warm beneath her as she seemed to float.

He loomed over her, licking his lips clean of her blood, then lowered his body against hers. Her chest rose and fell fast, her throat tightening. She needed to have him closer to bring her back to reality. More tears rolled down her face and into her hair, but still, she couldn't seem to speak.

He cupped her cheek. "It takes time for the effects to wear off."

"Effects?" she repeated in a small voice.

He lowered himself to rest his head between her breasts. "Taking blood and energy like that requires dark magic." He pushed the strap of her dress and grasped her breast, fondling it.

She ran her fingers through his hair, closing her eyes as she smiled.

20

PLEASURE

The sound of trickling water woke Namika, and she rolled to her side, hand reaching out. But the space next to her was empty, and she opened her eyes. Light glowed from behind the bathroom door, and she relaxed, guessing Adam was taking a shower. The memory of what they'd done swam in her mind, and she pressed her face into the pillow. Lust filled her so suddenly that she pressed her legs together to keep the throbbing at a low thrum, but it just seemed to heighten.

She swung her legs over the bed and placed her hand against her chest; these weren't her emotions. The desire burning through her body was likely Adam's. She tiptoed to the bathroom door and rested her hand against the doorknob. It would be wrong to peek, but the building craving pushed her forward.

Light streaked into the room as she opened the door a few inches and looked inside. Adam was indeed in the shower, his back turned to her. Water ran down his back, over his muscular rear, and down his strong legs. One arm braced against the tiles, while the other moved in a rhythmic motion. She swallowed hard at the sight. Every muscle rippled as he stroked his cock, and as his sexual desire built, she felt it within herself.

Her hand slid between her legs, cheeks burning when remembering she wasn't wearing any panties. The throbbing grew, and she glided a finger over her nub, shuddering at how sensitive it was.

Adam stopped, his back straightening as though he felt her eyes on him. Part of her wanted to run back to the bed and pretend to be asleep, but another side of her—one buried deep inside—wanted him to see her like this. To see what he'd do.

He turned towards the door slowly, like he didn't want to look back and see that he'd imagined her lust. His eyes glowed crimson, the vertical pupils barely slits as he locked gazes with her. Her breath hitched, but she didn't move; not to remove her hand from the doorknob or from her mound.

Without looking away from her, he turned off the faucet and exited the shower. He didn't bother covering up, and her mouth dried at the size of his erection. He was so endowed. She'd never had a cock of that size inside her. What if he didn't fit? What if it hurt too much?

He slowed his steps as though sensing her fears and doubts, but she pushed open the door wider; a silent invitation to come closer. And he took that invitation. She could feel her heart pounding against her chest as he slid his hands up her arms until he reached her shoulders. Gently, he took the straps and pulled them down, revealing her breasts. He cupped one, tracing his thumb on the underside; a sensitive area she didn't even realize she had.

He grabbed the material hanging around her hips, pushing down slowly. Like he was giving her the chance to change her mind. She wiggled a bit to help take off the dress, and it fell to the floor, pooling around her feet. Never in her life did she feel more naked and vulnerable. Standing naked, her hair falling loose past her shoulders— her only covering—while Adam stood in front of her.

She trembled, overwhelmed with a mix of lust and nervousness. He picked her up and walked to the bed, the candles on the nightstands flickering to life as the bathroom light switched off. The room was warm from the fireplace, the flames dancing on the other side of the glass.

He sat on the bed and placed her between his legs, her back turned to him. He kissed her shoulder, and tiny goosebumps rose along her skin. His energy wrapped around her, warmth spreading through her body as the feel of his power flickered along her skin. He slid his hands from her sides to her breasts, cupping them as he kissed along her neck. She traced her fingers along his arms and closed her eyes, leaning back into him. His cock pressed against her spine, and her breath came faster. When he nipped at her neck, she gasped at the sensation. Pressure built from deep inside her belly as he rolled her nipple between his thumb and finger, his breath tickling her shoulder.

Scraping sounds of the nightstand drawer caught her attention, and she gaped as it opened on its own. A small tube flew towards them, and she tried to duck out of instinct. He chuckled, his chest vibrating against her back as he opened the cap. She read the label, and her pulse sped when she realized it was lube. Shame filled her at needing it, and he slid his mouth along her ear.

"If I feel any kind of self-disgust from you again, I'll put you over my knee and spank you," he whispered.

She whimpered at the thought; both scared and aroused. He squeezed the tube, lathering his fingers with lube until they glimmered in the candlelight. He slipped a finger into her opening, and she arched; it felt good with the lube. At this angle, his thumb pressed against her clit, and she shuddered as he pumped in and out. Slowly at first, but he picked up speed, the lube dripping onto her ass.

"I want you to hear this," he growled. He pushed his hand against her mouth, her head pressed against his shoulder. "Listen now."

He thrust his fingers into her faster, moving so fast her mind fogged at the building pressure. Every pump slapped against her soaking wet pussy, the noise filling the room. She arched, her feet digging into the mattress as an orgasm crashed against her. He removed his hand from her mouth and brought the fingers he'd been using on her to her lips.

"Be a good girl, and clean them for me."

She was sure her body would catch fire, but as much as the idea embarrassed her, she wanted to please him. Opening her mouth, she licked his fingers, the taste a mix of the lube and her own cum.

In a blur of movement, he flipped her onto her back and hovered over her. Adrenaline tingled throughout her body at the sudden position change. He kneeled at her feet and grasped her ankle.

A lecherous smile filled with pointed teeth curled his lips. "Spread your legs for me, buttercup."

Her breath hitched, and she trembled.

"I can smell your fear." He kissed the top of her knee, and she relaxed. "Talk to me."

"You're huge," she blurted.

He grinned wolfishly. "Stroking my ego won't help."

"I'm scared it'll hurt."

"I give you my word. I'll be gentle. Do you trust me to keep my promise not to hurt you?"

"Yes."

"Then lie back and relax."

She rested her head against the pillows and opened her legs, heat burning her face.

"Having you spread like this, makeup streaks on your face, gushing wet, and yet you're still shy and blushing." He moved his head towards her thighs. "You're perfect."

And he went down on her again. And again. This time, using his fingers, his mouth, and his tongue. She climaxed more times than she could count, her voice raw from screaming.

ADAM RESTED on the bed next to her. His irises changed to the warm brown she was used to, staring at her in silence.

Without a word, Namika got up and trudged to the bathroom door. She used the toilet, then grabbed a washcloth from a pile sitting atop a shelf. Her mind strayed as she ran the cloth beneath the warm water.

Adam.

The way he acted with her was more than lust. Yet, while she wanted him to care for her as more than just someone to protect, the thought scared her. Demons rarely loved, and when they did, it brought nothing but destruction.

Opening her legs, she placed the washcloth against her privates and sighed as her muscles relaxed. It was beyond mind-blowing when he used his mouth, tongue, and fingers on her... inside her. She frowned as she rinsed off the cloth. He hadn't even had sex with her. What about his pleasure?

She switched off the light and stepped into the darkened bedroom. Adam's gaze followed her as she walked to the fireplace. The flames flickered, and she shivered at the chill in the air. She stood still, not ready to return to the bed yet.

His power tingled along her body as he approached, and she smiled as he wrapped a soft blanket around her shoulders.

"You should get some sleep," he whispered in her ear.

"I'm not tired right now."

"Then I haven't done right by your needs. Yet." His words were filled with promise for more pleasure. If she'd have him.

He walked past her and sat in the armchair near the hearth, his naked body like a work of art. She returned to the bed and grabbed the lube on the nightstand. Her heartbeat raced in her chest as she approached him, fixated on his erect cock. Keeping the blanket over her shoulders, she straddled him, her legs resting on his thighs. Her clit throbbed as the heat of his shaft pressed up against it.

She flipped the top off the tube and squeezed a generous amount of lube into her hand before closing it again. Slowly, she wrapped her fingers around his shaft, moving up and down to lather a good coating. His eyes lit red, a deeper crimson than usual.

Lifting herself, she rubbed his cock between her folds. A soft moan escaped her as she rose higher against his thighs, placing the head at her opening.

He grabbed hold of the armrests, and the wood splintered beneath the material, his pupils thinning as his energy coiled. She placed her hands against his chest, his muscles tensing beneath her fingers as she pushed down on his erection. It stretched her, and she stopped a few times, letting herself adjust to his girth.

She tugged at his wrists, and he let go of the armrests, following her lead as she pushed his hands against her breasts. He cupped them, and she pushed herself down, sheathing his cock deep inside her. She whimpered at the feeling of fullness, and a shudder traveled down her spine as he straightened, pointed teeth barred.

"If you torture me any further, I'll start to think you're secretly a demon." He groaned as she moved her hips from side to side.

"Had to pay you back for this evening," she breathed, pushing the blanket off her shoulders as sweat beaded along her forehead.

He gripped her ass, following her rhythm as she rode him. Nothing too fast, but every thrust slammed deep inside her, and she moaned with each one. He cupped her breast and brought her nipple into his mouth, sucking as she leaned closer to allow him better access. She cupped his cheek as she picked up speed, and he stared up at her.

Her heart raced. "I need you to take me. Hard. Please," her voice came out with a desperate plea she'd never heard from herself.

He draped his arms around her waist and got to his feet as she yelped. In seconds, he laid her on the mattress, bending her knees up. She threw her head back as he thrust his cock inside her, not giving her a single second to adjust to his size. Yet the sliver of pain mixing with the pleasure shook her core, and she moaned. He pumped inside her, slamming into her deeper each time. She raised her ass, meeting his every thrust, and clutching her thighs to hang on.

A mind-shattering orgasm took her, and she pressed her hand over her mouth to muffle her scream. He yanked her wrists away with a growl and pulled out. The sudden loss of being filled left her lost, but fear froze her to the spot as he loomed over her, his irises glowing like the depths of Hell.

"You'd deny me those beautiful screams of yours?" he asked with a cruel smile. "I think not." He grabbed her wrists in one hand, pinning them over her head. "Now then. Let's try this again."

He lowered himself enough so her knees fell onto his shoulders, and embarrassment filled her at being so exposed as he bent her body over so her ass was in the air. He pushed his cock into her, and a whimper tore through her. At this angle, he was balls deep, hitting a spot that sent orgasms crashing against her faster than she could keep up. She cried out, cursing him and begging for more as her throat throbbed and her ears rang from her own screams.

"Yes. Just like that," he groaned.

He pulled out, then spun her onto her stomach. She moaned when he lifted her hips and plunged his shaft inside her, pumping furiously like his life depended on it. The lube and cum streamed along her thighs, the sound of their wet slapping skin louder than her screams. He grasped her breast and pushed her up against his chest as he slammed into her. He grunted, sinking his teeth into her neck as he spilled his seed inside her. She clutched at his arm, the sound of him swallowing her blood so surreal, it was like she'd left reality. His fingers released her hip, and he moved to her clit, rubbing as he thrust a few more times inside her, and she came. Again and again.

When he pushed his hand against her back and pushed her onto the bed, she gripped the blankets. If he planned on fucking her anymore, she might die.

She bit her lower lip as he gripped her ass, then rubbed his thumb against her tight hole. He pushed in a little, and she gasped.

"Have you ever had anal sex?" he asked, moving his hips so his cock hit a spot that made her shudder.

She stiffened, swallowing hard. "No."

He pulled out slowly as he pushed his thumb inside her ass instead. She moaned as his cock sprung out of her, then he pulled out his thumb. Her trembling body fell limply as her muscles had turned to mush.

"Sleep in tomorrow." He kissed her cheek, then pulled the blankets over them both.

Wrapping his arm around her, he pulled her close, and she drifted off to sleep, lulled by energy cocooning her.

21
———

HUNGER

$\mathcal{N}$amika read through the incantation to summon Lokesh for what felt like the hundredth time. Adam had insisted he'd perform everything, but she wanted to learn it as well, in case something happened.

The night before lingered between them in silence; the first time had been to feed. The several other times had been for pleasure. She still didn't know how to feel about it.

Adam spoke to Shiriki about the information they'd found out about with Sebastian, and although Shiriki asked about the library's location, Adam stated he didn't know since he purposefully didn't check their surroundings. When the subject of the reaper portal came up, Shiriki looked grim.

"Reapers can lend their magic to other beings, and some are powerful enough to use the *Fosid* Rune... controlling ghouls and even creating them..." He glowered at the wall. "One reaper comes to mind, but he was imprisoned over forty years ago."

She looked up from the printed copy of the ingredients. "Fosid Rune?"

"The symbol that hid your presence from demons," Shiriki said, not looking at her; like he was lost in thought.

"And the reaper you think matches the description... Are you sure he couldn't have escaped?"

This time, Shiriki looked at her, and she stiffened. Adam had told her the night before not to speak with the Viscus demon unless answering his questions, yet here she was, questioning him again.

Like that went so well last time.

He clasped his hands behind his back. "If he somehow escaped the God of Shadow's prison, word would have spread across all realms, worlds, and everywhere in between."

She nodded quickly. "Okay."

Adam shot her a warning look, but turned his attention to Shiriki. "Any news from Haku about the surveillance video?"

Namika stared at the incantation again, but this time, she concentrated on the conversation. She hadn't seen Haku since they'd left the CrowBar in Ottawa, and Adam hadn't once mentioned he'd tasked him with anything related to the curse.

"I cornered him the other day about that," Shiriki said in a sly tone.

She did her best to suppress the shiver that shot down her spine; Shiriki sounded a bit too happy about the word *cornered*.

"And?" Adam asked.

"It seems there was a... *malfunction*, and all the data was erased. Backups were corrupted as well."

Adam let out a frustrated sigh. "I expected as much. I am still waiting to hear back about the cameras in the industrial area where we were attacked, but I'm not holding much hope for those, either."

"I am interested in seeing that location," Shiriki said with a smile. "Perhaps you can show me where it occurred?" It sounded more like a command than a question.

"Of course." Adam bowed, then stared at Namika. "Stay here. I'll be right back."

She nodded; she didn't like being excluded, but she understood they might want to speak about private matters without her there.

The door closed with a click, and she leaned back, still holding the paper with the incantation in her hands. The night of the summoning approached, and Namika waited impatiently for it. She just hoped Lokesh would answer her questions.

She stood up and rummaged through the room until she found what she was looking for. The reaper had mentioned an item that wasn't on the list of ingredients, but he'd said the God of Shadows would tell her anything she wanted if she offered it, along with the sacrifice.

Jutting down two dozen bacon cheeseburgers on the list seemed comical, but if it gave her a better chance, it couldn't hurt.

The door creaked open, and Namika looked up as Linda stood at the entrance. She seemed a bit more disheveled compared to her usual pristine look, the sunglasses adding to someone who had partied too hard.

"You're here," Linda said with a big smile.

Namika frowned. "Er...yeah." She approached the demon and pointed at the sunglasses. "Had a good time at the restaurant last night?"

Linda nodded. "I actually spoke with that reaper. We hit it off, and you'll never guess what."

Her pulse raced. "What?"

"He gave me a potion that makes it possible for you to

eat while you're cursed." Linda grabbed Namika's wrist and tugged. "Come on, I got you some food so you could try it out."

Namika tried making sense of the situation; something felt off, but she couldn't put her finger on it.

Still, she didn't argue, so she let Linda lead her out of the room and towards another part of the hallway she'd never noticed before. They stopped at the only door, and Linda pushed it open.

The smell of croissants and jams reached her nostrils, and Namika's stomach growled loudly, burning and twisting in pain. It was like the smell of food suddenly reminded her body that she hadn't eaten since she'd been cursed.

Namika stepped inside, and Linda closed the door behind them. A sturdy table stood in the middle of a small room with a few chairs surrounding it. The light above looked like a mini chandelier, the rose gold and hanging crystals giving the place a fancy feel.

She bit her lower lip as she pressed her hands against her abdomen to ease the pain. "I don't know..." The last time she'd eaten flashed through her mind. The taste of the food turning into ashes in her mouth, burning her tongue, wasn't something she wanted to experience ever again.

Linda sat at the table, slouching a bit. "You haven't tried in a while. And this time, you have a potion." She fished inside the purse hanging from her shoulder and pulled out a small vial of lime liquid. "Sebastian said it would help to keep you from deteriorating faster."

Namika took the vial and uncorked it. The smell was pleasant, almost like a mix of peaches and mangoes. She arched an eyebrow. "Is it the whole thing, or do I take a certain amount? How long does it last once I take it?"

Linda's smile widened. "It's the whole thing, and it'll last until you break the curse."

Letting out a breath, Namika used her magic to glide along the liquid, checking to see if anything stood out as dangerous. When nothing seemed bad, she brought the opening to her lips and downed the potion in one gulp. It didn't taste great, but she'd definitely had worse.

"Do... I have to wait a while before?"

She shook her head almost exaggeratedly, rapidly back and forth. "Nope. You can eat right away if you'd like. I imagine you must be excited to finally be able to. I tried to pick things I thought you'd enjoy."

Namika frowned. If Linda was acting weird because of her hangover, it must have been one heck of a party.

It took a few seconds of muttering encouragements to herself, but she eventually trudged to the food. She sniffed the homemade jam and smiled at the delicious-looking strawberries. Not bothering to be modest, she grabbed a croissant and ripped it open. She spread a good helping of the jelly inside, not at all ashamed of how much she put in. Her mouth watered as she bit down.

She slumped in a chair, chewing slowly. One after the other, she ate the muffins, biscuits, and even a few scones, despite usually not caring for those. The more she ate, the hungrier she got, like she couldn't get enough.

Ripples appeared along the walls, and Namika frowned as she stared around the room. It blurred, and her body swayed as though she sat on a waterbed. Everything morphed, the walls bleeding from the neutral grays to weathered concrete. The chandelier vanished, leaving behind a swaying lightbulb with a chain hanging from it. Namika blinked, her heart speeding at the thought that this was another vision of the Inferno. But there weren't the usual flames. Or the red vines.

But something was definitely wrong.

"What's..." Namika turned towards Linda, but froze, her mind trying to make sense of what she was seeing.

It wasn't Linda.

THE NAKED CORPSE of a woman sat limp in the chair where Linda had been only seconds ago. Her long blonde hair covered her breasts, but the symbol carved into her torso was all too familiar.

The Fosid Rune.

The smell inside the room suddenly caught up to Namika, and her stomach churned. She bolted to her feet, staggering back at the sight of the table. Body parts lay scattered across the surface, some with bite marks, chunks missing from them. With a shaky hand, she wiped at her mouth, and an overwhelming tremor coursed through her entire body at the blood smeared on her palm.

She leaned over to the side as she threw up. The pain burned through her throat, and she cried as thick black liquid choked her. She gasped as her stomach heaved. She couldn't breathe. Clawing at her throat, she was desperate for even a bit of air.

Human flesh. The curse was taking hold, and she'd die any second.

She dropped to her knees, heaving as more black liquid oozed out of her mouth. Sobbing, she pounded the cold, hard floor with her fist. It wasn't fair. She'd been so close to breaking the curse. They'd gotten the ingredients and the incantation. Why did this have to happen?

A burning sensation filled her, like someone had set her on fire from the inside, and she staggered to her feet. No. She wouldn't allow herself to die like this. Besides, she was still starving. Hunger seemed to push her forward as she walked around the cobweb-infested room, looking for a way out. Lights shone through multiple cracks of boarded windows, but she continued walking along the walls, determined to find the door.

Without thinking, she grabbed hold of the doorknob and yanked it so hard, it tore off. She kicked against the metal door, and it ripped off its hinges, falling to the ground. It wasn't cold outside anymore. It wasn't any type of temperature, really.

She glanced down at herself and raised her arm. The skin had turned gray, the black veins beneath the surface pulsing in sync with her hatred. She shook her head, trying to reach deep within for her magic. This wasn't her. It was the curse poisoning her mind.

Like when Adam had been attacked.

She had to find Adam. To go back to the Dragon's Lair. Maybe if Shiriki was still there, he could stop the curse—even if temporarily again.

She glanced at the street name and frowned. "Sutherland..." Not that it was much help, since she wasn't familiar with the city. In front of her was a train yard, huge and stretching from one end to the other.

How was she supposed to ask for help looking like she did? No coat and wearing slippers. And an arm that looked like it belonged to a monster. She didn't even know what the rest of her might look like.

Standing still wouldn't get her anywhere, so she proceeded a short distance and looked down both ways. One led to more of an industrial area and a bridge, while the other side had buildings that looked like they fit downtown.

Her footsteps crunched against the snow as she walked along the side of the road. She pushed her graying arm against her chest, trying her best to cover it with the other arm, and keeping her head down.

Voices caught her attention, and her pulse sped as two men walked in her direction. She wasn't about to take any risks of being seen if the rest of her had warped into monstrous attributes. She crossed the tracks and headed towards the trains filled with shipping containers, hoping to avoid attracting attention to herself.

She approached a few discarded vehicles and leaned against the side of a van to keep upright. Her stomach churned at her reflection in the window. The white of her left eye had turned black, and half her face and neck were the same gray as her arm, the black veins beneath her skin contrasting.

Panic filled her mind, and she dashed away, heading for nowhere, but she needed to run farther. She'd turned into a horrifying monster. The body parts on the old table flashed in her thoughts, and she grasped her head, squeezing to get the images out. Bile burned the back of her throat, and she dry heaved, trying to get rid of everything she'd eaten.

The wind blew harder, and she lowered her head as her vision blurred. She hit something solid and staggered back, but a hand caught her wrist, keeping her from falling. Her heart hammered as she tried figuring out a way to run off before the person noticed there was something wrong with her. But her mind was blank. She tugged against the grip, and when she could get loose, she looked up.

Mekaisto. The demon king himself.

He looked as terrifying as she remembered, despite being in his lowest demon form. His blood-red eyes glowed brightly. The vertical pupil focused on her. His jet black hair fell to his shoulders, strange black smoke coiling around him.

"Namika, so glad I found you," he said in a gentle voice that meant nothing good. "Imagine my surprise when Shiriki informed me that you had vanished without a trace." His grip tightened on her wrist, and she shook as his lips curled over his pointed teeth.

A voice inside her mind screamed that he was there to kill her. To drag her to the Inferno himself. At the thought, darkness rose inside her, pushing against the usual warmth of her magic, and instead, replacing it with fury. A void wrapped around her core, and she wrenched free of his grip, her vision turning sharper than ever.

She lashed out a blast of energy at Mekaisto, determined to survive. She wouldn't let him take her.

He moved to the side, arching an eyebrow as though amused by her attack, but everything about the power rippling from him told her he was angry. Fire flashed along the trains, melting the snow as steam rose. She backed up and raised her hands, throwing magic against him, but he deflected every hit like they were nothing more than unwanted insects.

She gritted her teeth, focusing her energy into her hands, then slamming them against the gravel. A shockwave blew across the rocks, shattering them apart as they flew at Mekaisto.

It slashed at his arm, making it bleed. Everything seemed to freeze around them as he stared at her, evil swimming behind his eyes. Darkness coiled, smoke turning alive as it squeezed her body, lifting her in the air. A hand shot through the darkness, and Mekaisto wrapped it around her neck, his sharp fingernails digging into her skin.

This is it.

Her breath created small puffs of white, but soon she could barely see any of them as he tightened his grip.

"Now then," he cooed as he pulled her closer. "Are you finished with your little tantrum?"

The darkness spilling within receded against her magic, and her mind cleared. He released her, and she dropped to the ground, coughing as air filled her lungs. Mekaisto loomed over her, his glower deadly.

Her head felt like it splintered as he broke through her mind. He wouldn't be able to see anything——a gift that mystics possessed to protect themselves——but he could certainly hurt her. She pictured herself eating the pastries, but slowly, they were replaced by body parts, and she gagged. Leaning against the snow-covered pavement, she was desperate to throw up. She coughed and spit, wiping her tongue. Tar-looking liquid coated her fingers, and she shook her head, crying. She screamed, unable to stay inside her own body; she needed out. Digging into her flesh and muscles, she clawed at her insides, her shrieks filling her ears. But she didn't care. The thought of having eaten human flesh was too much.

"Stop." The word was simple, yet so strong that she paused.

Her pulse throbbed inside her ears, making her feel like she was drowning. Someone took her hands in theirs; she trembled at how bloody they'd turned, and the wound in her abdomen gushed.

She looked up at Adam, her breathing slowing.

His expression was nothing but understanding, and she calmed at the warmth in his gaze.

"I've got you."

22

TRANSFORMED

*N*amika sat cross-legged on the sofa, rocking back and forth. Her mind continued breaking, the image of body parts circling her mind. From time to time, she shook her head, trying to get the thoughts out, but it didn't work. Mekaisto stood nearby, watching her as though ready to intervene again if she lost control.

The door burst open, and Namika held her breath as her best friend marched inside. She hadn't seen Celina in months—not since she'd come to see Namika at the CrowBar to explain everything that had happened.

Celina dashed to Namika and pulled her into a tight hug. "I'm so sorry. It'll be okay."

"How can it be okay?" Namika asked in a sob, shaking her head as she pulled away. "Look at me. I'm not even... I'm a monster."

Celina placed her hands on her hips and turned a deadly glare on her husband. "Why the hell would you tell Adam to keep my best friend prisoner indefinitely without even telling me about it?"

"I suppose I should have given Namika her freedom

instead?" He took a step forward, the shadows on the walls following him. "And then what? Venatores are being hunted by vampires and rogue demons who despise their kind."

"I could've talked to Namika, explained things so she wouldn't feel abandoned. Instead, you kept me in the dark *again*," she hissed through gritted teeth.

The demon king actually looked remorseful for a second. "You had your hands full with our son. I did not wish to overburden you."

Celina pointed a finger at his chest. "For your information, I'm perfectly capable of being a good mother and a good friend."

He grasped her hand and pulled her close, his gaze softening. "A wonderful mother, yes." He kissed her palm. "I was going to tell you about Namika eventually, but you seemed overwhelmed."

Namika's pulse quickened, surprised at the sudden gentleness in Mekaisto towards her friend.

"Kai, let me handle this." She pushed her red hair behind her ear. When he didn't move, she motioned her hand as though dismissing him.

He vanished from sight, and Namika stared at her friend.

Celina grasped Namika's hand and gave it a gentle squeeze. "Apparently, I've missed quite a bit since I last saw you."

Namika let out a bitter laugh. "You have no idea."

And so Namika told Celina everything. From the moment she'd worked during evenings at the CrowBar, to discovering the change in orders from Mekaisto instructing Adam to keep Namika prisoner. The attack by the lost soul and the vampire, who was hell-bent on finishing the job. Shiriki's involvement, and finally, the feelings she had for

Adam and what they'd done last night. When she told Celina about the corpse and body parts, Namika shuddered.

"This is all my fault," Namika said. "What am I going to do? I'm a monster. And now, the curse has probably progressed to where I don't have much time left at all. All because I was tricked by a stupid cloaking spell I should've recognized." She shook her head. "I'm going to die and burn in the Inferno forever." The sound of her heartbeat thrashed in her ears. "I've felt what it's like there in visions since being cursed. I can't..."

"One thing at a time," she said with a gentle smile. "First, tell me if you want me to get Kai to throw Adam in a dungeon and turn Shiriki to dust *before* I rip my husband a new one."

Mekaisto materialized back inside the room. "You called, dove?"

Celina rolled her eyes, but didn't seem surprised at his sudden reappearance. "Is there anything you can do to help her? I don't want her sent to the Inferno. It's not fair."

"As Namika was likely already informed, this curse falls under the realm of the God of Shadow, Lokesh. I cannot interfere in this, dove."

Namika nodded. "I've got what I need to summon him, but I don't know if I've got enough time left after I..." At the thought of eating human flesh again, she pressed her hand against her mouth, trying to muffle a sob.

Celina placed a hand on Namika's shoulder, but Namika pushed it away. "No. I can't... I want it out of me. I feel it inside of me. The people." She brought her knees up to her chest and pressed her face against them, bursting into tears.

The sounds of voices and footsteps seemed to mix. People were arguing about something, but nothing made sense. After a few minutes, silence fell, and she felt Adam's energy envelop her in warmth.

She stared up, letting the tears fall. More emotions added to her sadness, but she wasn't sure which were hers anymore.

Adam sat down next to her, but she continued to glance towards Celina and Mekaisto, who sat across from them. Shiriki lingered near the fireplace, leaning against the wall, watching.

"Namika," Adam whispered as he cupped her face. "I saw what was inside the abandoned building," he said quietly. "You're having trouble coming to terms with what happened."

She pressed her lips together and nodded.

"I understand." He slid closer. "The first time I drank human blood and consumed their energy, I felt... filthy. Like I'd done something so morally disgusting that my own body was tainted forever."

"That's... how I feel," she said, her voice cracking.

"Eventually, I reminded myself that I wasn't a human performing these actions. I was a demon. Like a lion or an alligator may eat a human being, I was just another kind of predator." He pushed her hair from her face. "In that moment, you ate what you did as a ghoul. Not as another human."

Her mind seemed to slow a bit, trying to accept that information. "I... don't understand how I left here. Unless..." She frowned, recalling how they'd walked down a corridor Namika hadn't noticed before. "I think the cloaking spell also created the illusion of a hallway in this basement, but it was actually a reaper portal. Which is how I ended up elsewhere."

"What happened exactly?" he asked, his tone patient.

She glanced at Celina, who gave her an encouraging

nod. Mekaisto narrowed his eyes; something in his gaze felt like he was trying to figure out why he couldn't search into Namika's mind.

"After you left with Shiriki," she cleared her voice when it cracked. "Linda..." She quickly turned to Adam. "Linda! Where is she? Is she okay? Have you heard from her?"

Namika wasn't sure why she cared so much about the demon's wellbeing; maybe she'd grown fond of her?

"She's still out looking for Elijah..." Adam frowned after a few seconds. "I can't sense her."

Celina arched an eyebrow. "Demon Barbie is missing? No big deal..."

Namika stiffened, her hands curling into fists. "Linda isn't nice most of the time, but she's been a great help to me during the last few days."

"Oh..." Celina averted her gaze as her cheeks heated. "I'm sorry. I didn't mean——"

"No. It's okay. I just..." Namika let out a breath. "She's been helpful, despite complaining about it, you know?"

Adam placed a hand on Namika's arm and gave it a small squeeze. "I'll put word out to find where she is, but in the meantime, can you tell us the rest?"

"I followed someone who looked like Linda. It was probably a cloaking spell, but I'm still not sure how, whoever did this, was controlling a corpse like that," she said with a shudder.

Shiriki straightened. "The corpse in the abandoned building with the rune carved into her looked like Linda and was moving around?" He seemed morbidly curious about that.

Namika nodded. "Yes, and it spoke in her voice and everything."

Shiriki shot an inquisitive look towards his king, but Mekaisto remained silent.

"Can a cloaking spell do that?" Adam asked aloud, not directing the question to anyone specific.

Namika shrugged. "I've never heard of one that could do that. I think it was likely a combination of different ones." She let out a breath, the memory of what had happened still too fresh in her mind. "I... I followed it into a corridor in this basement, but I think it was a reaper portal again." She had trouble focusing; it was like the events were replaying too quickly.

Celina shifted in her seat. "Can this wait a bit?"

Mekaisto shook his head. "This needs to be addressed and dealt with."

"Yes, but giving her an hour won't hurt."

"It has the potential to cause her to recall things not as clearly." Shiriki kept his gaze locked on Namika. "Besides, like sawing through a live victim's bone, it is better to stay still and let it happen."

Namika gaped at him. "Is that your version of ripping off a Band-Aid as quickly as possible to get it over with?"

He grinned, and she recoiled at the thought. Celina shot a glare at Shiriki, but didn't comment. With a sigh, Namika shook her head.

"I know it's better to talk about it while it's still fresh in my mind. I'll be okay," she said to Celina with a small smile.

Adam brushed her hair from her face. "Take your time."

"Linda—the corpse... It said it spoke with Sebastian." When both Celina and Mekaisto looked confused, she added, "Sebastian Ecter. The reaper we met with who gave us the information on how to summon the God of Shadows."

Mekaisto cocked his head. "And how did you manage

to get him to speak with you? And about something like that?"

Celina frowned. "What do you mean?"

"Reapers are secretive, but no one quite like the Ecter family," Mekaisto said, the growing interest in his expression making Namika nervous. "It is not impossible to have spoken with him, but for him to share secrets? He would never have done that unless..."

Shiriki suddenly perked up. "Oh ho. So that is what you have been hiding, little Venatore." He gripped his hands behind his back. "Or should I say, little mystic?"

Namika trembled as both Mekaisto and Shiriki stared at her with interest. She knew neither of them could steal her magic away since it did not belong to their realm, but she wasn't sure if being branded by Adam changed that.

"First, you hide that you were a Venatore, and now I find out you're a mystic?" Celina said, crossing her arms and giving her a mock-sad face. "Anything else you're not telling me? Secretly an alien? Part of the Illuminati?" she finished with a grin.

Namika relaxed a bit, relieved her friend was taking the news better than Adam had. "Nothing else, no. I swear."

Mekaisto arched an eyebrow at Adam. "You do not seem surprised... Something you forgot to report?"

"It was not something that concerned our realm, so I didn't think it was pertinent to inform anyone," Adam said with a slight edge in his tone.

The darkness around Mekaisto coiled out, shadows slithering across the walls. "I do not remember giving you leeway to decide what constituted something worth reporting or not," he growled.

Celina placed a hand on his arm. "We keep telling Namika we need to hear about what happened, and then we interrupt her constantly."

"The corpse said the reaper gave her a potion that would let me eat since I haven't been able to since I was cursed. Food turned to ash in my mouth the last time I tried. It took me to a room with a spread of food. I took the potion and started eating, thinking it worked, but..." She took a deep breath, then let it out. "Everything just... the cloaking spell stopped, and I realized I was somewhere else, that Linda wasn't actually Linda, and that the food was..." She shook her head, and Adam wrapped an arm around her and brought her close.

"It's alright now. Deep breaths," he breathed.

"Kai?" Celina tugged on his sleeve. "There must be something we can do to help break the curse. Even if it's not in a direct way."

"They seem to be handling it well enough on their own," he said with a chuckle as he stared from Namika to Adam. "No, dove. There is nothing we can do. The gods keep to themselves and rarely share their knowledge with the rest of us. The only way to break the curse is to summon Lokesh and ask directly."

Celina arched an eyebrow. "Why can't we... I don't know, go see Lokesh in whatever realm he's in? Besides, I thought there were two worlds, and one realm separated into three parts. Now you're telling me there's another one?"

Shiriki put out his hands, and what looked like a hologram floated in the midst of the room. "A second realm exists, separated from both worlds." Darkness swirled, and small stars materialized, spinning. "Voross is a realm so wide it could be considered a world of its own. One section is reserved for beings who died or were destroyed and judged evil. Lokesh rules over that dimension."

"Wouldn't that be the Inferno?" Namika asked, mesmerized by the image.

"Voross is a place where the dead who have sinned must remain and make up for what they have done. There is no rest there until they prove they are worthy of it." He flicked his hand, and flames erupted as red vines slithered. Namika pressed against Adam, and he held her tighter. "The Inferno is where souls go after they've made a pact with a demon."

"But I've never done that," she muttered through her teeth.

Mekaisto nodded. "True, but you were marked by one who was, and that lost soul is draining your life away with each passing day." His lips curled into a grin worthy of his title. "There are always loopholes."

"That wasn't a necessary comment," Celina shot at her husband.

The hologram changed, and silence fell in the room. White and golden lights twirled like they were part of a fountain, and a sense of peace surrounded Namika.

"Another section of Voross is where beings who are judged as good can go rest. What humans call Heaven, depending on their beliefs. This area is referred to as Lyoran. A place for people with kind hearts," he murmured, a look of longing in his gaze as he glanced at it.

Thousands of questions flew through Namika's mind, yet she couldn't seem to utter a single one. The holograms vanished, and Shiriki turned his back on everyone, staring into the fireplace. "Time is ticking, Adam. Do not let her time run out, or you will spend eternity regretting it."

He vanished before Namika made sense of what the Viscus had said. She blinked a few times, her chest tightening. The thought of never seeing him while she suffered caused her magic to splinter a few walls, and she nibbled her lower lip.

"Sorry," she whispered, forcing herself to regain control.

"Destroy the entire building for all I care." He nuzzled her neck. "Just don't hide from me."

Celina grinned, and Namika's cheeks heated at her friend's knowing look.

Mekaisto got to his feet. "One last matter to discuss."

Adam stood, stiff as a board. "Please, she didn't——"

"Don't worry," Celina said as she stood next to her husband. "I already spoke to him about it."

"What...what is it?" Namika asked as she joined the rest of them, keeping close to Adam.

"This is the first and last time you get a pass for attacking me. Next time, I will show you the Inferno is a pleasant fate in comparison to what I can do."

The hairs on Namika's nape rose, and Celina nudged him hard in the ribs, although it didn't seem to affect him at all.

"No, you absolutely won't, Kai. Never threaten her again like that." She crossed her arms. "Promise me."

He brought her close and grazed the top of her head with his lips and smiled. It wasn't cruel or scary, but a genuine smile. "I promise you will need to convince me better than that. Perhaps a bit more begging on your part?"

She tried to nudge him again as her face turned red, but he laughed as he caught her arm. After some squirming, Celina pulled away from him and went to Namika.

"I'll research and ask around to see if there's anything we can help with." Celina hugged her. "And I'll figure out a way for you to be able to contact me directly."

"Thank you for coming," Namika said. "And for listening."

NAMIKA HOVERED in the bathroom's doorway, peaking inside like her worst enemy was waiting for her. Despite Adam telling her she was beautiful no matter what, she hadn't found the courage to look at herself in the mirror. Her arm was still gray, the black veins beneath contrasting against the flesh, and her hand still had the curved claws. She assumed what she'd seen quickly in the van's reflection window was still the same as well.

The door opened, and Linda strolled in. "I was told you wanted to see me, so of course, I came as soon as I could to your beck and call," she said in an annoyed voice.

At the sight of the demon, Namika rushed to her and hugged her tight. "You're okay. You're still okay."

Linda stiffened. "Have you lost your mind?"

Namika quickly remembered how she must look and back away while averting her gaze. "Oh, sorry. I just... I thought you were dead."

Linda blinked a few times. "Still here..." She quickly gave a shrug, then motioned toward the doorway. "So, what were you doing standing in front of the bathroom? Do you need a nightlight or something?"

"I... I haven't seen what I look like yet. Not clearly, anyway."

With a huff, Linda grasped Namika's chin and raised her head. "You're being such a baby."

"Stop!" Namika tried wrenching away, but Linda's grip tightened, and Namika winced.

"Your appearance changed, so what? You're still the same scared, self-righteous bitch you've always been, aren't you?"

Namika stopped trying to get away and gaped at the demon. "Was... was some of that a compliment?"

"Just facts." Linda waved her hand dismissively before grabbing Namika's wrist and marching into the bathroom.

Before she could react, Namika stood in front of the mirror with Linda standing next to her. Half her face on the left was gray with the same black veins, most coiling around her eye. The pupil was still dark brown, but the white of her eye was pitch black. Her neck was the same, and she had a feeling that most of her body on that side looked just as warped.

Tears welled in her eyes as she brought her hand to her face. It wasn't her in the mirror; it couldn't be.

Linda stared at Namika through the reflection. "You look badass."

Namika burst out laughing, half sobbing at the same time. "Sure," she said with a smile. Yet, she looked at herself differently this time; Linda was always brutally honest with her and had no reason to sugarcoat anything.

Still, it would definitely take time to get used to it.

23

ON HER OWN

dam pulled up in front of a tall garage door. Wind blew against the car so violently, Namika was sure it would topple it over. Tiny snowflakes blew around them, and she shivered at how cold it looked outside. After a few seconds, a loud cranking sound resonated around the empty lot, and the door rose. Once it was around halfway up, he drove inside, and she squinted at the sudden bright lights around.

They stepped out of the car, and she looked around. The building used to be an old factory, and its open concept design was one she'd never seen before. Multiple floors were visible on each side while the center was empty; several large trucks could park inside and still have room for more.

A man approached and bowed deeply, his blond hair falling forward. "Good to see you again, boss."

"Phillis," Adam said with a curt nod. "This is Namika Strang." He motioned towards her, and Phillis arched an eyebrow.

"No offense, but I prefer hunting ghouls. Having them

brought to me for slaughter seems a bit mean," he said with a wink.

She averted her gaze, pushing more hair in front of the left side of her face to try hiding away the monstrous appearance. Sudden movement caught her attention, and a feeling of cold expanded in her core as Adam grabbed Phillis by the face, Adam's palm covering his mouth.

"Shut your mouth, or I'll shove molten lead down your throat." Adam growled as he raised his free hand, and smoke billowed around it.

She rushed to the other side of the car and grasped Adam's arm, tugging so he'd look at her. Something in his gaze burned with darkness she hadn't seen in him before, but his expression gentled at her sight. Adam let go of Phillis, and the man quickly staggered back, bowing deeply.

"I apologize. It was a poor attempt at humor on my part, and it won't happen again."

Adam glanced from Namika to Phillis, the smoke surrounding his hand growing darker. "Do you accept his apology?"

"Yes." She nodded. "It's okay. Please." The last thing she wanted was for someone to die because they'd insulted her.

Phillis' shoulders relaxed, and he straightened. "I thank you for your mercy, miss."

The smoke vanished, and Adam walked towards the trunk of the car. "Did you get what I requested?"

"Yes. One of my men is bringing it over," Phillis said, still eyeing Adam with trepidation. "He'll be here any minute."

Adam grabbed things from the trunk, and Namika approached the man.

"So what is it that you do for Adam?" she asked, trying to break the awkward silence.

A small smile touched his lips. "I'm head of the cleaning crew in this city."

"Oh, so you're the one Adam had me text after we were attacked by ghouls?"

He nodded. "Yeah. That one was quite the massacre. Took hours to clean everything, and while trying to get first responders off our backs."

The trunk slammed shut, the sound echoing around the vast room. Both Namika and Phillis jumped at the sudden noise, but Adam didn't comment as he placed the duffle bag he'd grabbed on the cement flooring.

Adam pulled out the vase and held it out at arm's length. "Hold your breath," he instructed.

She did, and he uncorked the top; shrieks escaped from within, followed by a mixture of black and white smoke. It stopped within seconds, and Adam gave her a quick nod to let her know it was clear to breathe again.

"What the heck was that?" she asked.

"The powder inside this vase is made up of the bones of creatures that live inside the Silence area of the Dark Realm." He slid his hand inside and pulled out a handful of dust.

The powder fell precisely as he walked around, creating the circle necessary for their protection. She approached the discarded bag and grabbed a small white candle from inside. They needed the light source to read the incantation, but the instructions were clear in their warning; no light was to be left behind afterward. No explanation as to why, but she wasn't about to question it either. She lit the wick and placed the candle in the middle of the circle, careful to step over the powder every time.

Adam slipped his hand into his pocket and pulled out

the medallion Sebastian had given them. Even at a distance, she could feel the hum of magic.

She glanced up at Phillis. "Do you have a bowl or anything I could put two dozen burgers inside?"

His eyebrows shot up, and he opened and closed his mouth. "Is that... a code for something? Blink twice if you need to get away from my boss."

Adam shot him a glower that warned he was already walking on thin ice, but when she laughed, both men relaxed a bit.

She pulled out two of the bacon cheeseburgers they'd bought before heading here. "I'm serious."

"Er... yeah. Let me go find something. Hang on," he said, holding up a finger as he stared around before rushing away.

Sitting on the floor, she busied herself with pulling out the cheeseburgers from the duffle bag. By the time Phillis returned with a large plastic bowl, she had unwrapped a couple.

"Thanks," she said, taking the bowl from him and placing the food inside.

He gave her a curt nod before turning towards Adam. "My guy should be arriving any minute with what you requested. I'll go meet up with him and bring him here *asap*." And without waiting, he vanished in a blur of movement.

A smartphone ring went off, and Adam pulled out his device with a frown. "Who is this?"

He let out a frustrated sigh while taking the phone away from his ear, then tapped the screen. Static and noise filled their surroundings for a few seconds before a familiar voice echoed from the other end.

"I'm glad I caught you before you started the summoning," Sebastian said, sounding grave.

Her heart skipped a few beats as she slowed her task, her stomach churning at the thought that something was wrong. Had they missed something?

"And how would you know we haven't already started?" Adam asked, glancing around as though trying to see where the reaper could potentially be hiding.

Sebastian scoffed. "Because you would've called me screaming that it didn't work." There was a pause, and a small ding vibrated from Adam's phone. "I've sent you a photo. The instruction page I sent you had more about it on the other side. I hadn't noticed until I reread a larger part of the book to double-check."

Adam tapped the screen, his eyes moving side to side as he read. His jaw clenched as he stared at Namika. "Apparently, only one person at a time can summon the God of Shadows. One medallion for one question." He narrowed his eyes at the device. "How convenient that you missed the first part..."

She stiffened; she would have to do the summoning by herself.

"Look, it's not like I had time to research beforehand." Sebastian's voice sounded just as annoyed. "If you don't believe me, then do what you want. But the medallion will be used when you summon Lokesh. Whether it works or not."

"And I suppose you can't provide us another one so we can make sure?" Adam said, his voice dripping with sarcasm.

Another pause. "I don't think you understand the rarity of a reaper's medallion," Sebastian said in an icy tone. "Just like a demon to undervalue everything."

Adam's grip on the device tightened, and he glared at it as though trying to murder Sebastian through the phone. He closed his eyes for a few seconds, then reopened them, suddenly looking calmer. "This isn't some trick?"

"No. I don't care what you lose in all this, but if Namika fails because of you, then I'll be pretty pissed off. She doesn't deserve to go to the Inferno, and it's why I gave her my medallion. I wouldn't suddenly decide to sabotage her now."

Namika got to her feet, holding the bowl. "I appreciate that, Mr. Ecter. Thank you."

"Do you have the two dozen bacon cheeseburgers I told you to get?" Sebastian asked.

"Yes. We have everything," she said, trying to sound brave, but her voice shook.

"Then you'll be fine," he said in a gentle tone. "Mr. Ashton. Once the summoning is completed successfully, I ask that you text me to let me know. Or I'll come looking for Namika myself to make sure she's alright." And without waiting for a reply, the line ended.

Adam put away the phone, cursing under his breath about reapers being the bane of his existence. Namika put the bowl of burgers in the circle, then approached him.

"I'll be fine. I've read the incantation, and I know the steps."

He took her hands in his, bringing them to his mouth. "I wanted to be there with you. To protect you throughout it all." He kissed her fingers, his gaze boring into her. "Summoning him is... frightening."

"As opposed to me attacking your king?" she said. "I've seen his true form when he attacked the Venatore headquarters. I think I can handle the God of Shadows as well."

"It's not your strength, I doubt, but my own. The thought of standing by... not being able to help if you need me..."

She slipped her hands from his grasp and cupped his face. "You'll be here waiting for me, and that's all I need to know to feel safe."

The sound of footsteps approached, and they turned as another man walked towards them. He held a squirming figure wrapped in a blanket strung over his shoulder, not looking like it bothered him in the least. Like it weighed nothing.

Phillis caught up to the man. "I told you to wait," he hissed through his teeth.

The man shrugged before dropping the load to the floor, and a loud grunt sounded from the bag. "Look, I've got things to see and people to do," he said with a smirk. "Besides. I did my job. I delivered." He kicked the bag, and his smile widened when the person inside screamed.

Namika stiffened but stayed silent. She didn't know who the newcomer was or who was inside the bag; the last thing she wanted to do was embarrass Adam.

"Good work, Revel." Adam glanced at the squirming person, then fished into his jacket pocket to take out a thick roll of money. "Don't spend it all in one place."

The man took it. "Okay, *Dad*."

Phillis punched Revel in the arm, and the man's eyes turned silver as he snarled at the demon. "Back off."

Namika's eyebrows shot up; Revel was a vampire. She hadn't expected Adam to work with them since the two races didn't get along.

"Enough." Adam's voice was calm, but the commanding tone wasn't to be ignored. "Thank you for your assistance."

The vampire shot a curious look towards Namika, then walked away.

Adam turned to Phillis. "Linda is currently patrolling

the parameters. I want you to join her to cover more ground."

"Yes, sir." Phillis' blue eyes bored into her. "I'm sorry again for what I said when we first met." He bowed deeply. "It was a pleasure to meet you, miss." Without uttering another word, he vanished.

Adam strode to the bag and pulled out a man. His face was bloody, one eye puffed up in dark shades of red and purple. With his wrists and ankles tied, he couldn't do much, and the gag in his mouth stopped him from saying anything.

"Before you ask, because I know you will," Adam said, glancing at Namika with a grin, "this man was recently released from prison because his victims were too afraid to testify against him." He crouched in front of the man, staring at him with amusement. "He enjoys hurting children and telling them he'll kill them and their parents if they tell anyone about what he does." Adam straightened. "I figured you'd prefer I choose a sacrifice that deserved death."

Namika stared at the man as his nostrils flared and he squirmed harder. With a small nod, she turned away, not wanting to look at him; she didn't pity him, but instead, a darkness within wanted to rip him apart herself.

Adam dragged the man near the circle, and when he tried wriggling away, Adam smiled in a way that sent shivers down her spine. A long dagger materialized in Adam's hand, and without hesitation, he stabbed the blade into the man's leg. The weapon impaled through the limb and anchored onto the cement floor as he shrieked. Blood pooled beneath, and the man's muffled screams filled the room.

She let out a shuddering breath, trying to focus on her task despite the noise. Taking the folded paper out from her jeans pocket, she unfolded it with trembling fingers. She swallowed hard at the thought of meeting the God of Shadows. What if he refused to answer her question? But this wasn't the time to second-guess anything. This was it. They'd know how to break the curse. It had loomed over her for what seemed like forever, and with everything else that happened, it felt like she'd never get to this moment.

Adam pulled her into a hug, and she gasped; she hadn't noticed his approach, too lost in her own thoughts. She held him close, burying her face into his vest, breathing in his scent and calming herself. It would be okay. He would be here, waiting for her once it was over.

She pulled back and smiled up at him. "I'm ready."

24

UNEXPECTED

Namika walked to the circle, needing to do this before she'd overthink everything even more and get too scared. She took a seat in the center of the circle, making sure the candle was directly in front of her for easy access. The flame flickered, and she focused on the incantation, doing her best to ignore the man's whimpers.

She read the words; it wasn't a language she knew, but it was familiar enough to a few others she'd learn. Darkness surrounded her, and she leaned forward a bit towards the candlelight so she could continue reading. Once she got to the end, she folded the paper before shoving it hastily into her pocket. She placed the medallion in front of her. It hummed on the floor, the tiny vibrations making it glow green every few seconds. The powder surrounding her bubbled to life, turning to a golden color. It turned to liquid that slithered forward, warping into symbols, as though alive. It fizzed and smoked, then froze.

The ground shook, and she pressed her hands against the surface to keep from toppling. Thankfully, the circle was wide enough so that if that happened, no part of her would be out.

Greenish and black mist seeped closer, but as soon as it got close to her circle, it stopped as though hitting a barrier. The man's muffled screams echoed, but she was too focused on what was happening up ahead to pay attention to him.

A large platform rose, golden steps appearing one by one as the smoke swirled thicker. Her breath hitched when a massive throne came into view, the figure sitting on it masked by the fog. But she could feel the energy from him and guessed it was Lokesh. Skeletal creatures trudged along the room, but none of them seemed to notice anything had changed.

Part of the mist dissipated, and Lokesh leaned forward on his throne. His eyes glowed like emeralds, but with no whites or pupils, it was difficult to tell where he was looking.

She cleared her throat. "God of Shadows," she called out, relieved her voice didn't shake. "Accept my gift to what is most precious to you."

The man tried squirming away, making a slow crawl towards their circle like a wounded snake.

Lokesh lifted his scepter, then slammed it three times on the floor. The platform vibrated, and a growl filled the room. Namika's muscles tensed as a creature stalked forward from the shadows, teeth bared. It was the size of an elephant but had the shape of a mix between a bear and a wolf. Its long snout poked at the man screaming through his gap, sniffing as though figuring out if it was edible. Drool dripped from its mouth, and with a snarl, it closed its mouth over the man's torso.

Namika looked away as her stomach churned.

Gurgling sounds filled the air, and the crunching that could only be bones sent bile to the back of her throat. With trembling hands, she grabbed the bowl and knelt so she could better place it outside the circle. "I also offer this as a token of gratitude."

The beast stopped right in front of the barrier, its hot breath blowing against her as she trembled. She shuffled back, trying to put some distance, but it didn't seem to matter; it towered over her as it bent its head and sniffed a few of the burgers. It gobbled them, licking the inside of the bowl once empty.

Lokesh got to his feet, the scepter vanishing into smoke as he walked down the steps. He wore what looked like armor fit for a king in greens, gold, and blacks. Even his long black hair rippled in different colors, as though golden lights shone through.

The creature sat, tail wagging, billowing wind and smoke. With its ears to the side, it looked like an innocent—though enormous—puppy, and Namika smiled. Lokesh rubbed the side of its face.

"Who's a good girl?" he asked in a baby voice. "You are, Starlights. You're a good girl," he said, using both hands to scratch the creature's head.

Namika's eyebrows shot up, and she gawked at the scene.

Lokesh turned to her. "Now that the formalities are out of the way, let's talk," he said, sitting on the floor in front of her.

She stared at Lokesh, trying to figure him out. At first, he seemed to be the way she had pictured the God of Shadows who presided over Voross. But after? Not so much.

Starlights lay down next to the god, licking her lips

from time to time. When she continued staying silent, Lokesh grinned. He leaned his chin against his knuckles, his gaze locked onto her.

He traced a finger along the floor, and the medallion shone. "Sebastian's medallion." His smile widened. "That certainly explains why you brought the extra food. He knows it's Starlights' favorite." The medallion stopped glowing and vanished.

The air stilled as she tapped into her magic, allowing it to flow outwards. Not in a display of strength, but so she was honest about what she was.

"A mystic afflicted with the Vokri curse? Interesting."

She leaned closer. "Can you tell me how to break the curse?"

"You know how it works, right?"

"Shi..." She wasn't sure if she should mention the demon king's second in command. "If it had been a random attack, I would've turned into a ghoul right away. But in my case, it was likely targeted because the person knew my name. It has to be a blood relative, right?"

His eyes bore into her. "Immediate family only. The blood relation needs to be strong for a curse like this to take hold."

"Wait... you mean like my parents?" The words took a few seconds to sink in. "That's impossible."

"Yes. Parents, siblings, or children." He cocked his head. "Are your parents still alive?"

"My mother is... I don't have a sibling..."

"And your father?" he asked quietly.

Her throat seemed to close shut, and she tried swallowing through the lump. "It has to be a mistake." She blinked back tears. "My father never made a deal with a demon..."

Yet the night her grandmother and father were

murdered replayed in her mind. All those years, she'd been sure the demons had said how they were there for revenge against her mother. What if her mind had invented that to protect herself from the truth? What if her father had actually negotiated with a demon that caused their deaths? But he never would've cursed her to this fate...

If he made a deal, maybe I didn't know him as well as I thought after all...

She let out a breath and met Lokesh's gaze head-on. "How do I break the curse?"

"In reverse." When she frowned, he chuckled. "The lost soul who cursed you did so by carving your name into your own flesh."

She traced the faded scar below her shoulder. "My name was written? Which one?"

"It doesn't matter. Names change throughout our lives. Some more than others." He got to his feet, towering over her. "Find the lost soul and carve his name into his flesh."

Namika stood as well. "Thank you."

"One little thing you forgot," he said, and pointed at her feet. "You were supposed to blow out the candle right after the incantation."

She glanced down. "Oh, right..." she muttered, then stared back at him as she arched an eyebrow. "Was that... important?"

"Light creates shadows, and..." He raised his hand, and the shadow around the candle shot up, wrapping itself around her neck. She screamed, gripping the sudden solid form as it raised her off her feet. "I'd say it was important, yes," he said as a wicked grin spread across his lips.

She trembled as she stared at him; she'd messed up.

The shadow wrenched her less than an inch away from the barrier, and her breathing sped up.

"Since one of my offspring is the first mystic, out of

respect for them, I will forgive your mistake." His emerald eyes seemed to shimmer. "I will also tell you a secret. A loophole to this curse."

Her grip around the shadow's solid form tightened, and she blinked a few times. She wanted to say something—anything—but she couldn't seem to find her voice.

"If the time comes, and you've failed to break the curse, there is one way out." The amusement left his expression, and instead, darkness fell across his face, creating skull-like shapes. "If you take your own life, the curse will not be completed. You'll be dead, obviously, but you won't be condemned to the Inferno."

She swallowed hard. "Can you...tell me how long I have left?"

"Not long. A few days at best." He cocked his head. "You have your answer. Now go break the curse." And with no additional words, he vanished.

Namika staggered as the shadows disappeared with him, and she gasped. The factory reappeared in place of the realm of Voross. Adam approached, but she held out her hand, needing a few seconds to wrap her mind around everything. Tears burned her eyes as she went through all the information Lokesh had told her.

Her own father had cursed her. After everything she'd gone through already, hadn't she suffered enough? Even years later, her family's death still haunted her.

"It's...my father..." Her shaky voice turned into a sob, and she welcomed Adam's arms around her, holding her close.

She calmed down faster than expected and was able to tell Adam everything the God of Shadows had told her. Well, almost everything; she kept the part about taking her own life to herself.

A strange new determination burned inside her; it was time to break the curse and get her life back.

"What's next?" she asked.

25

A CONNECTION

Namika paced around. "Something's been bothering me since Toronto."

"What is it?" Adam asked as he put away what was left of the summoning.

"How did the vampire know where to find us? We were in Ottawa when he first attacked me, but he followed all the way to Toronto not long after we arrived?"

He chuckled as he grabbed the candle. "It couldn't possibly be because my company name is written in giant letters on the building?"

"I mean, yes. But it's more than that. How did he know that's where we went in the first place?

He kept his gaze down as he continued cleaning up. "Well, we have already established this vampire is likely getting help from a reaper."

"Okay, but that still doesn't explain how either of them keeps tracking us down." She shook her head. "We get to Winnipeg, and suddenly we're being sent into traps? They even got into the Dragon's Lair without getting noticed, and sent that..." she shivered at the memory of that day, "corpse with the cloaking spell. We're missing something."

When he stayed quiet, she narrowed her eyes at him. He placed the empty vase inside the duffle bag and zipped it up. By the time he finished, she was staring at him with her arms crossed. "You're keeping something from me."

"Smart women are the most dangerous of creatures," he muttered, the corner of his mouth curling into a half-smile. "I don't know for sure, but I'm guessing it has to do with the curse."

She slid her hand to her shoulder, despite being unable to feel her scar beneath the thick coat. "What do you mean?"

"There's likely a connection between you and the lost soul, and this vampire... or reaper, is using it to their advantage."

"Wait, so you think they're using the curse to track me?" she asked in a small voice. All of her childhood lessons had been about masking herself to the world, and the idea of being followed didn't sit right with her.

Adam grabbed the duffle bag and swung it over his shoulder. "Maybe it's not the only way to use that connection, though..." He muttered the words, as though speaking to himself. He put the bag inside the trunk of the car. "A lot of magics are two-ways."

"You mean I could potentially track the lost soul?" Her pulse sped at the thought. "But how? I don't even know where to start to learn how to do this."

Before he could answer, Shiriki materialized near what was left of the protective circle. Adam bowed, and Namika took a few steps closer to the vehicle.

"You are still both alive," Shiriki said. "The summoning went well, then?"

Adam shot a warning look towards Namika, and she understood to keep quiet about her having to do it solo.

"Yes. We have the answer about how to break the curse," Adam said, leaning back against the trunk.

"Good." Shiriki smiled. "Mekaisto is summoning you to court in order to report your latest findings."

"Now?" Adam straightened. "Can't it wait?"

"Why? Do you have plans at this very moment?" Shiriki asked, cocking his head.

"Namika only has a few days left before the curse is completed and she dies." Adam's hands curled into fists. "I can give Mekaisto an update once she's cured."

Something in Shiriki's smile turned deadly. "Your answer to the king is that he should... *wait?*" His sinister laughter filled the room, and Namika's pulse sped as Shiriki's silver pupils shone. "It was not a request."

Adam's gaze darkened as he took a step forward. "And what if I refuse?"

Namika dashed to Adam and grabbed his arm, shaking her head. "It'll be fine," she said quickly, glancing between the two demons. "You said it yourself. We have a few *days*. Not hours or minutes. Go to court and tell your king what we learned. Please."

Adam seemed to calm down a bit, but she wasn't sure how angry the other one was at that moment.

She swallowed hard as she faced Shiriki, trying her best not to tremble. "Lokesh gave us a lot of information, and some of it was... upsetting. We're both still getting to terms with all of it."

Shiriki's energy rippled around him, but he seemed amused again.

Adam placed his hand on Namika's. "Linda will escort you back."

Seconds later, Linda appeared in the room and bowed low to both demons. "You called me?"

"Drive Miss Strang to the Dragon's Lair, and keep on guard," he ordered.

Linda shot a grimace at the car. "You couldn't have picked a nicer vehicle? This thing looks like it's at least five years old."

Adam's jaw clenched. "That's the point. An expensive car would attract attention."

"Fine, fine." Linda waved her hand dismissively. "But if I see anyone I know, I'm blaming you for ruining my reputation." She got into the car, and the garage door ground open. A blast of freezing air blew inside, and Namika tried to warm herself by rubbing her arms.

He reached inside the trunk and pulled out a navy scarf. With a smile, he wrapped it around her neck. "Better?"

Her heart seemed to swell, and she nodded. "Yes, thanks." Her breath appeared in the small white puffs. "I'll try figuring out that reverse connection thing in the meantime."

He nodded as he closed the trunk, and without another word, disappeared in a quick flash of movement.

Shiriki took a few steps forward, and she stiffened. "Reverse connection?" he repeated.

She wasn't sure if she wanted to share anything with him, but he likely knew a lot about different magics, even if these belonged to a different realm than his own.

"Adam thinks that the curse is creating a connection between me and the lost soul, and they're using it to track me wherever we go. So maybe there's a way for me to use that same link to find the lost soul."

He suddenly appeared just a few inches from her, and she gasped, pressing herself against the car. "Not impossible," he said, then pointed at her chest. "If you push that magic of yours aside, it will ease access to the darkness from the Vokri curse. Use it to locate what you require."

Her pulse sped. "I... never mentioned the name of the curse."

"Oh?" His smile widened over his pointed teeth. "You or Adam must have mentioned it before."

"I only learned it now from Lokesh..." She gawked at him, anger mixing in with the fear running through her blood. "Have you known the name this whole time? What else do you know?"

"Perhaps, one day, you will find out." He winked, then disappeared as well.

She really wished demons would stop hiding so many things all the time. He was probably withholding a lot of information, all the while helping them to the bare minimum. With a few choice words muttered under her breath, she opened the passenger door and slid inside into the warmth.

Linda glanced at her as she put the vehicle in drive. "Everything good?"

"As good as it gets," Namika said with a sigh, leaning back against the seat.

The car jolted forward, and soon enough, Namika was lost in thought as the scenery blurred past. Heaviness weighed down against her, and she closed her eyes, trying to regain any semblance of energy; she was just so tired.

A white light flickered, and she stared down at herself. Except, she wasn't really her anymore; it was like she was looking into the core of her body. A ball of light shone within a cage, and a strange sadness filled her. She had unlocked the door to her magic to heal Adam, but the prison remained within. Unable to completely break free.

She tugged at her outstretched arm and frowned when

something held it in place. Barbed wires crisscrossed from her limb, blood streaming down her gray skin. Darkness swirled around, and she drew her hand towards herself, pulling the wires with it. Fear warned her not to proceed, but she brought the infected limb closer to the cage and slid her fingertips along the sharp edges.

Namika gasped as her eyelids flew open. "Whoa, wait... Shit."

"What the fuck? Are you trying to make me crash or something?" Linda snapped, tightening her hands on the wheel. "You can't just scream like that."

"I was...screaming?" Namika asked, but didn't listen to the demon's response. A red light shone from her chest, forming a straight line ahead. She blinked a few times, her mind catching up to what was happening. "Can...can you see it?"

"See what? You losing your mind in real-time?"

Namika didn't dare move too much. "This is going to sound insane, but I think I tapped into the curse's magic. There's a light pointing towards its location because I'm pretty sure I connected to it."

"Seriously?" Linda glanced from Namika and back to the road. "I mean, I overheard you and Shiriki talking about something like that, so it doesn't sound impossible."

"Turn right!" Namika shouted as the light suddenly twisted towards one side.

The tires screeched against the road, and Namika slammed into the side of the door, nearly hitting her head against the window.

"Bit more warning next time," Linda said through gritted teeth. "What are we doing, anyway? Adam gave me an order to bring you back to the Dragon's Lair. Not chase after some magical connection light thing."

Namika continued staring ahead, trying to anticipate

the light's trajectory. "The God of Shadows said I only have a short time remaining before the curse takes hold. I need to find the lost soul and carve its name in its flesh before then."

"Sucks to be you." Yet Linda's tone didn't seem to match the words.

Namika let out a groan. "What about Adam? You know as well as I do what happens if I end up going to the Inferno. That's why you were so pissed off at me for dragging him into this." She pointed ahead. "I don't know how long I can hold this connection or even if I'll be able to do it again. This might be our only chance."

"I still can't disobey an order without a plan," Linda said, but she didn't turn the car around.

"We follow the light. Find the lost soul's location." Namika's heart skipped a beat. "Left here!" She grabbed hold of the seatbelt to keep from ramming against Linda as the car turned once more.

"Fine. We locate it, and that's it. We don't do anything until Adam returns from the Dark Realm and joins us."

Namika nodded. "Works for me."

As they turned onto the perimeter surrounding the city, Namika leaned forward, focusing up ahead as they approached a white truck. The light shone straight through it, and she frowned, unable to see if it had curved at all.

"Pass the truck," Namika said, waving her hand to the side.

Linda pushed against the pedal and drove the car forward. The light swayed slightly, and Namika gasped.

"It's in the truck." She pointed at the vehicle. "The lost soul is inside there."

"Well, fuck," Linda spat as she changed lanes and drove behind it again. "Now what?"

"Can we stop it somehow?" Namika was leaning

forward so far, she felt like she might jump out of the windshield.

They were so close.

Linda shook her head. "No. The plan was to find it, not intercept or anything like that."

"What if we lose track of it? It probably senses I'm right here." Panic filled her mind with each passing second. What if the reaper suddenly appeared inside the truck and yanked the lost soul out of there?

Can reapers create portals within moving vehicles?

She wasn't about to wait and find out. Pushing her energy into her hand, she outstretched her arm and focused on the back wheel of the truck. It twisted, then snapped off, slamming the vehicle down in one corner. Sparks flew as it dragged, and Linda cursed under her breath.

The truck drove over the tiny median. Incoming cars skidded to the side, tires screeching. Horns blasted as a vehicle hit the side of the truck and rolled into traffic. Namika gasped as two more cars swerved into them.

A crunching sound resonated throughout the vehicle. Her neck felt like it snapped on impact, and she clenched her jaw.

Silence.

Then screams.

Namika blinked a few times, staring at the crumpled hood. The smell of burned rubber filled her nostrils, and she released a quivering breath. Multiple vehicles were scattered across the highway, some parked at odd angles, while others were crumpled beyond recognition.

People darted out of their cars, running to help the victims. A few held their cellphones up, recording the disaster.

Sirens echoed from a distance.

Linda leaned towards Namika and undid her seatbelt. Blood dripped along her hair, but she didn't look too bad considering the state of the car.

The back door of the truck rolled open. Ghouls jumped onto the vehicles, smashing the windshields and denting the metal in sickening crunches. People screamed, running from the monsters. But the ghouls were faster.

Namika squinted, trying to make out what was happening in the darkness; the only lights were from the street lamps and headlights. The monsters ran across the highway, chasing people down. One jumped onto their car, and Namika lowered her head as shards of glass exploded from the windshield.

She threw herself out of the car and staggered away from it as the ghoul turned its attention towards her. Her magic filled her extremities as it tried to heal her wounds, but she barely paid attention.

It lunged, but Linda intercepted it, sending it flying across the road. It fell limp on the pavement, face bloodied beyond recognition.

The demon shot her a burning red glare. "You've really fucked up this time."

As though on cue, strobe lights from first responders flashed from both directions, heading to the catastrophic accident. Namika's pulse sped. How would they cover this up?

She shook her head, pushing her fears away and focusing on what was crucial. The lost soul was likely still inside the truck, and she wasn't about to let it run off after everything.

Namika created a ball of nonlethal energy within her palm as she was ready to strike at whatever else came at her. She didn't want to kill her father before breaking the curse. But after?

All bets were off.

The passenger door of the truck opened, and a woman stepped out. Her eyes glowed in the familiar whites of vampires, and she snarled when she stared at Namika. But Linda didn't give her the chance to do anything. The demon slammed her against the truck. Over and over until her body seemed to have lost all its bones.

A few people screamed at the sight while running off, still holding their devices up in the air to record.

Another ghoul lept out towards Namika, and she blasted it at the monster. It screeched as its flesh cracked, and it exploded in a cloud of ashes. The dust flew away in the billowing wind as the lost soul jumped out before she could aim. Her magic crashed against the side, and she clenched her jaw.

It straightened, and Namika's mind suddenly seemed to catch up to the realization.

Dad.

Tears filled her eyes as she stared at him—or what was left through the burns and decomposition. He looked less like a monster than the first time they'd come face to face. Obviously, he was gaining more of Namika's life force. The left side of his face wasn't gray anymore, but the flesh was reddened and blistered, as though still burning.

"How could you?" she said through her teeth.

He bared his fangs, but she didn't care. Her mind numbed as she pushed away at her emotions. She swung her arm, and he crashed into the truck, denting the metal.

The static of two-way radios cut in and out as first responders tried communicating through the chaos. It wouldn't be long before they'd reach the truck.

Flicking her wrist to the side, Namika spun her father, so she'd have access to his back. Her magic flickered; there wasn't much time left. Her hands shook as she pressed the claw-like fingernails of her cursed hand into his back. It was her or her father; she wouldn't go to the Inferno because of her father's choices. She carved into his skin, repeating that to herself over and over as he screamed.

Once the name Azuma was etched, Namika backed away, panting. He fell to his knees, trembling. She stared down at her bloodied fingers, waiting for something—anything—to happen, but the curse remained.

Her blood froze within her veins when a sinister laugh echoed, and he straightened. He turned, his eyes turned pitch black, his lips curling into a monstrous smile.

"You failed, and your time is almost up," he said in a shrill voice.

He lunged, and she ducked out of the way, her hands and knees scraping against the pavement. She winced at the pain, her heart hammering as Linda materialized in front of her, shielding her from her father's attack.

A green light burst near the truck, and a figure stepped out. Their hooded cloak hid most of their features, but the energy rippling from them was strong. Namika staggered to her feet, but before she could act, the newcomer grabbed the lost soul and pulled him back into the portal.

It hadn't worked.

Lokesh had lied, and with hardly any time left, there would be no escaping the Inferno.

26

FAULT

amika stood in self-pity for what felt like an eternity. But no matter how much time went by, it wouldn't change what she had to do. The alternative was too horrifying.

The pain and agony. Fear beyond anything.

She wrenched her coat off and rolled up her sleeve. There was only one thing she could do. And she had to do it fast. No thinking or she'd back out.

She pressed her claw-like fingernail against her wrist, blood pooling around the point. Then...nothing.

She frowned as she stared around; nothing moved. Everything had gone silent. Time itself seemed to have frozen.

The environment changed, and she stared around at the most beautiful scenery. White arches and columns stood on a reflective marble floor, translucent curtains undulating in a small breeze. She arched her neck, looking at the nebula shining above her; each star twinkling brighter than the other.

Footsteps approached, and she spun.

She met with a pair of the bluest eyes she'd ever seen. Like the clearest ocean in a land of fantasy.

"There you are," the person with the blue eyes said in a soft tone. They didn't smile, but there was a gentleness about them.

"Who are you?"

"I am the first mystic. Offspring of Lokesh, God of Shadows, and human, Vera." They bowed, their black hair falling in a cascade of shimmering lights. "My name is Sorin Respor."

"Why...are you here?" She glanced over her shoulder, trying to find the accident site, but it had vanished.

"My father informed me that one of my own was cursed, and so I did not hesitate to find you."

"Lokesh tricked me," she said in a trembling voice. "It didn't work."

Sorin shook their head. "How do people wind up in the fiery depths of the Inferno?"

"A deal with demons."

"And do you truly believe your father would have given his soul like that?" A small smile curled their lips.

"No. But there's no one else it could be."

They approached Namika. "Your father and grandparents are in Lyoran, at peace."

"So it wasn't him. That's why breaking the spell didn't work." Her mind was working fast, trying to keep up with her thoughts. "But my mother is still alive——"

"Perhaps it is time you see her."

Namika blinked, and she was suddenly standing in front of Sorin. At this angle, mountains were visible in the distance, clouds touching their peaks. The sky looked like a galaxy, and she couldn't help but feel a strange calmness.

She looked back into Sorin's gaze. "My mother is sick. She doesn't recognize me anymore."

"You have made allies with demons, have you not?" They cocked their head, their hair shimmering in what looked like starlight. "One in particular once had a connection to the Venatore group, and could look into your mother's memories."

Her heart skipped a few beats.

Shiriki.

He'd been the one who had given Venatores their powers ages ago. Would she really allow him to look into her mother's mind? Did she even have a choice?

Namika's stomach clenched as though she were falling.

The smallest of smiles touched Sorin's lips. "Before you go, I will grant you a gift."

Sorin put out their hands, and white light flowed from their palms. Namika's soul burst from her, the threads moving towards the first mystic. She shuddered at the sight, but didn't feel any danger this time. Not like when Sebastian had looked into her.

Slowly, Sorin pressed their index fingers together, then pulled, creating a beautiful string of golden light. It floated towards her and attached to her core, along with the others. Her magic seemed to warm, and she exhaled.

"What...is that?"

"The curse has changed some of your physical attributes, which will make it difficult for you to navigate in the human world as you are. This magic will help you cloak your appearance."

"But if I break the curse—"

"The transformation is permanent." A sad expression crossed their face. "You will carry this curse, broken or not, for the rest of your life."

Tears rolled down her cheeks, but she wiped them away. It didn't matter what she looked like. Not while she still had to deal with saving her life and soul. The sound of screaming reached her, and she frowned.

"I paused time, but the spell is wearing down." Sorin glanced over her shoulder. "Be cautious of him."

The falling worsened. Her surroundings changed, and she gasped. White puffs obscured her vision as she panted. She was still standing in the middle of the highway.

Someone yanked her to the side, and her chest tightened as she stared at Adam. He grabbed her wrist, staring at where blood still dripped along where she'd tried cutting herself. The fury behind his gaze wasn't easily missed as he stared down at her. Her heart pounded as she met his gaze.

"Can I explain later?" she asked.

His energy pressed against her, and she staggered. He stared at her as though fighting too many emotions at once.

"Fine." His voice was husky, like his throat was tight.

He led her to the side of the highway and pushed her towards Linda, who caught her before she fell to the ground.

Shiriki appeared next to Adam, his expression stony. More static rang through the air, and he turned his head, his pupils glowing pure white. Electricity ran across the vehicles; every headlight and lamp post exploded in angry blue sparks. People screamed, rushing in different directions, but they all hit an invisible barrier.

"Who is responsible for this?" Shiriki asked in a deadly tone.

Namika raised her hand slowly. "I am. It was an accident, I didn't——"

"I do not recall asking for an excuse." Shiriki's voice sliced through the air, and Namika took a step back. He turned his attention to Linda, his lips curling into an angry smile. "You were given an order to drive her back to the Dragon's Lair. You disobeyed."

Namika took a step forward, shaking her head. "No. Her priority as my personal servant is always to help break the curse. She made it clear that we'd only find the location of the lost soul and then wait for Adam."

Adam crossed his arms. "Let me guess. You didn't follow through with the plan?"

She shook her head. "I panicked. I was——"

"Enough." Adam stared at Linda. "You will return to the Dragon's Lair. I will deal with you later." He took a step towards her, energy rippling from him. "If you fail to follow my command again, I'll send you to Mekaisto for reeducation."

Linda let out a forceful breath, but quickly bowed and vanished without a word.

People in the crowd got into their vehicles, trying to break through the barrier, but it wouldn't budge.

"So many casualties..." Shiriki said in an amused tone.

Namika's pulse sped as she glanced from the demon to the people desperate to escape. Adam shot her a glare as he pulled out his smartphone, but Shiriki raised his hand.

"No," Shiriki said, his tone final.

Adam arched an eyebrow. "We need the cleaning crew to fix this before more first responders show up."

"Namika is responsible for this mess, and as her owner, it falls on you to clean it up," Shiriki said with a smile.

Adam stiffened, but slipped the device back into his pocket without arguing. "I see."

"And she will watch, so she never forgets that her actions have consequences for more than just herself." Shiriki grabbed her arm and pulled her closer to the barrier.

She didn't dare try to wrench away from his grip; she

had the feeling if she did, he'd likely take a chunk off her skin. Still, Adam stood, unmoving, as he stared at Shiriki. It almost seemed like he was raging an inner battle as to what to do next. After a few seconds, Adam grasped her chin and forced her to look at him.

"Don't look away."

He walked through the barrier, black and red smoke billowing around him. It hid him from view, but his energy continued pouring out from him in waves. Power blasted as the smoke rose into a tornado, blood-red embers circling the sky above. Adam stepped out, a trail of red tendrils following his every movement; like his shadow was as alive as he was. The smoke turned into dark red serpents, lashing at everything around them, teeth ripping through anything they touched.

Her heart hammered in her chest as he came into view. His gray hair fluttered in the wind, longer on the sides. He raised his hands on either side, his black pointed fingernails looking like they could slice through anything.

The energy was his, but it was so much more powerful.

A large vehicle appeared amongst the blackened particles, smashing against the highway and sending pieces of cement flying. They hovered for a second, then slammed back into the ground. People scattered, screams and cries filling the air.

Her heart hammered as she recognized a gasoline tanker. "Wait... What——?"

"No witnesses," Shiriki whispered in her ear. "They all get to die because of you. And Adam gets to be the one to do it."

Tears blurred her vision, and she tried wiping at her face, but Shiriki grabbed her hair and wrenched her head back. It forced her to continue looking at the scene unfold in front of them.

Red electricity sparked into a ball in Adam's palm, and for a second, he seemed to hesitate. She opened her mouth, trying to find her voice again so she could beg him to stop. But he aimed at the tanker and blasted it.

Flames engulfed the vehicle, and the detonation that followed seemed to happen in slowed time. The sound of the explosion resonated a few seconds after the actual blast, sending a roaring fire across the highway. A giant fireball rose, burning in the night sky and illuminating the horror all around. Burn survivors cried out in pain, crawling along the pavement. Strewn across the road, the charred remains of victims were visible as the smoke dissipated. The flames seemed to turn into liquid as they pooled along the vehicles, setting them ablaze with everything else.

The barrier vanished, and Shiriki released Namika. She dashed towards Adam, wincing at the heat of the fire surrounding them. As she approached, Adam slowed his steps, his red eyes burning into her; his stony expression was that of a stranger. Without a word, he walked past her, and she fell to her knees, hitting the ground hard

What have I done?

THE CLEANING CREW busied themselves with the cleanup, organizing their stories, and even setting up a trailer where a few people worked on computers. Likely to remove what had been recorded live during the initial crash.

Namika did her best to wipe away the blood on her wrist, but the deep cut was taking time to heal. Shiriki glanced at the wound, and something about him changed, like his usual amusement had vanished.

"Given up?"

"Lokesh said it was a loophole," she muttered. "Taking

my own life seemed a better alternative than ending up in the Inferno."

"I doubt Adam will understand it that way." Shiriki glanced towards where Adam stood. "Killing yourself without so much as a word to him." His eyes burned in what seemed like white flames. "Or maybe there was nothing of importance to say in the end?"

Fire continued rising towards the sky, the black smoke darkening the occasional sparks of light. The car Phillis had brought Adam was parked behind him, hazards blinking. She couldn't see his expression at that distance, but his power crashed against their surroundings. Angry wasn't the word she'd use——she wasn't even sure what to describe it as. He'd returned to the form she was used to seeing; the human one. The one that didn't remind her he was a monster.

Shiriki walked away, heading towards the car; she followed closely, fidgeting with her fingers as they approached. As soon as Adam was within earshot, she went straight to the point, explaining what happened. From going after the lost soul, to damaging the truck, to forcing it to stop. The failed attempt to break the curse, and her decision to use the loophole Lokesh told her about rather than be sent to the Inferno.

"I suppose there's a reason you decided not to go through with it." Adam crossed his arms, the emotional distance between them seemingly getting bigger.

"Sorin stopped time and spoke to me..." She took a deep breath. "They told me my grandparents and father are in Lyoran. That I need to ask my mother how it's possible for a lost soul to have cursed me. But she has dementia..." She stared at Shiriki, trying her best to keep eye contact. "And that's why I need your help."

"Interesting. You wish for me to look into her memories?" Shiriki asked in amusement. When Namika nodded, he grinned. "Very well."

Her heart sped. "Is there a way to get a flight out now? Or——"

"I have a better idea," he said with a smile that sent shivers down her spine. He turned his attention to Adam. "Do you remember the building where a vampire party turned into a massacre a few years ago?"

Adam nodded. "Hard to forget that place."

"Head there." Shiriki opened the back door of the car and slid inside.

Namika's stomach churned at the thought of him sitting behind her like that——not that it would make any difference if he wanted to cause her any harm. The wind picked up, and motion caught her attention. Her gaze settled on the white sheets over the burned corpses. All these people were dead because of her, because she couldn't wait to break the curse and follow the plan.

Adam opened the passenger door and waited in silence. More than anything, she wished she could fish inside his mind to find out what he was thinking. She got inside the car, and once he slid in, he pulled the car onto the highway. Shiriki leaned forward, and she pressed herself against the side, trying to put some distance between them.

He turned the wheel, and the car screeched to the right, taking an exit towards downtown. Images flashed in her mind, tires peeling against the asphalt, desperate to stop in time. She clutched the seatbelt at how fast he was driving, barely making any of his stops. Her heart hammered in her chest at the thought of being in another accident. It would be her fault again.

She glanced sideways at Adam. He was upset, and that was her doing, too. He'd had to kill innocent people because they'd seen too much. Because she had been careless. Selfish. Tears blurred her vision.

They weren't far from their destination; they pulled up into the private lot of a condemned apartment building in less than fifteen minutes. She wished Shiriki hadn't been with them since she wanted to talk to Adam about what had happened. Wanted to apologize for what he'd been forced to do. But what could she really say that would make any of it better? And she'd have to eventually talk about how she was about to kill herself without an explanation. After everything they'd gone through together, she owed him so much more.

They stepped out of the car. Snow mixed in with the wind, whipping at her skin like knives.

Adam eyed the vehicle. "Phillis rented this under the company's name."

"What a shame," Shiriki said with a shrug as he walked towards the building.

His hands curled into fists, but he stayed silent as he followed the Viscus demon. Namika's shoulders slumped as she dashed after them; Adam hadn't even bothered to make sure she'd been following. He didn't care about her at all anymore. Glass crunched beneath her boots, the ground uneven. A gust of wind fluttered a pile of trash bags, and she jumped at the sudden sound and movement. Her pulse wouldn't slow since the accident.

Not an accident. I caused it.

The fencing around the building sagged, a few spots only held up by abandoned, turned-over shopping carts. The chain links uncoiled as Shiriki approached, creating a hole for him to step through without having to slow his steps. She glanced behind them, terrified they'd be spotted, but the streets were deserted at this hour. It was likely around three in the morning, and with most of the bars closing an hour ago, there wasn't much risk of getting seen.

The door creaked open with little fuss, and they stepped inside. Rusty mailboxes at the entrance were all dented and broken into, leaving behind discarded nests and rodent droppings. Cockroaches scattered at the sudden invasion, and Namika rubbed her arms, trying to get rid of the goosebumps crawling along her skin. She was suddenly so itchy.

Shiriki glanced around before focusing on the stairs leading to the basement. "Ah, this is where I left it." Without explanation, he went down.

Adam followed, kicking some broken drywall to the side to make an easier path. The building groaned as though contesting having visitors inside after so long. She glanced up above, nervous that the whole thing would suddenly collapse on them. How long ago had this place been condemned? And why were they even here?

When she got to the bottom of the stairwell, the squish of the soaked carpet caused a slight give in the floor, and she lost her balance. Adam quickly caught her by the elbow, steadying her. The tension between them was so thick, it was as though the silence was a living entity. Her mind worked a mile a minute, desperate to explain herself so he wouldn't hate her after what he'd been forced to do because of her. But no words came to mind.

She coughed at the potent smell of mildew, eyeing the mold splotches on the walls; this couldn't be good to breathe in. Spiderwebs hung amongst the pipes running across the open ceiling, and she did her best to avoid walking beneath them. She didn't think it was possible for it to feel colder down here than outside.

A shimmer caught her attention, and her stomach

tensed as she approached a familiar place. The room with the filing cabinets in Shiriki's dwelling.

"So you *do* see it," Shiriki said with amusement.

Adam arched an eyebrow. "Let me guess. You saw this place in my storage room at the CrowBar, didn't you?"

She nodded; there was no use denying it since they'd obviously figured it out. "I'm not sure why I can sense it, though."

"Mystics have a different range of skills for their magic," Shiriki said as he approached the room in question. "You happen to see through veils."

"Wait..." She took a few steps towards the shimmer. "Does this mean, if I step into this place, I'll be back in Ottawa?"

"Exactly." Shiriki's smile widened, showing pointed teeth. "And back inside my home."

She recoiled at the thought, but it only made him look more amused. Still, she wasn't about to complain about not having to get on another plane. This kind of travel would definitely come in handy. She glanced at Adam, waiting for some sort of sign from him that it was safe for her to step through. He stared back at her, and after a few seconds, gave a curt nod.

Stepping through the shimmering air was like a strange silken velvet washing over her. By the time she stood in the filing room, an uneasy feeling filled her to the core, but she wasn't sure why.

"What's the name of the care home where your mother lives?" Adam asked as he pulled out his smartphone. She gave him the name, and once he tapped his screen a few times, he looked back up. "Visiting hours start at ten in the morning. Meaning we have around six hours to wait before we head out."

Shiriki glanced at the door, and less than a minute later,

the old woman Namika remembered by the name of Hilda came limping inside.

"You're back already?" When her gaze landed on Namika, her eyebrows shot up. "Don't tell me you dragged this poor thing through the Dark Realm to get here faster." She shot a glare at Shiriki, and Namika nearly begged for forgiveness on the woman's behalf out of fear of what the Viscus demon might do about the disrespect.

But Shiriki grinned. "Do not worry yourself. Namika here is full of surprises." He stared at the floor as though looking through it. "Prepare the guest bedroom on the second floor."

Hilda frowned. "Two bedrooms?"

Adam shook his head. "No. I have to keep an eye on this one."

A part of Namika wanted to snap back at him, but her shoulders slumped in defeat instead. He was right; she was always making stupid mistakes.

Shiriki took out a pocket watch and clicked the top part so it opened. "I have things to take care of before we leave in a few hours." He turned to Hilda. "You may retire for the rest of the morning." And without saying anything else, he disappeared.

27

PAIN

*H*ilda showed them to the guest bedroom, then busied herself with preparing fresh sheets and blankets for the bed. Namika's pulse sped at how the wooden bed frame was made—like a four-poster, but without any of the material atop. Each pole had cuffs hanging from chains anchored into the wood. She wished more than anything they'd have gone back to the CrowBar instead.

Adam stared into the old-fashioned fireplace, and flames blazed to life, roaring like they had been alight for hours. It warmed the room, but Namika still felt a different kind of chill.

"If you require anything, ring the bell, and I'll come up," Hilda said, pointing towards a small golden bell with a rope hanging from it.

Once she left, silence seemed to press down into the room. Namika mentally prepared herself to face him, but when she turned, he stood inches from her, and she yelped. He backed her up, and before she could find the words, he cuffed her wrist to one of the wooden poles of the bed.

She gaped at him. "What are you doing?"

His eyes narrowed on her, and she swallowed hard. Without a word, he left, slamming the door behind him; the frame splintered.

Her pulse quickened as she tugged against the restraint. Even her magic didn't work against this, and she had the feeling that was on purpose. Anger bubbled up inside her as she pulled harder; the wood bent slightly. She clenched her jaw, then rammed her shoulder into the pole as hard as she could. It cracked with the first collision. Snapped with the second one.

The top part of the four-poster crashed onto the mattress, and her heart pounded in her chest. Still, despite the fear of consequences for what she'd done, the fury burning inside her was stronger. It overtook her senses as darkness seemed to wrap around the core of her magic. She grabbed the wooden pole and yanked it until it ripped off, splinters falling to the floor.

She slipped the cuff from it, but froze when Adam marched into the room.

Their gazes met, and she tightened her grip on the pole, instincts kicking in for defense.

"I told Shiriki to buy it in metal instead of wood," he said in an amused tone. But something dark danced behind his eyes as they turned red. He shut the door, the frame hanging at a strange angle.

"You didn't need to lock me up like that," she said in a hushed voice, trying her best to control her anger.

"Considering the last time I left you alone, you managed to make all the wrong choices." He pointed at the collapsed bedframe. "Even cuffed wasn't enough to stop you from acting irrationally."

She used the pole to motion at the doorframe. "That's the pot calling the kettle black."

Yet, the images of victims crying out in agony as they tried to escape flashed through her mind. And Adam had been forced to do it. Because of her. She didn't deserve forgiveness.

He wrenched the makeshift weapon away from her and threw it to the side. It hit the shelf, sending it crashing to the floor. "Was it worth disobeying my orders?"

She wept, her cheeks wet with tears, and she shook her head. "I know it's my fault that all those people are dead. And that Shiriki made you do it." She stared up at him, the lump in her throat choking her. "I'm so sorry you were forced to do that because of me. I'm sorry."

"You think I'm upset because I had to dispose of witnesses?" His tone was laced in ice, and she suddenly saw him as a stranger again. "No, buttercup. I don't care about them. I've killed more people than I can count throughout my six hundred plus years."

Her breath hitched at his indifference. Where was the man who was warm and affectionate? Or was his mask slipping to reveal the demon within?

"Then... why are you mad at me?" she asked quietly.

He manifested right in front of her, and she stared up at him, heart hammering. Reaching behind her, the cuff loosened with a click and fell onto the bed. She rubbed her wrist, but he grasped it, tracing his thumb over where she'd cut herself.

"You acted recklessly. Causing an accident like that on the highway. You're lucky there wasn't more traffic." He shook his head. "What if you had accidentally killed the lost soul? The cure to the curse would've died with it."

Her chest squeezed. "I panicked. I was terrified of losing it while we were following. If I could sense it, then it likely could do the same for me."

"You were impatient," he said through gritted teeth. "And immature."

She narrowed her eyes. "I'm sorry I didn't make choices you approved of," she said, her tone laced with sarcasm. "But I don't appreciate being locked up like that. You—"

His red irises swam with more than fury; like everything he'd contained since finding her with a bleeding wrist was being released.

"You don't appreciate it?" He repeated in a hiss. "Is that so?"

"I'm—"

"Sorry?" He scoffed and paced the room. The walls splintered as he passed, getting wider with each step.

"I thought breaking the curse wasn't possible anymore." She took a deep breath. "I carved my father's name in the lost soul, and it didn't work."

"So you decide to kill yourself without even talking to me?" He bellowed, his irises turning bright red.

"What difference would that have made? It's not a choice for you to make," she shouted, her hands curling into fists.

"Choice?" His lips curled over his sharp teeth as he gave her a dark smile. "You think your choices are really yours after I branded you?"

Black smoke circled him, then lunged at her. Red embers sparked within as they wrapped around her torso, and she yelped as he lifted her a few inches off the ground.

"Put me down right now," she snapped, squirming. "You...stupid demon."

He placed his fingers beneath her chin, raising her head slightly so they were at eye level with one another. "Using a naughty word to insult me? You must be truly angry with me." He leaned closer. "I'm honored."

Her shoulders slumped. "If I had told you that my only option left was to kill myself, it would've made things a lot harder."

"A lot more than leaving me without a word after everything?"

His words stabbed into her. The same thoughts had crossed her mind more than once, but she didn't have a choice at the time. "You don't think I feel horrible about it?" she asked quietly.

"Apparently not enough." His voice had deepened like it was coming from the depths of the Inferno itself.

The smoke vanished, and she staggered back until she hit the wall. He leaned his forearm against the wall, his face inches from hers.

"You didn't tell me about the loophole Lokesh shared with you because you always planned to kill yourself, didn't you? Why else would you have hidden that information from me?"

"You think I fought this entire time only to... what? Just kill myself for fun?"

"It certainly didn't take much for you to jump on the opportunity."

"What do you know about it?" She pointed at him, wanting nothing better but to poke him in the chest. "You're a demon. You don't have to worry about being thrown into the Inferno. I'm sorry you can't understand why I'd rather kill myself."

"I understand too well," he said through his teeth. "It's how I became the first Sanguis demon all those years ago."

She searched his gaze, trying to get the story, but he turned away like he knew what she was doing. He didn't go far, though, and she grabbed his arm.

"Adam——"

He wrapped his arms around her and held her tight

against him. "When I saw you standing there, blood dripping from your wrist like that..."

"I'm sorry, Adam. I really am," she sobbed against his chest as he hugged her close. He rubbed her back, then kissed the top of her head.

He grasped her chin and slanted his lips over hers. His anger, passion, fears, and darkness all expressed in one kiss. What felt like a second and an eternity passed, and when they pulled away, his gaze had somehow become brighter.

"I'll never give up on you. Even if I have to send every one of my children to stay in the Inferno to shield you from its horrors while Shiriki tortures me."

Her emotions seemed to swirl within, a mixture of both happiness and fear at his words. His own feelings mingled with her own, and she expelled a quivering sigh. A declaration of love from a demon?

She wiped her tears as she pulled away, forcing a smile. "Sorin gave me a gift."

Closing her eyes, she reached within herself. The new thread he'd created floated towards her, and she touched it; a golden glow flowed through her grayed fingers, turning them back to normal. When she opened her eyes again, Adam gawked at her.

"Not a cure?" he asked, although his tone suggested he didn't dare hope that was true.

"They said any changes caused by the curse are permanent. Whether broken or not." She stared at her arm. "This allows me to cloak myself so that I can stay in the human world. And it doesn't feel like I'm using much of my magic, so it's not draining me or anything."

"That's good." He slipped off his jacket. "Don't feel like you need to hide your appearance from me, though. You're beautiful in every form."

Her pulse sped, and again, fear seemed to course

through her veins. They'd been getting closer on an emotional level for some time. Why was she scared at the prospect? It had been innocent flirting at first, lust even. Love was different. With a demon, it was eternal; they didn't let go of those they chose. She was a mystic, but mortal.

And suddenly, her terror made sense. Would he turn her into a demon? A demon's obsession—their possession—knew no bounds.

She desperately needed to change the subject again. "About Linda..."

"What about her?" He pulled off his tie.

"You assigned her as my personal servant, right?"

"I did," he said slowly, as though unsure of where she was going with her point.

She crossed her arms. "Well, considering she serves as my personal aide, she has to follow my orders when we're alone."

He let out a sigh. "Yes, but there are limits—"

"And she respected those." She took a step closer to him. "I told her I didn't know if I'd be able to access that connection to the lost soul again, and that I was running out of time. Both of which were true..."

He frowned. "But?"

"I also may have made it sound like time was running out faster than a few days, and reminded her that you'd be tortured if I failed." Saying it out loud filled her with guilt. "Linda also made sure that I was clear about only finding the location. I'm the one who broke the wheel off the truck and caused the accident. None of it was her fault."

The faintest hint of a smile touched his lips. "Don't worry about her. I figured she wasn't the one who'd been so reckless, knowing too well what happens to those who are seen by humans... I didn't punish her, nor will I."

Namika's shoulders relaxed. "Oh, good. Thank you."

"Linda would hate to hear you defend her like this." He went over to a small compartment built into the wall and slid it open, revealing a hole.

She approached, eyeing it. "What's that?"

"Laundry chute." He pointed at her clothes. "Throw them down, and Hilda will have them washed in time for when we visit your mother in a few hours."

"We're guests. I'm not making her do my dirty laundry for me."

"She's paid to do chores like that. Besides, if you show up to a care home wearing filthy clothes, I doubt they'll let you visit." He pulled the covers back, then rearranged the pillows so she could rest her head at a better angle.

She smiled; he kept his back turned on purpose to give her privacy. She pulled off her boots, then undid her pants before stripping to her panties. She let out a sigh as she took off her clothes; it was becoming too much of a reoccurrence lately.

Once she stood in only her underwear, she slowed, realizing she had nothing to change into. He likely expected her to wait for her washed clothes in bed. But was he expecting anything else to happen? She finished removing her clothes, throwing them all down the chute, then trudged towards the bed.

Sliding beneath the covers, she relaxed at his gentle gaze.

"I need to make a call, but I'm not leaving the room. Try to rest."

Her heart sank, but she nodded. He didn't trust her after what she'd done. She pressed her head against the pillows, wishing she could sink inside and disappear. But instead, she closed her eyes, listening to the sound of Adam's voice as he made his call. A few times, he used languages she didn't understand, and only once did he use the one that sent chills crawling along her skin.

Minutes ticked by, and although she was exhausted, she couldn't fall asleep. Her mind was going over what she'd say and do over when she'd see her mother until it turned into this weird script. The heater clanked as the room warmed, and she let out a breath. She knew it was cold outside, but it was an oven inside.

Material rustled, and she opened an eyelid only by an inch. Adam took his clothes off, and her pulse quickened at seeing him naked. The hard ridges of his muscles reminded her of their first night together, but her chest squeezed as her fears and doubts slithered into her mind.

Her gaze settled on the V-shape of his muscles, like an arrow pointing the way towards a treasure. She swallowed hard, ignoring the heat in her face as she locked eyes with him. He got in bed with her, but kept his distance.

She placed her fingers on his jaw, and he closed his eyes as though her touch sent him into a place of bliss. Slowly, she slid them through his hair, smiling when they stuck out in a few places. He took her hand in his, kissing her palm and staring at her as something other than hunger danced behind his gaze.

As though he wanted to possess her.

He leaned in and kissed her. His fingers glided along her shoulders, tracing a path along her neck, then settling at her throat. She pressed her hands against his chest, and their lips parted. He stayed inches away from her face, and she stared into his red irises. They were so beautiful up close; reds, maroons, and specks of his warm brown colors mixed together.

She swallowed hard, her body trembling as he pulled the sheet. It slid over her breasts, and a few goosebumps covered her skin as it scraped over her sensitive peaks. He kneeled, and her breath hitched at his engorged erection, bobbing against his navel. Her pulse throbbed between her legs, wanting to feel him inside.

His hand slid along her sides until it reached her breast, and he cupped it. She felt a tingling sensation on her skin as her breath came faster. He lowered himself and lapped at her hard peak before wrapping his lips around it. She shuddered as he sucked, a soft moan escaping her lips.

She ran her hands along his shoulders as his muscles rippled beneath her fingers, his powers sizzling at the edge.

His erection pressed against her abdomen as he shifted his body, and she froze, heart hammering. Slowly, he pulled her against him so her back was nestled comfortably against his chest.

"We don't need to go any further," he said, his tone steady.

"Do you need to... feed, though?"

He turned her head to the side, so she'd look at him. "Feeding isn't the reason I want to touch you."

"Really?" When he frowned, she turned back towards the pillow, her cheeks heating. "I mean... because we have to use... lube, it must get annoying to be... with me, no? Makes everything more complicated..."

"First of all, being with you is as close as I'll ever get to feeling paradise. And this"—he kissed her neck—"is also sex. Not just penetration and orgasms."

He pulled her tighter against him, and with no clothes between them, his skin against hers was beyond bliss. More than sex and lust, it was intimate.

She slid her hands along his arm. "I enjoy this... a lot," she said, trying to find the right words.

He glided his finger behind her shoulder. "Tell me. Why a buttercup?"

She closed her eyes, recalling the yellow flower tattooed

on her skin. "My grandmother brought some seeds from Japan when they moved to Canada. She planted them all over her garden since they were her favorite." The sea of golden flowers wavered in her memory, and she let out a sigh.

When he smiled, butterflies filled her stomach.

Am I falling in love with him, too?

28

ESTRANGED

It took a while for Namika to get out of the car; she kept stalling, trying to find a reason not to go inside the care home. How long had it been since the Venatores had put her mother here? Namika couldn't remember at all. And never once had she visited her mother.

The cold air blew against her, and she breathed in the humid air she'd gotten used to throughout the years; Manitoba, in comparison, was a lot drier.

Adam gave her space, allowing her all the time she needed. Shiriki, while patient, just seemed amused, as always, about the whole situation. Despite the Viscus demon's human appearance, he still somehow looked menacing.

They approached the building, outdoor tables and chairs pushed against the walls, signaling the end of summer and spring. The windows were large, allowing natural light to shine through, but with the gray skies overhead, it didn't seem to make much of a difference.

Namika caught sight of a familiar face she hadn't expected to see.

Haku.

The last time she'd seen him was when she woke in a cell below the CrowBar after Adam had branded her.

It seemed like a lifetime ago.

He stood out, as always, with his crimson hair and multiple piercings. When he noticed their group, he straightened and bowed deeply.

"Did you bring it?" Adam asked, slipping his hands into his jacket pockets.

The demon nodded, handing a yellow wallet to Namika. "Here."

Her eyebrows shot up as she took it.

"Haku is the one I called a few hours ago. I told him to grab it from your room at the CrowBar and meet us here." Adam motioned with his head towards the entrance of the building. "You'll likely need to show ID before they'll let you see your mother."

Namika swallowed hard, but nodded. This was it. Somehow, the prospect of seeing her mother again after all these years was scarier than anything else she'd done in the past few days. Would she recognize Namika?

Choosing not to wait any longer, she secured her grip on the wallet and stared at Haku. "Thank you for bringing this all the way out here."

She knew that, as a demon, traveling the distance of about half an hour by car wasn't anything difficult, but she felt she had to show him thanks. Something about seeing Haku after everything that happened seemed like things were coming full circle; that the end of this ordeal was finally almost over.

Haku arched an eyebrow, but grinned. "Yeah... no

problem." He turned to the other two demons and bowed once more. "Was there anything else, Master?"

"No. You can return to your tasks."

"Yes, Master," Haku said, then vanished in a blur of movement.

Adam slid his hand along her lower back as he leaned forward. "Let's get inside."

"Oh yes," Shiriki said, gray eyes gleaming, matching the wintry smile curling his lips. "I can't wait to see what we find in that mind of hers."

Namika wanted to snap back about this not being funny, but she saved her breath; he wanted a reaction, and she wouldn't give it to him.

"After you." Shiriki opened the door and waved her inside.

She clenched her jaw and marched inside the first section of the double doors. When she reached out to open the next one, Adam pulled it open for her as well, and she suppressed a groan. She was already on edge, and having both of them opening doors for her like that was grating on her nerves.

No. I'm just angry at myself.

Guilt filled her, but she curled her hands into fists and walked on. The front desk stood in the living space for the residents, but with no employee there, she took the time to look around. A few people sat in chairs, reading or conversing. A small modern fireplace encased in black glass gave the place a warm feel, but there was still something... sterile about the space.

A woman appeared from around the corner, and her eyebrows shot up. "Hello," she said, standing at the desk, "how may I help you?"

Namika shuffled closer, holding her wallet against her abdomen as her stomach churned. "Hi..." She cleared her throat, her chest squeezing. "I'm here to see Winona Cross. Please."

"Miss Cross has had no visitors in quite some time," the woman said with a smile. "She'll be glad to have company." She typed a few things on her computer, glancing up towards Adam and Shiriki every so often. "May I have a piece of ID, please?"

Namika unzipped the wallet and pulled out her driver's license. After a few seconds, the woman handed the card back to Namika.

"And how are you related to Miss Cross?"

She swallowed, trying to get rid of her dry mouth. "I'm her daughter."

Something in her gaze turned icy. "And this is your first time visiting her?" she asked.

Namika stiffened, but nodded, too scared that if she spoke, she'd burst into tears. Adam approached, the glare in his eyes sending Namika's pulse racing.

"Is there a problem here?" he asked in a low voice.

The woman quickly shook her head. "No... I..." She cleared her throat. "And they are...?"

"I'm her partner, and this is our friend," Adam said in a slicing tone.

Still, Namika glanced over her shoulder at Shiriki and nearly burst into laughter; friend? Before she could wrap her mind around the thought, the woman pointed at the red sign on a nearby table.

"If you haven't already, please use the hand sanitizer, and then I'll show you to Miss Cross' room."

Namika pushed her palm against the pump once, allowing a good amount to land in her hand; part of her was terrified her curse would somehow spread to others if she didn't disinfect enough. The cold wetness of antiseptic foam stung a few areas on her skin, reminding her of where she still had a few healing cuts.

They walked down the corridors in silence, each step somehow bringing more dread to Namika. What if her mother panicked when she saw Adam and Shiriki? Would she recognize them as demons? She'd been a Venatore her whole life and likely noticed things other people wouldn't.

Namika grasped the wooden handrail along the wall, slowing her steps. "I don't know if I can do this," she whispered as tears burned her eyes.

The employee had continued forward, Shiriki following close by while Namika's heart seemed to beat inside her throat. Why couldn't she face her mother?

Because I've left her here alone.

Adam grasped her shoulders. "You can."

"But what if... she doesn't recognize me? Or what if she does, and she asks why I've never visited her before today?" She grasped his wrists. "The first time I'm here to see her, and it's because I need something? What kind of daughter am I?" she asked with a small sob.

"The kind who was hurt as a child." When she didn't calm down, he grasped her chin. "And one who was busy fighting a war against the forces of darkness."

She laughed, shaking her head. "That's not funny." She relaxed a bit, focusing on a special events board filled with colorful papers. "I feel so guilty."

"I know," he said, taking her hand in his. "But don't decide what happens before it even does. She might be angry that you haven't visited. Or she might be happy you're here and not even care about the past." He led her forward. "You won't know until you see her."

By the time they caught up with the employee, she looked uncomfortable, standing close to a door as Shiriki grinned at her. She quickly motioned to the room, then left as fast as her legs could carry her.

"She seems frightened..." Shiriki said with a chuckle.

She rolled her eyes. "Can't imagine why."

He glanced over her shoulder at Adam. "Stay outside, and guard the room. Make sure no one comes through."

Her pulse quickened. "Wait. Why does he need to guard anything?"

"Because it would be problematic if someone walked in and saw me in my form." He took a step closer, his silver eyes flashing for a second. "You don't want a repeat of this morning now, do you?"

She glanced back at Adam, tensing at the thought of being alone with her mother and Shiriki. Still, she nodded. "Okay... can I go speak with her alone before?"

"Of course," Shiriki said with a smile as he motioned his hand towards the door.

Taking a deep breath, she grasped the handle, then turned it and walked in.

The room seemed to vanish as she laid eyes on her mother. She sat on the edge of the single bed, muttering to herself, rocking back and forth. A few times, she let out a swear word, then shook her head almost violently.

Namika's chest squeezed as she approached the bed, the smell of fresh linens reaching her nostrils.

"Hi, Mom," she said in a small voice.

Her mother stopped rocking and looked up at her daughter. "It's about time. I've been waiting for my glass of water since yesterday."

Namika glanced at the end tables on either side of the bed; a glass of water stood full on one of them, untouched. Forgotten. She quickly grabbed it and handed it to her mother.

"I'm sorry it took so long," she said with a lump in her throat.

She took a few sips, then gave it back. "Why are you here? Come to steal my possessions?"

Namika's shoulders slumped; her mother's mind was further gone than she'd thought. Would Shiriki still be able to find information in there? What were they even looking for? She wished Sorin had been a bit more forward; they told Namika about asking her mother why carving her father's name into his flesh hadn't worked, but nothing more.

Her mother pointed towards a few framed pictures on the wall, and Namika's pulse sped; there were none of her. None of her father. Just a few photos of members of the Venatores who Namika recognized. It shouldn't have surprised her; the group had always been the most important thing in her mother's life.

Namika grabbed the single chair in the room and dragged it towards the bed. "I have a question I'd like to ask you."

The door shut with a snap, and she turned as Shiriki stepped inside. "A few questions, actually."

He put out his hand towards Winona, and she took it. "Open your mind to me." He grasped Namika's hand before she could think, then motioned towards her mother. "Take her hand."

Namika did as she was told, shivers running down her spine as energy rippled from Shiriki; touching him seemed to call out to something deep inside her, like something was desperately trying to crawl out.

He stared at Winona. "Tell me about your family."

The room flashed in white light, and Namika felt like she was falling.

29

A MOTHER'S SECRET

*W*inona's eyes seemed to gloss over, filling with white until they turned milky. She smiled, her whole body so relaxed, Namika was worried she'd fall off the bed.

A second chair appeared—this one larger and more comfortable-looking—and Shiriki sat.

"Tell me about when you met Azuma Strang," Shiriki said, his voice soft, almost lulling the very air around them.

Her mother blinked a few times. "I was eighteen. He was nineteen. I got pregnant and was forced to marry him." She shook her head. "I didn't want to marry outside the Venatores, but it was a one-night stand, and I wasn't allowed to get rid of it."

Namika's stomach churned at hearing her mother despise her before she was even born. Yet, something wasn't adding up in her mind, and she couldn't figure out what it was.

Winona beamed as she stared at Shiriki. "But it was meant to be. I was supposed to have him. My son. Jayce."

"Jayce?" Namika repeated, mouth agape. "I... had a

brother?" Suddenly, things seemed to be falling into place and making more sense. He was the one who'd cursed her.

"He was powerful and a natural leader," she said with a nod, completely ignoring Namika. "At fifteen, the higher-ups in the group even gave him more responsibilities. They recognized his ambition to climb within the ranks."

Shiriki cocked his head. "Ambitious enough to sell his soul to a demon?"

Winona's jaw clenched. "So what? He did what he had to. The other members were jealous of how powerful he was."

Namika frowned; it was likely because of the deal, but she wasn't about to say that. It seemed, in her mother's eyes, her brother could do no wrong.

"Then what happened?" Shiriki asked.

"Everything was perfect. So what if a few kids went missing? Most were from the Lumen group, anyway. Or homeless children. No one missed them." She shrugged.

Shiriki's eyes glowed brighter. "Children for the demon to eat, correct?" When she nodded, he grinned. "And what did your son get in return?"

"We were at war!" she yelled. "Demons were killing us and Lumen constantly. So before this demon killed any, he let Jayce take their powers for himself. Not like they were going to use it after they died."

Namika thought for sure she'd be sick. "All that power for what? What would be the point if the cost was his soul?"

"The deal they had was supposed to last a lifetime," she said as tears rolled down her face. "The demon was only supposed to gain his soul once he died of natural causes. But Jayce said the power he took from the others would make him immortal." She shook her head. "And then, when my sweet Jayce was sixteen, I got pregnant again. I was so... angry at Azuma for it. He knew I wasn't allowed to abort. And this one..." She fixed her gaze on Namika. "This one was a mistake."

Despite not liking what she was learning about her mother, hearing her say that still stung. She let out a breath. "What happened to Jayce?"

"The demon tricked my poor baby! He was killed at eighteen."

Shiriki chuckled. "What is more natural than human death because they took on more than they could chew?"

Namika had a brother, but she couldn't remember him. She would've been two years old when he died. His soul was devoured by a demon, then sent to the Inferno until he escaped. All because he was power-hungry.

"Is that why my father took me away? To protect me from that kind of life? So that history didn't repeat itself?"

"Your father was a coward," her mother spat. "Ran away when our baby boy was murdered. I didn't care, though. He took you with him. Good riddance." She leaned closer as though suddenly realizing who Namika was. "You were too much like your father. A mystic and a Venatore. Trying to be more powerful than your brother before you were even born."

"It was never a competition," Namika snapped back.

"Your grandmother had to cut out more than you know." Her mother grasped Namika's wrist and pulled her closer. "You don't even know how powerful you are, do you?"

Her breath hitched. The memory of having her soul-mate thread severed flashed through her mind, and she shivered. Pushing the thought away, she focused on her goal.

"That's enough. I have the answers I needed." She got

up and paced the room as Shiriki brought them back from the strange realm they'd been hovering in.

Shiriki straightened, his white hair brushing against his shoulders as he leaned forward. "You may not find yourself in Hell, but Voross will have a special place waiting for you." His lips twisted around his jagged teeth, and Winona screamed.

The room flashed once more, and her mother rocked a bit, murmuring about extra items. "... Eve's things got mixed in. Don't want it."

Namika's chest squeezed at hearing her old name, but curiosity burned at her mother's words. "It? What got mixed in?"

Winona stared at Namika like she was seeing her for the first time, but stayed silent. The hiss of air flow overhead turned on, sending a blast of warmth. But Namika only felt cold.

Her mother pointed towards the nightstand. "It isn't mine, but she left it behind. Only thing she brought back with her when her useless father and grandmother died."

Namika opened her mouth to say something nasty, but Shiriki raised his hand for silence. "Where is this item?"

Winona got to her feet and trudged to the nightstand in question, then pulled open the bottom drawer. She grabbed something, then returned, throwing the item on the bed. The small teddy bear Namika's grandmother had made for her bounced on the mattress.

Namika hadn't seen it since she'd moved out. The little yellow bear still held a small topaz between its paws; her birthstone. Before she could pick it up, Shiriki took it, examining it like it was the most interesting object in the world.

"That is what she meant..." he said in a hushed tone

before turning to Namika. He handed her the bear, a sinister expression on his face.

Still, she took it, and as soon as she did, the gemstone burst into a golden light. Namika yelped as it seeped into her fingertips, but didn't let go of the plushie. She let out a shuddering breath once it stopped, then looked back at Shiriki.

"What was that?"

Shiriki grinned. "Did something happen?"

She glanced back at the teddy bear, her heart racing. It wasn't a bad feeling, but it felt like something familiar had reconnected with the core of her magic, and she wasn't sure what to make of it.

It also didn't help that Shiriki continued staring at her like this was the most fun he'd had in years. Without even a last look or word to her mother, Namika left the room, her heart heavy.

Jayce. Her brother. And he'd been the one to curse her.

Namika barely registered Adam asking her what had happened as she strode down the corridor. She needed to leave this place. Away from her horrible mother. Leaving her to rot here didn't make Namika feel too guilty now.

The sudden temperature change as she stepped outside felt like it pulled her away from her thoughts, and she slowed her steps. She searched her memories for any semblance of the brother she once had, but there was nothing. Was he ever home when she was little? Had they even met? Had he held her as a baby? Played with her at all? It all seemed impossible.

Adam reached her quick enough and pulled her close. Against the cold. Against the world hand its cruelties.

"I heard everything," he whispered. "Are you alright?"

She nodded, but wasn't sure if she was lying even to herself. But it didn't matter. She knew the lost soul's name, and this time, she wouldn't fail in breaking the curse.

She turned her attention to Shiriki. "What would it take for you to help us hunt down my brother?"

Adam grasped her arm. "You can't be serious."

"Very." She kept her focus on Shiriki. "But there would be a condition."

He burst out laughing, leaning against the outer wall of the building. "A condition to assisting you? Oh, the prize better be exquisite, or I'll think you're insulting me."

"You won't kill my brother before I've broken the curse. After that, drag him to Hell for all I care."

"And in exchange?"

"You want your sentence reduced or removed?" She crossed her arms. "I'll tell Celina how you helped, and push for her to change her mind."

Shiriki's smile didn't fade, but his eyes flashed silver. "How interesting." He glanced past her shoulder at Adam. "I see why you chose this one."

Adam's hold tightened on her, and she placed her hand over his arm.

"Do we have a deal, then?" she asked.

Shiriki's smile widened. "Done."

RETURNING to Winnipeg took no time; using the veil between Shiriki's dwelling and the condemned apartment building was way faster than a plane. Even a private one. Once they were back at the Dragon's Lair, Adam pulled out his smartphone. After a few seconds, he stared around with a frown.

"What's wrong?" Namika asked as she slipped off her coat.

"I can't reach Linda... And I can't sense her anywhere." He frowned. "Again."

Shiriki shrugged. "She is likely in the Dark Realm." He'd gone back to his demonic form, and a chill shot down Namika's spine at his silver eyes. There was always something evil lurking behind his gaze.

Adam still seemed like something bothered him as he tapped the screen a few more times. "In that case, I want Haku here. I'll get him in touch with Phillis so they can round up more—"

Shiriki grabbed Adam's phone, then threw it to the side. It hit the floor with a clatter.

"Out of the question," Shiriki said with a smile, but there was something dangerous about it. "If more of us are involved, it could be seen as a declaration of war on reapers or even vampires."

"The king gave us permission to break the curse," Adam said through his teeth.

"Yes, but that is why you and Namika can fight this. Even including me in this may be seen as crossing the line between a personal fight and a war between races."

Namika moved away as Adam and Shiriki continued speaking. Not that it mattered since they'd started speaking in demos. And she wished they'd stop. She enjoyed hearing different languages—even if she didn't know it herself—but this was the one that sent chills all over her body.

She grabbed the cellphone from the ground, hoping it wasn't cracked. To her surprise, the screen was still unlocked, and a new message from Linda had popped up. "Linda texted you back."

Adam glanced over Shiriki's shoulder at her. "What excuse does she have for disappearing, then?"

She was surprised he'd allow her access to his phone

like this, and her heart seemed to swell at the trust he showed her. Tapping on Linda's contact, Namika arched an eyebrow at a link that was sent with no other context. Without thinking too long about it, she pressed her index finger against it, and it opened a video.

Her stomach churned as someone clawed at their surroundings in what looked like a wooden box, smoke and flames licking their flesh. A fingernail chipped off, the underside bloody as they screamed.

"The screams are familiar," Shiriki said in a bored voice. "Is that Linda?"

"Linda?" Namika repeated as her mouth fell open. She looked back at the video, her hands trembling "They're burning her alive." Stomach acid seared the back of her throat. "Oh god. We need to save her. We need—"

Adam took the device from her hands. "Namika—"

"No. This is my fault. Again." She pushed her hands against her abdomen, recalling all too well what the vampire had done when he'd found her at Adam's penthouse. "She's suffering because of me. Because she was helping me on the highway. He has her. I know it's him."

"You mean the vampire? Why do you think—?"

"I lied when I said I hadn't been hurt when he attacked me in Toronto. He stared me right in the eyes with a smile and stabbed me. He enjoyed it." She released a trembling exhale. "He told me to make sure I died quicker this time."

Shiriki chuckled. "Sounds familiar, somehow…"

She shot him a glare, but turned back to Adam. "He has Linda, and now she's—"

"It's live. We can still get to her on time." He pointed at the red button showing a live feed in the corner, then tapped a volume icon, and silence fell. He seemed calm, but the pain and fury behind his gaze somehow made

Namika feel better; she knew Adam would do everything he could to save her.

"Any way to trace it?" she asked, looking away from the blistering fire.

"Maybe, but it would take too long."

She tightened her ponytail and paced. "My mother mentioned something about my grandmother taking something from me when she severed my soulmate thread." She rounded on Shiriki. "You seemed to know what she meant when the gemstone from my bear shattered," she said, marching to her discarded coat and pulling out the tiny plushie from her pocket. "I felt magic. What was that?"

"You expect me to know?" Shiriki asked in an overly innocent tone.

Her hand tightened around the teddy bear as she moved closer to the Viscus demon. "I know you do."

Shiriki approached her. "And so do you." He placed his hand out in front of him, and the room vanished.

She was alone again, within herself. As she had done before when searching for the connection with the lost soul. With her brother.

"That cage inside of you," Shiriki's voice echoed around her. "Unlock it now that you have all of your magic once more."

She reached out towards the golden bars, but hesitated.

"What are you afraid of?" he asked.

Her fingers hovered near the metal, their reflection warped. She'd been told her whole life to hide what she was. A mystic, a Venatore. Her grandmother taught her to keep secrets, and her mother told her never to speak about her father and his side of the family. In the end, she'd always felt like she was no one; that she wasn't allowed to be someone. Had she really been so powerful that her own grandmother—someone she'd trusted above all others—took part of her own magic away from her? Would she ever be able to trust anyone? Maybe she could, but the first person she needed to trust again was herself.

Taking in a deep breath, she let go.

The bars bent and snapped, allowing her magic to flow through her. The filaments turned golden, crimson glowing along their edges. Images flew through her mind: a one-story building. It looked like a warehouse of sorts with a beige exterior and dark red trimmings. She counted six garage doors, and before she could see more, Linda's burning body flashed in front of her. Namika gasped, trying to look away, and when she did, the lost soul lunged at her.

Namika opened her eyes and screamed.

"I've got you." Adam grabbed her arms and steadied her. "What happened?"

"I saw where we need to go. Linda and my brother are at the same location." She tried describing it, but with neither of the demons from the area, it didn't help.

When she was about to swear using the worst word she knew, a familiar light glowed from her chest, disappearing straight through Adam. The same line that led to her brother a few hours ago.

"It's back," she whispered, as though nervous that she'd scare it away by speaking too loudly.

"What—"

"The light. The one that connects me to my brother through the curse," she said, pointing at her chest. But before she took a step towards the door, it faded, then disappeared. This time, she let the word slip.

"Fuck," she yelled. "We need to find them. Now."

Adam's eyebrows shot up, but he didn't comment on her swearing. Instead, he tapped his screen again and put the phone out in front of him. "We don't know the area, so let's call someone who does."

After a few seconds of ringing on speakerphone, a familiar voice came through the other side. "What can I do for you, boss?" Phillis asked in almost a sing-song tone.

"We're looking for a specific building. Warehouse, beige outside with red trimmings. One floor."

There was silence, then. "That sounds like the place I had to send some of my guys the other day because a ghoul was loose inside Polo Park. Luckily, it was late at night, so there weren't too——"

"Where is it?" Adam's words sliced through the air, and even Namika recoiled a bit.

"Hang on to your breeches, boss," Phillis shot back.

Adam glared at the phone. "You're by far the most disrespectful of my children."

"But you still love me," the demon said in the same singing voice. There was a ding, and Adam tapped the screen. "Sent you a street view photo of the place. Is it the same one you're looking for?"

Adam tilted the device so Namika could see better; it was exactly the right place. "Yes, that's it. Where is it?"

"Did someone crush your balls, sir? Your voice is suddenly higher..."

"I swear, Phillis——"

Another ding. "I texted you the address. Jeez... no sense of humor."

Without waiting, Adam ended the call, then checked their destination. "Only about ten minutes from here."

"Let's go." She didn't wait, grabbing her coat as she headed for the door. Shiriki blocked her path, and she nearly ran right into him.

"I will meet you at the location." He glanced at Adam.

"I suppose being burned alive is a good excuse for Linda not answering your summons?"

Namika's hands curled into fists, but Adam wrapped an arm around her, holding her back as she tried lunging at the Viscus demon. She tilted her head to the side and met his gaze. His silent message told her not to take the bait.

Slowly, she relaxed in his hold, letting out a breath. When neither of them said anything, Shiriki vanished.

30

—————

ATTACKS

inutes later, their *borrowed* vehicle screeched to a halt on a back road to the warehouse in question. Namika instantly recognized the building she'd seen in her vision, and her pulse quickened. "That's the place."

She darted out of the car, only to spot Shiriki and Haku standing nearby. Her heart raced at the sight of the two demons. She was surprised Haku had been allowed to accompany them after what Shiriki had said about not starting a war. Either way, she was relieved to have the extra help to save Linda.

The thought of her brother and what she had to do to break the curse lingered in her mind, but getting to Linda in time was suddenly more pressing.

Haku bowed his head. "Master."

Shiriki leaned against the chain-link fence, his long black coat fluttering in the wind. Even in his human appearance, he looked like someone she'd avoid, even in daylight. He'd tied his blond hair in a loose ponytail, but his gray eyes were familiar.

She didn't trust Shiriki with a ten-foot pole, but she couldn't afford to be picky. Not with everything at stake.

Adam surveyed the area in question with a frown. "Still too many workers at this time of day."

She knew he meant too many witnesses, and her stomach churned at the memory of the perimeter. So many innocents, killed because of her. How would she ever make up for it? She pushed the doubts from her mind and focused on her goals.

Save Linda. Find Jayce.

Once the curse was broken, she'd dedicate the rest of her life to finding the victims' families and trying to make up for what she'd done. But first, she had to survive.

She stared around. "We can't wait, though." She pointed towards the front of the building. "What if we go to the primary place of business? We could pretend we're looking to buy something. Or maybe need directions?"

Haku shook his head. "There are security cameras everywhere. This place is more secure than some prisons. They'd see us coming."

"If this is their place of operation," Adam said, "then there're likely a lot of ghouls in there. We'll need the element of surprise."

Shiriki straightened, then pointed at Namika. "Any new tricks since fully unlocking your magic, little mystic?"

Heat filled her at being called out, and she narrowed her eyes on him. Still, she searched her newfound powers; she'd always been gifted at cloaking herself, and maybe she could use that to somehow sneak inside.

A truck drove into the main yard, and they watched as it backed in towards one of the garage doors. It rolled open, and familiar energy rolled along her skin.

"Ghouls. They have ghouls in there," she whispered, pointing at the vehicle.

A plan formed in her mind, and as insane as it was, she was sure it would work. And that it was their only chance at keeping the element of surprise.

"What are you thinking of?" Adam asked, taking her out of her own head. "You look like you've got an idea..." He didn't seem happy at the prospect, but he fell silent, waiting for her to explain.

"I'll go back to my true form that shows the curse, and when they start bringing in the ghouls, I'll join their group. I can blend in with them, and because I'm good at cloaking myself, it's likely no one will notice I'm not just another ghoul."

Adam's jaw clenched, but before he could refuse, Shiriki chimed in, "And once you're inside?"

"I'll find the main security area and switch off their system."

Haku tapped his chin. "It's possible. There's likely a security guard, though, or someone overseeing all these cameras, so you'll have to take them out." He grinned. "If you have a phone, I can walk you through how to disable it without anyone taking notice right away. It would give us the time we need to get inside."

"There are too many things that could go wrong," Adam said in a low voice.

"As opposed to if we barge in?" Namika asked, crossing her arms over her chest. "We don't have time to discuss other options. We still need to find Linda once we're in there." She pointed at the truck. "And they're going to start bringing them in any second, and I need to be there when they do. Please trust me with this, Adam."

"I trust you," he said without a moment's hesitation. "It's the other ones I don't. But you're right..." His eyes flashed red. "Just know that if you end up getting hurt, I'll rip apart everyone in there for good measure." He pulled out his cellphone and handed it to her with a small smile. "Stay safe."

Butterflies fluttered in her stomach as she nodded, then slipped the phone into her jeans. She slipped off her coat, doubting that ghouls needed anything to keep warm, but she regretted it pretty soon as the freezing wind sliced across her skin. Still, she clenched her jaw and continued around the fence.

She allowed her magic to not only cloak her but also let go of the thread Sorin had given her to hide her true form. Pushing some of her curls in front of the normal side of her face, she glanced around, making sure she wouldn't be spotted ahead of time.

A crowd of twenty-something ghouls gathered near the garage, and she slipped in between them, blending as best she could. A few people approached holding long metal rods that looked like cattle prods, and ushered them inside. Namika glanced around, trying to figure out why the creatures were so tame; every other time she'd encountered them, they were violent monsters.

One staggered to the side, and that's when Namika spotted it. A bracelet with a blinking red light around the ghoul's wrist. She did her best to look at the others, trying to glimpse their arms; most wore the same strap. Did it control them somehow? Make them act more like brainless zombies?

As they continued shuffling through the warehouse, Namika caught sight of a door marked security guard, and her pulse quickened. She needed to get away from the group without being seen, but with the people herding them like cattle, it would be difficult.

When they turned a corner, she slipped in between the shelves, cloaking herself with as much magic as possible.

Everyone passed by without looking at her, and her shoulders relaxed. It had worked. So far.

She crept up to the security guard's door, glancing over her shoulder every few seconds to make sure there weren't any stragglers who could catch sight of her. The door wasn't fully closed, and she slowly pushed it open.

It was dim inside the large room, and warm. Multiple screens showing every angle of the place stood atop one another over a filthy desk. Food wrappers and cans were left scattered across its surface, crumbs left behind everywhere.

A man in a uniform sat in a cheap computer chair that looked like it was made of plastic. He glanced at the screens from time to time, but seemed more focused on the video playing on his smartphone while he ate chips.

This would be too easy.

She put out her hand in front of her, aiming for the guard's head, and blasted energy forward. It hit him, and he slumped over the desk, unconscious. At this angle, it looked like he'd fallen asleep on the job. She closed the door behind her and craned her neck, trying to see the rest of the room, but it was dark. With a sigh, she grabbed Adam's smartphone, tapped the contact for Haku, and brought the device to her ear.

"You're in?" Haku's voice asked from the other side.

"Yeah. So, how do I disable this thing without alerting everyone?"

After asking a bunch of questions about the makes, models, serial numbers, and more technical things Namika didn't understand, she made her way back to the main control panel at the desk. He instructed her on which settings to click and the buttons in order, and she couldn't help being impressed at how skilled he was at all this.

Although she had no idea how old he was; maybe he had been learning these things for years.

She glanced at the screen, watching as the crowd of ghouls was moved from the main part of the warehouse to what looked like a trapdoor. They opened it, and they began filing down as though there were stairs. At the angle the camera was, and with the way everything in the main room looked the same, she couldn't tell where it was, though.

Everything shut down, and she straightened. "Okay, everything seems good to go."

"Perfect." And without another word, Haku hung up.

A figure materialized by her side, and she yelped.

A ghoul.

She sent a blast of magic at it. It hissed, pressing its hand against where part of its face melted. Her pulse sped as she bolted to her feet, trying to escape, but the ghoul caught her.

When it smiled at her, something in Namika's mind snapped.

Not a ghoul. Another lost soul.

Despite hitting it several times, it dragged her farther out of the room. Finally, with a kick, she got free. Her head hit the pavement, and the room spun as she blinked fast. She sat up, rubbing her head and ignoring the throbbing pain.

It leaped forward, and she gasped. It clawed at her face, slashing across as she shrieked. Blood streamed down her cheeks, warm against her clammy skin. She reached into her core and focused the energy there for a few seconds before releasing it in a halo.

It grabbed her ankles, yanked forward, and she fell. She tried kicking, but its grip tightened, claws digging into her flesh. A light flickered up ahead when it pulled her down a corridor with ease, and her heart pounded against her chest. The sound of flames roared, mixing with the smell of something burning. Or cooking. Neither were good signs.

They entered a large room, and her blood seemed to freeze in her veins. Charred bodies hung from meat hooks above, and taking up most of the wall space was a massive oven. The door was opened—the fire inside licking at the side of the metal grates.

"Time to burn," the lost soul said in a cracking voice.

Her eyebrows shot up, and she turned onto her stomach, clawing at anything she could reach. It continued dragging her towards the oven, the heat burning her feet through her boots.

"Adam!"

An invisible force slammed into the monster, forcing it to let go of her ankle as it was thrown backward into the oven. Its shrieks filled the room, and she crawled away until she reached the wall. She pushed her trembling hands against her ears, needing to block out the horrific sounds.

Someone grabbed her, and she screamed, desperate to push them away.

"Namika," Adam whispered.

She stopped fighting and took a shuddering breath as she was met with his red irises. With a sob, she held on tight to him. He held her close, allowing his energy to coil around her. She pushed her face into his chest. "I was... so scared," she cried.

He pulled her to her feet, then cupped her face. "I'm here now."

"They're in the basement. There's a trapdoor in one of the rooms," she said, panting.

"Stay close," he whispered to her.

She suppressed her magic so they wouldn't be found

too quickly, but she found out fast how useless that was. A trail of body parts lay scattered in the corridor. Blood and gore splattered the walls and ceiling, making her wish she could close her eyes while walking through the horror house.

"Did...Shiriki do this?" she asked.

"Who else?"

She let out a sigh. "Did he have to leave such a mess?"

Adam's eyes turned red as he scanned a few doors. "He can't help himself."

Namika slowed to where a bloody torso was left behind. She grabbed Adam's jacket sleeve and tugged.

"This was a human." She turned her gaze on him, the industrial lights buzzing overhead. "He's killing humans, too."

"Did you expect any different from him?" He shrugged. "You're the one who asked him for help."

She gritted her teeth. "I didn't want him to kill them—"

"They likely work for the vampire behind all this if they're here. What does it matter if they die?"

"We don't know for sure. They could be victims." She glanced at the maimed body, her stomach churning at the sight. "I thought he'd help us. Not himself."

"Then you don't know him well," he said with a bitter smile. "Come on. The faster we catch up to him, the faster we can ask him not to kill so brutally."

She wanted to point out she didn't want them to be killed, period, but Adam was right. If they were here, they likely worked for the vampire. The smell of blood reached her nostrils, and she shuddered as they continued forward, picking up the pace.

It probably smells delicious to Adam.

"Here," Adam said, motioning to an old metal trapdoor. This was the way in, and every step they took toward finding Linda, time pressed against them. They had to get her out.

"We need to hurry," she said, rushing forward. "Is the video still live? Do we still have time?" she asked as she tugged on the handlebar of the trapdoor.

It creaked open, and she let go with a wince as a jagged piece sliced her palm. Shiriki appeared, catching the door before it slammed against the side of the wall. He took her hand, and a white light appeared beneath the cut, pushing her skin together.

He let her go. "Clean the blood off, or they'll smell you before we make it down there."

"Did you have to kill everyone in here?" she asked coolly as she grabbed a discarded rag from one of the nearby shelves and wiped her palm as best she could.

He didn't turn, but his energy slammed against her, and she staggered back. His hair turned white, and a strange aura rippled around him as though readying himself to attack.

Adam placed himself next to her, his own powers filling the surrounding air.

"Never mind—forget I asked," she muttered. "Can we go now?"

Shiriki turned his head to the side, a cold smile twisting his lips over his pointed teeth. "Yes." He stepped inside, but after a few seconds, vanished.

She dashed forward, staring below, then rolled her eyes; he really enjoyed disappearing on people. Letting out a shuddering breath, she followed Adam down the steps, into darkness.

31

BROKEN

Footsteps echoed, and Namika froze mid-step as the floor nearby cracked. Part of it crumbled into a deeper part of the basement, sending dust billowing into the air. She coughed, staggering back until she bumped into Adam.

She approached the edge where the floor had collapsed. "Long way down. Or it's pitch black. Or both." She peeked over her shoulder at him. "Is there a way to contact Shiriki and find out if——?"

Something wrapped around her ankle, and she yelped as it wrenched her down. Her heart lodged in her throat as she fell, her stomach clenching as panic flooded her mind. She hit the bottom and whimpered as pain throbbed throughout her body. Silence accompanied her, and she stiffened.

Ghouls ran forward, and Adam appeared in front of her. "Don't move," he commanded.

She did, pressing her lips together as blood droplets formed. The ghouls slowed but didn't retreat fast enough, as he sent his powers in every direction. The droplets morphed into blades, scraping along the cement walls, hitting at anyone in range. They tore through flesh and bone, the ghouls' screams echoing.

Namika got to her feet and then sent her magic around them. When nothing came back, she let out a frustrated groan. "I can't find Linda anywhere." The thought that they were at the wrong location made her feel nauseous.

A ripple of energy glided along her skin, and she turned towards a large garage door. It was half-open but with no sounds coming from the other side, she approached.

Adam grabbed her arm, holding her back as he raised a finger for her to wait. He crouched, staring beneath the door, then motioned for her to follow.

The room itself looked like something used to be manufactured here. What had they been making underground? She frowned, still unable to figure out why there was no smoke coming from the building. With an oven that big, it had to be coming out somewhere.

Figures stalked out of corners and from behind old machines. At least fifty ghouls surrounded them.

"There's a lot more than I thought," Namika muttered as she stared around.

"I'd be disappointed if there were less."

Violence and bloodlust. No matter what, Adam was still a demon.

A few lunged at them, and Namika released her magic just in time. It hit two in the face, slamming them into other nearby attackers. Movement caught the side of her vision, and she spun as Shiriki materialized into view. He crouched on the side of a railing, smiling ear to ear.

"Help would be great," she called out as she bolted out of the way from a ghoul lashing out at her.

She tripped it so it ran right into Adam's bloody wall, slicing the ghoul in half.

"You seem to be handling it fine."

She narrowed her eyes. "You're supposed to help. That was—"

"The deal, yes." He straightened, balancing on the railing like he was on a flat surface. "You never specified who I am supposed to help."

"Does anyone actually like you?" she asked through gritted teeth.

He laughed at that, shaking his head. "No. I believe most tolerate me."

"At best," she muttered before turning to the fight. "So, who are you helping right now?"

"Myself."

A large machine roared to life, and she jumped, her pulse throbbing in her ears as she stared at it. Debris and old objects were brought forward on a conveyor belt, only to end up being crushed into a fine powder. She swallowed hard, hating that with so much noise, they'd have more issues.

Adam threw a wave of crimson blades, and it crashed against a dozen creatures. Their screams echoed through the vast room, but their voice died out as they were destroyed.

A hundred ghouls rushed inside the room, and her eyes widened. How had the vampire made so many already? How many humans had he murdered and maimed?

Adam glanced at Shiriki. "I suppose you won't be of any help until it's convenient."

Shiriki shrugged. "Convenient? No. I cannot participate in the killing of these ghouls by law as Mekaisto's second in command." He crossed his arms as he leaned against the wall.

"Wait. If there are this many ghouls, then there's likely other people as well. Maybe this is where they're also turning them into these monsters." She turned to Shiriki. "I need you to check the rest of this place. If you find any prisoners, please help them get to safety."

Shiriki jumped from the railing and onto the floor near a few bodies left maimed by Adam's powers. "I suppose that is an acceptable task," he said.

"And don't hurt or kill any of them," she quickly added.

"Whatever would make you think I would do that?" he asked in a mocking tone before vanishing in a blur of motion once more.

More ghouls attacked, and she created a shield around herself, stopping most of them from being able to slash at her.

The remaining ghouls stopped attacking, watching in silence as footsteps echoed from above. Namika stared up, and her stomach churned.

A figure appeared along the top railing, leaning forward. His face was covered by a blank white mask, but his energy was familiar enough that she guessed it was the vampire.

Rickie.

"You can destroy as many as you'd like, but I'll keep sending out more," he called out in amusement. His voice sounded unfamiliar, and for a second, she wasn't sure anymore if it was really him or not. Yet his power was definitely the same.

Noise creaked from higher up, but before she could react, a few ghouls fell from the ceiling, then slammed into Adam. They sent him flying across the room and onto the conveyor belt.

She dashed towards Adam, her heart racing, but the

pressure against her knocked the breath out of her lungs. Falling onto the floor, she gasped for air, but every intake sent more pain through her.

The vampire pressed his foot against her spine, and she winced, a small scream escaping her throat.

"Just watch him be crushed. Once my ghouls devour him, I'll destroy what's left."

The corners of her vision darkened as it became harder to breathe. She turned towards Adam as he tried fighting off hundreds of ghouls, pinning him against the conveyor belt. The machine crushed the objects, its teeth nearing Adam with every second.

Rickie wrenched her to her feet, pressing her back against his chest, an arm around her, keeping her still. Plans flew through her mind faster than she could keep up with, but one thing stuck.

She allowed the darkness that waited by the surface and released it. This time, she knew better what to expect, and as soon as her teeth changed, she sank them into his arm. The taste of copper filled her mouth, and she had to not gag as she ripped out a chunk of his flesh.

He screamed, throwing her away from him as hard as he could.

She slammed against the wall, and blood dripped into her left eye. But the usual pain wasn't there. Or she couldn't feel it. Golden filaments surrounded in crimson light wrapped around her body as she staggered up to her wobbly legs.

"You bitch," he shouted.

The machine continued its low crunching sound over bones and debris, turning her attention away from the vampire.

She touched the blood streaming into her eye and

pulled her fingers away. Filaments followed, wrapping around her clawed fingernails.

More ghouls ran into the room.

"Bring her to me," he hissed at them.

They lunged at her, and she raised her arms to the side, the lights slicing through them like warm butter. Splattering to a pile of gore, she smirked as Rickie took a few steps back, as though surprised by her sudden powers.

She focused on Adam and pulled deeper into the darkness from the curse. Lost souls joined in the fray, and Namika's brother was amongst those attacking Adam, so she'd have to be careful not to kill Jayce before she broke the curse.

The filaments flew out, wrapping around Namika's brother and yanking him out of the attacking group. Jayce gasped, squirming as Namika lifted him into the air.

"You're not going anywhere," Namika whispered in a voice that didn't sound like her own.

With her free hand, she aimed at the group Adam was busy with and let go of everything she had. All the control her grandmother had taught her as a child. Shadows separated from the filaments, and they aimed for the creatures. They passed through their bodies as they shrieked, maimed from the inside out.

Most turned to dust in a matter of seconds, and Adam took the opening. He ripped off the heads and limbs of the ghouls closest, destroying them before they even hit the floor.

The machine came crashing against Adam, and Namika screamed, pushing her powers to try to shut it down. But it didn't matter.

Adam put his hand up, holding it in place before it even touched his head. The machine smoked and ground against the force, stopping it. Sparks flew, and it shook as he pushed against the descending teethed ceiling.

She smiled, relieved he was okay. But she couldn't linger. Jayce had to be dealt with. It was time to end the curse.

With a small flick of Namika's wrist, the filaments rammed him against the floor repeatedly. The cement cracked, and soon Jayce couldn't even scream as his body turned into a limp puppet of broken bones.

Jayce whimpered, and Namika arched an eyebrow. "Oh, good, you're still alive. Kind of." She spun her brother to his stomach and sat on his body.

With her fingernails sharp as knives, she etched Jayce's name into the ghoul's flesh. There was a soft wail, but within seconds, he stopped. Something inside her snapped, and the exhaustion she hadn't realized had weighed her down vanished.

The surrounding filaments turned black, pulsating with what looked like smoke as they surrounded her. It lifted her up, and she suddenly felt light as air. Her soul burst from her chest, the threads glowing so brightly she was forced to squint. The dark magic of the curse merged with her mystic powers, turning each thread to gold with what looked like black strings along their edges.

The filaments encircled her faster, moving in a blur. She put out her hands towards her soul, and it slammed back into her. It didn't hurt, and as all the magic returned to her body, she felt more powerful than ever. Her feet touched the ground once more, and she breathed out.

The curse was broken. She'd done it.

"This isn't over," Rickie shouted from above.

She looked up from where he stood near the rafters. He pushed a blackened box, and to her surprise, it fell to the floor without smashing into pieces. It had to be made of metal with the sound it made hitting the cement. She didn't go near it, but Rickie took the opportunity of her distraction. By the time she stared back at him, he'd summoned a dozen blades, each black and swirling as though made from smoke.

Someone flung themselves in front of her. The blades impaled Adam through the back, and her scream caught in her throat as blood gushed out of his mouth. He leaned against her, and they both fell to their knees as his body convulsed. She quickly pushed all the healing magic she had into him, helping him close the wounds. But it wasn't working.

Rickie was about to send more weapons flying at them, so she placed herself in front of Adam and created a shield. They hit against the golden light, each blade creating sparks as it came into contact with her energy.

A familiar portal appeared behind him, plunging the room into a green hue. Someone came through wearing the same blank mask. Namika guessed it was a woman since they wore a black laced dress that had a gothic theme to it. She was petite as well, her head coming up below Rickie's chest. Was she a teenager?

She grabbed the vampire, muttered something, then wrenched him back into the portal.

Namika turned back to Adam as his wounds finally started closing properly, and cupped his face. "Are you okay? Tell me you're okay."

He smiled. "I'll be fine as long as you are."

A small cry escaped her throat as she pulled him close, continuing to heal him with all the magic she could muster.

The cover from the box creaked open, and it slammed against the floor, resonating loudly in the space around them. Namika's pulse sped as Linda crawled out, covered in what looked like soot, her blonde hair singed in a few places.

"Took you long enough," she muttered with a cough. A few places on her arms were covered in red blisters, and it seemed she was having trouble healing.

Namika let out a half-cry, half-laugh. "You're okay."

"Do I look *okay*?" she spat, grabbing a strand of her hair and letting out a sigh. "I'm gonna kill them for this."

Adam got to his feet. "Did you see what the vampire looks like? Or the reaper?"

Linda shook her head as she did her best to dust herself off. "No. Ghouls grabbed me while I was out looking for Elijah. They're the ones who dragged me into this stupid box, then threw me in the fire." A small shudder ran through her, but she looked ready to murder as her eyes glowed red. "When I find them..."

"We will," Adam said, the promise of pain dripping in his tone as he stared back up to the empty railing above.

32
______

FAMILY

Namika stretched, finally feeling like she had caught up on much-needed sleep. A week had passed since she broke the curse, and she'd spent that time sleeping and eating. Although after so many days, she was getting tired of being laid up.

Placing the pillows more comfortably behind her, she sat back just as the door opened, and Adam walked in. He held something in his hand, but at the angle he stood, she couldn't make out what it was.

"How are you feeling?" he asked with a smile as he approached the bed. He sat on the edge of the mattress, staring at her with worry in his gaze.

She nodded quickly, then pointed at the potted plant in his hand. "I'm fine. What is that?" she asked in a breathless voice. It was the most beautiful foliage and flowers she'd ever seen. Each flower was a different pastel color and almost glowed in the dim lighting of the room.

He grinned, clearly proud of himself, as he lifted it a bit higher so she could see it better. "This is an *elios*. A plant from the other world." He handed it to her, and she took it carefully.

"This is... breathtaking," she said, beaming at him and then back at the elios. Its leaves were rounded and a pastel purple, giving it a surreal look. "Wait." She stared up at him. "What do you mean 'from the other world'?"

"I wanted to give you a gift, so I went to Pyralis and purchased this." He motioned at the plant. "There aren't many left since they used to be grown by elves—"

"Elves?" she echoed, blinking a few times to make sure she wasn't dreaming.

He nodded. "They went extinct several thousand years ago." He touched one of the flowers, and it wiggled as though happy. "The elios that remained were cultivated by vampires, and they've kept them growing under strict supervision since they're rare."

"And you...bought one?"

"Yes. For you." He pushed her hair behind her ear. "You mentioned you enjoy taking care of plants."

She searched her memories for when she would've told him that, and her eyebrows shot up as she recalled. She'd told him during their first flight when he'd been trying to distract her.

"You... remembered that?" she whispered, tears filling her eyes. No one had ever gotten her such a thoughtful gift. She brought it closer to her chest, swallowing the lump in her throat.

He pulled her into a hug, careful not to squish the plant between them, and she let out a shuddering breath.

"Was it too much?" he asked in a quiet voice.

She shook her head, smiling ear to ear as she pulled back to look at him. "Thank you, Adam. So, so much."

He took the flowers from her and placed them on the bedside table. "I'm happy you like them."

She slid her hand along the mattress next to her. "Want to lie down with me for a bit?"

He arched an eyebrow as he tugged at his tie, loosening it. "Have I ever refused such a request for you to ask?"

Heat filled her face as he stripped off his clothes, and even despite the dimness in the room, his naked body was as clear as if all the lights had been on. His energy tingled along her skin, and she locked gazes with him as he stretched out next to her.

"I need you," she whispered.

His irises turned red, and she lost herself inside the beautiful, deep crimson as he searched her. "I'm not expecting anything in return for the gift—"

"I know. That's not why I want you," she said, tracing her fingers along his lips.

He slanted his mouth over hers, and she gasped. He thrust his tongue between her parted lips, making love with his mouth as his hands explored her body.

Pulling away from her, he grabbed the lube and slathered a good amount on them before slipping his hand between her thighs, tracing along her skin, never once breaking eye contact. Goosebumps crawled along her skin as her pulse throbbed in need, and she spread her legs wider. Her breath hitched when he slid a finger between her swollen lips, then pushed inside her opening.

She arched her hips to meet each thrust, moaning when he added a second finger. He picked up his pace until she hovered over the edge. The sound of his hand slapping against her skin as the lube rolled along her thighs was so erotic, she barely dared to breathe.

"Please. I need you inside," she panted.

He grasped her chin, not slowing his pumping inside her.

"I want to see you cum all over my fingers, buttercup," he said in a husky voice.

He curled his fingers, hitting a spot that made her feel like he set her nerves on fire. She closed her eyes, holding her breath as she came so close.

"Look at me." His voice was commanding, and she obeyed quickly.

His rhythm increased even more than she thought possible, and with a shattering cry, her orgasm crashed on her in spasms. She barely had a second to think before he was on top of her, spreading her legs wider.

Her limbs twitched as she stared down, anticipating him inside her more than she cared to admit. He fisted his cock and slid it between her lips. She was so wet, it slipped easily, sending shockwaves of pleasure every time it rubbed against her clit.

He slid inside, slowly, as though he wanted to enjoy every inch. She wrapped her legs around him, digging her soles into his ass, but all he did was slow down even more.

"Ah," she breathed as he pushed balls deep inside her. She was so full, and it was perfect.

He kissed her so gently, even when he slid his tongue between her parted lips. Sliding out, he kept the rhythm to a slow burn, in and out as he swallowed her muffled moans and cries with his lips.

Each stroke of his cock inside her sent her pleasure building, always so close to another orgasm. He nuzzled her neck, licking at a sensitive spot along her skin. He slid his hand beneath her ass, grasping it to use as leverage as he pumped harder inside her. She moaned his name and several curses.

He pulled out completely, then thrust his erection inside of her, and she threw her head back with a cry. It was quick and hard, but it's what they needed at that moment. To give in to an animalistic side and just fuck. He pumped into her, grasping her hips to slam into her. Intolerable pleasure sent her every nerve into overwhelming spasms, and she cried out with abandon. He thrust one last time, deep, then groaned as he released himself.

She buried her face against his chest, panting as he held her tight. He kissed her forehead, tightening his hold.

NAMIKA STARED at the sizeable crowd gathered in the hotel's hall. "When you said a dinner party, this wasn't what I had in mind."

"I like to impress," Adam said with a shrug. "Besides, we'll have our own private table, so it won't be as crowded."

"Private table shared with guests."

He grinned. "You know me too well." He pulled her against him, sliding his hand to her ass.

She gasped when he gave a light tap, then narrowed her eyes at him. "You better not pull that kind of stunt when the others arrive."

She stared around the room; it was another of Sebastian Ecter's businesses, and it catered to the supernatural beings like the restaurant where she'd met him. "You're sure it'll be okay? I mean, won't this place explode with the amount of powerful energy?"

He played with his cufflinks, averting his gaze. "They won't be here long enough for that to happen."

She gaped at him. "Are you telling me that could happen if they stayed too long?" When he didn't answer, she grabbed his tie and pulled him closer. "You're kidding me, right?"

He slid the tie out of her hand, then rearranged it, not

once breaking eye contact with her. "Do you need me to help ease your worries away with a distraction?"

"Don't call... *that* a distraction," she said as her cheeks warmed.

"That?"

"...sex," she whispered.

She turned her attention to the crowd and let out a breath. Haku was talking with a group of other demons, grinning as he said something. A few vampires were invited, and although everyone seemed comfortable enough, there was tension in the room.

Shiriki leaned against a wall to the side, watching in silence. Whenever someone caught his gaze, they scampered away as though they'd become victims.

Pressure built against her like a tidal wave crashing down, and she allowed her magic to surround her, using it as a barrier.

No one had to announce the guests had arrived.

The doors opened, and the room fell silent as everyone inside bowed low. Namika followed Adam's directions, staying straight until they'd approached. She forced her muscles to stiffen, the urge to follow everyone else's show of respect strong.

At the head of the group of guests, Mekaisto had chosen his lowest demon form, yet his powers still rippled from him like he was darkness itself. He wore a Victorian-style suit with black pants and a dress shirt, the dark red vest matching his irises.

Namika smiled when she met her best friend's gaze. Celina's black dress suited her, and the small amount of red lace at the hems matched what her husband wore. Even the baby in her arms was well dressed, and Namika grinned at the little black pants and a red dress shirt. The family was rarely seen together in the human world, and so this was their way of making a statement of sorts.

When they stopped in front of Namika and Adam, both hosts bowed low.

"Welcome," Adam said before straightening. "I'm pleased you could make it."

Celina's son shoved his hand into his mouth and bit down, blood and saliva dripping down his chin. Tears welled in his eyes, and he whimpered, his yellow eyes burning brighter as he pulled his hand out. The wound closed, but Celina sighed.

"Kai, you promised you'd do something about this," she muttered, grabbing a tissue out of a black bag slung over her shoulder. She wiped her son's mouth and hand, continuing with her muttering of her husband's excuses.

Mekaisto grinned. "Will you let me hold the bag, or are you still going to show your anger at me by being stubborn?"

"You know I don't like to swear in front of Fenrir, so don't tempt me," she shot.

Namika turned her laugh into a cough, averting her gaze when Mekaisto glowered at her, but Celina smiled.

Adam cleared his throat. "Let's sit, shall we?"

Shiriki materialized closer to the group, and Fenrir reached out his small arms towards him, a toothy grin spreading across his face as he babbled unintelligible words. Celina shot her son a look of annoyance before turning her attention to Shiriki.

To Namika's surprise, her best friend handed Fenrir to Shiriki, who took him in his arms like he was the most precious of treasures.

Namika opened and closed her mouth, unsure if she wanted to laugh or rescue the child. Shiriki's smile turned gentle, and she suddenly understood his request. He'd wanted access to the Dark Realm to see his grandson again.

"Celina," Namika said in a quiet voice, hoping no one would pay close attention. But it had the opposite effect. The entire group turned towards her, and she rolled her eyes. "Can we speak in private?"

Mekaisto muttered something in demos, which came out as a growl at the same time. When Namika flinched, Adam's energy burst forward, and both demons stared each other down.

Celina placed her palm on her husband's arm. "You promised this would be a fun evening."

He enveloped an arm around her waist and pulled her close. "Don't be long, dove."

Celina gave one last look at Shiriki, who was still holding her son, then followed Namika towards a door leading out. They walked in silence down a hallway until reaching a separate room where they could be alone.

Silence hung heavy for a few seconds until Celina broke it. "Genki?" *How are you?*

Namika smiled. It used to be how they greeted each other every morning in high school. Memories flooded her, and she became less nervous about her favor.

"Shiriki helped us when he came to the warehouse." Namika scoffed. "Well, once he felt like it. But I made a deal with him."

"You did what?" Celina all but shouted. "You made a deal with Shiriki? Are you insane?"

Namika grimaced. "Hey, you'll remember you did the same with your husband."

Celina pressed her lips together, then nodded. "Point taken. What's the deal?"

"That I'd get you to ask your husband to lower the number of years in exile." She glanced towards the door.

"And now I know why. There's a bond between him and Fenrir."

"I'm sure it's because he misses his laboratory from Hell," she muttered, crossing her arms, but it didn't sound like she believed her own words.

"Maybe a bit of both?"

Celina averted her gaze. "Fine. I'll agree to a lesser exile period. But getting Kai to agree will be Hell. Pun intended," she said with a small grin.

"Maybe you could offer something like occasional weekend visits for good behavior?" They both burst out laughing, and Namika shook her head, smiling ear to ear. "Well, you're the only one who can convince Mekaisto."

"I'm sure I can make a deal of my own with Kai if I have to," she said, her cheeks turning a slight shade of pink. It clashed against her red hair, but Namika pretended not to see anything.

They left the room, heading towards the hall with the guests. Namika sat next to her best friend while Adam took a seat between Namika and Haku. Linda had been invited, but she'd become obsessed with finding those responsible for torturing her and insisted she guard the area in case anyone came uninvited. Her chance to catch those she wanted to take revenge against.

Namika leaned towards Celina but glanced between her and her husband. "Can I hold your son after Shiriki?"

Celina beamed. "Of course." Without waiting, she stood and walked around the table to reach the demon. Without a word, Shiriki handed her Fenrir.

Celina returned to her seat, and Namika leaned towards Fenrir. "Hi there. Want to come to see me?" She held out her arms, and Celina handed Fenrir over.

His yellow irises shone, and when he smiled, tiny pointed teeth were visible. He babbled something and bounced. "You have such beautiful eyes, Fenrir. Look at you. Such a handsome boy." She placed him on her lap, surprised how well he held up his own body weight at his age. When he gripped her finger, she wiggled it. "Oh, and strong too."

When she glanced up, Shiriki was in deep conversation with Mekaisto, and Celina was looking at her son with so much love.

Once Namika had given Fenrir to Celina, Adam wrapped his arm around her and brought her closer to him. The food arrived, and they ate, talking with one another, and sometimes breaking into smaller groups.

"Was there a particular reason for this dinner party?" Mekaisto asked, a knowing smile curling his lips.

Adam nodded. "I'd like permission to hunt and kill the vampire responsible for cursing Namika."

Mekaisto arched an eyebrow. "That could start a war with vampires and nightshades... I will speak to their king and see if he would accept certain terms for an exception."

"Thank you, your majesty," Adam said, bowing his head. "Also, a reaper is very likely involved in helping this vampire, and together, they seem determined to create as many ghouls as possible."

"And cursing more people," Namika chimed in. "I saw at least one other lost soul."

Mekaisto drummed his pointed fingernails against the table's surface. "I give you permission to take care of those as well."

Adam turned to Haku. "I'm putting you in charge while I'm taking care of all this."

The demon's eyebrows shot up. "Wait... really?" He quickly straightened, then bowed his head. "Thank you, Master. I won't let you down."

Namika smiled, knowing how much it meant to Haku for Adam to trust him like this.

Celina glanced over her shoulder at Adam. "You better take care of her, or I'll drag you into Kai's dungeons myself."

Adam took Namika's hand, and she turned towards him. "I'll keep her close." He kissed her knuckles, his brown eyes boring into hers.

Namika's heart swelled. She felt like she truly had a family again.

ABOUT THE AUTHOR

M. A. Fréchette writes the darker side of romance.

Being an extremist, she loves both the dark aspects of life and everything sweet. All her stories are either set in Canada where she lives or in alternate worlds she made up while living within her imagination. When not writing, she thinks of the next scene or plot while enjoying video games. Although she has a fascination for monsters, with a bachelor degree in criminology, she understands there's no need to create the paranormal; humans are capable of inflicting nightmares of their own.

Please feel free to reach out through any social media. I truly love hearing from readers!

facebook.com/AuthorMAF

twitter.com/authormaf

instagram.com/authormaf

amazon.com/author/authormaf

bookbub.com/authors/m-a-frechette

ALSO BY M. A. FRÉCHETTE

A Demon's Love series

MY SOUL TO GIVE (book #1)

MY LIFE TO TAKE (book #2)

Unbroken series

A THOUSAND WORDS (book #1)

Standalones

STRINGS ATTACHED

www.ingramcontent.com/pod-product-compliance
Lightning Source LLC
Chambersburg PA
CBHW030529190726
48283CB00006B/1835